2.50

MW01598020

Truly the Devil's Work

THE CIRCUS SALMAGUNDI MYSTERIES

KIM BANNERMAN

FOX&BEE STUDIO

Truly the Devil's Work

Copyright © 2022 by Kim Bannerman

ISBN 978-1-7780567-0-3

ISBN (ebook) 978-1-7780567-1-0

All rights reserved. No part of this book may be reproduced or transmitted in any form or by any means, electronically or mechanical, including photocopying, recording, or by any information storage and retrieval system, without permission in writing from the copyright owner.

This is a work of fiction. All names, characters, places and incidents either are the product of the author's imagination or are used fictitiously, and any resemblance to any actual person, living or dead, is entirely coincidental.

This book was created in Canada.

For more information, contact kim@kbannerman.com.

Books by Kim Bannerman

The Lizzie Saunders series

Bucket of Blood

Mark of the Magpie

The Agony of St. Alice

The Circus Salmagundi Series

Truly the Devil's Work

The Vengeful Dead

The Sea Will Have

Other titles

The Tattooed Wolf

The Fire Song

Love and Lovecraft

The Blackwood Papers

Aeterna

To my grandmother, Alice Bannerman, who took me to the circus and told me wonderful stories but would not have approved of my tattoos.

Chapter One

Honoria and Calliope refused to speak with me, and frankly, I couldn't care less. We had nothing in common. Any communication attempted between us would result in idle chatter, and I've never been very skilled at small talk. In essence, their silence made my life easier.

But it bothered me, right from the beginning, that the sisters had so quickly assessed my place in the Circus Salmagundi as below their own. Maybe, without thinking too much upon it, I'd hoped that the rigid caste systems of the real world couldn't follow me into the land of acrobats and clowns, dancing bears and talking ravens, childhood delights and wonders, and that I'd be protected from social stratification by the magic of the circus.

Gertie helpfully corrected my mistake.

"Oh, no, Rose," she said, eyes full of pity, "The Gibson sisters are far, far, far above you."

Gertrude von Reigel had taken an instant liking to me when I joined the Circus Salmagundi and, like a hen protecting a chick under its wing, decided it was her responsibility to educate me on the particulars of my new life. She was a trick rider, a few years younger than me, and she hadn't been a member of the Circus Salmagundi for very long; perhaps she sympathized with my situation, or perhaps she liked the satisfaction that teaching a less fortunate creature can bring. Perhaps she was lonely and craved attention, however fleeting. Whatever her reason, it didn't matter. It had been a long time since someone had shown any warmth towards me and I appreciated the attention, plus Gertie knew all the gossip and she was eager to share it.

Gertie had rich brown hair tied up in a fluffy bouffant, a crowning glory of soft tresses and curls that harkened back to an early style and highlighted her high forehead, graceful brows, and sparkling eyes. From a distance, she was beautiful; balancing on the back of a galloping stallion, she became divine. But here, eating lunch together in the galley of the SS *Atropos*, it was easy to spot her terrestrial flaws. Her nose was a bit crooked; it must have been broken many years ago. She always painted her mouth a little too thickly and rouged her cheeks a little too brightly in an attempt to hide her sallow complexion. She could be kind if it served her, but she had a bit of a temper and she certainly lacked tact. Most of the time, Gertie didn't care about anything that didn't directly revolve around her.

She'd filled her teacup to the brim, leaving me with just enough tea to fill my own cup, half-way. She took the best slices of cucumber sandwiches and left me with one soggy triangle. Now, this was not to say she was greedy, per se, but unless you were one of her cherished horses, she didn't think of you as having needs of your own. It didn't occur to her that anyone else lived in the universe. Consequently, if you didn't get in fast with Gertie, you were left with the scraps.

She took one delicate bite of her sandwich, chewed and swallowed, before saying, "Anyone in the Ten-In-One tent is going to be at the bottom of the ladder, I'm sorry to say. No one respects the freak show. That's just natural." She counted out the layers of society using her sandwich as a guide: bread, cucumber, cream cheese, lettuce. "The Geek is at the very bottom, then come the rest of the side show performers, yourself included. After that comes the main tent performers. Now, Wanda and Bill were outsiders, so they're lower than me. I was born into the circus, you know, and that provides a certain amount of privilege." She beamed as she tapped her fingernail against the top piece of bread. "Then you have the owner; he's higher than anyone else. In this circus, Grover Scott is king, and don't you ever forget it!"

Truer words had never been spoken. Mr. Scott was the admiral of our shabby fleet, and he was a solid four-and-a-half feet of determination, grit and vexation, with a face like a pit dog and a constitution to match. You did not cross him, lest you find yourself marooned.

"So where does that stick the Gibson sisters? Are they cucumber or cream cheese?"

"Honoria and Calliope come from a most distinguished lineage! Their family wasn't circus, but vaudeville. And they don't debase themselves for applause; they have real talent! You've heard them: they have lovely voices, nothing cheap or carny. So," and she nestled her fingernail between the top slice of bread and the lettuce, "They sit just below the owner." She threw a smile in my direction that reminded me of a mother soothing a crying child. That singular expression told me to abandon all hope of aspiring to such lofty heights.

From my own pathetic sandwich, I picked a slice of cucumber from its blanket of soggy bread. It lay limp and cold between my fingers.

I sighed. I guess this was me.

"So, the Gibson sisters aren't happy being part of the Circus Salmagundi?" I asked as I ate it.

"Oh, of course not!" Gertie scoffed, "Why would they be? Before the war, they used to perform on stages across England and Europe. They're very far above all of us. Practically untouchable." She poked her finger at the remains of my sandwich. "Are you going to eat that?" Without waiting for a reply, she plucked it from my plate and devoured it.

This inspiring speech of Gertie's had occurred on May 1, 1920, the first afternoon I'd spent with the Circus Salmagundi. At the time, it struck me as harsh and rigid and wholly impractical, but in retrospect, Gertie's brutal advice turned out to be absolutely correct. The Gibson sisters were a pair of virtuous angels floating high above my blemished mortal coil, ascending into the stratosphere on wings made of song, and neither of them would speak a single syllable to me for a full six months. Over the summer, I'd come to know many of the other performers and roustabouts, but never them. Not a word. Not a peep!

But, like I said, I wasn't too bothered by the shunning. The rest of our troupe seemed happy to believe that the Gibson sisters were quality people, worthy of blind adoration, but I had better things to do with my time than fawn over them, praise them for their vacuous melodies, or fit myself into their ridiculous hierarchy.

Do I sound bitter? I probably am. I don't have a sweet voice or a fair face to earn my keep. Once upon a time I might have been young and pretty and conceited and vain, but those days are far in my past, and the year 1919 had left me a husk of my former self. Now, I'm scarred and tattooed, cynical and solitary, too old to marry and too stubborn to die. I live quietly on board the *SS Atropos* as we sail from port to port, from gig to gig, and keep mostly to myself, content to mind my own business.

So, suffice it to say, I was astounded when, early on the first morning of October, Honoria Gibson knocked upon the door of my berth and called out my name in a friendly manner, as if we'd always been the greatest of tillicums.

"Rosie? Rosie, my dear? Are you on board?"

We had sailed in late the night before, having come through a nasty squall on the Strait of Georgia, and frankly, I was exhausted from the stress and travel. I'd never been so relieved to see the lights of Victoria! As soon as we rounded Ogden Point, the nasty Pacific swells calmed and the boats stopped lurching, and our flotilla puttered passed the friendly entrance leading into the Inner Harbour, slowly and carefully. Just beyond the rocky turret of Macaulay Point stretched dark swaths of bucolic farmlands; it could be tricky to navigate without lights to guide us, especially when the tide was turning, the night was dark, and the hour was late. Before the lanterns of Victoria had vanished behind us, we turned into a small cove and docked at a rickety wharf belonging to a dairy farmer named Louis Buckley.

I don't know how Buckley and Mr. Scott had first been introduced but the farmer had invited us to set up our tents in his pasture and perform our show for five consecutive nights, starting October 2nd. Mr. Scott was grateful for the opportunity to play to these rural crowds, although he didn't have to say it: the circuit had proven difficult all summer and the whole of our troupe felt the same way. People still feared contracting Spanish flu. That anxiety had burned itself deeply into their habits, and even though the plague hadn't killed the same numbers this year as it had in '18 or '19, no one wanted to sit in a crowd or huddle together too closely. Most families avoided social events and parents dared not expose their surviving children to any risk. All summer long we'd played to half-full audiences and, frankly, the Circus Salmagundi needed whatever help it could get to stay afloat, every pun intended.

Mr. Buckley's invitation promised eager audiences from the surrounding villages and town-sites, and in return, all he asked for the rental of his land was a quarter of our profits.

How could we refuse? It might be the only opportunity to save us from utter ruin.

Our three ships docked at his wharf, which was really too small to accommodate us, but what choice did we have? The *SS Atropos* had once been a large tug, the *SS Decimo* had been a cargo ship, and the *SS Nona* had been an old steam ferry: none of the ladies were dainty vessels and the bay was not a large one, so to make space, the boats were lashed with ropes and bladders were strung between them to keep them from colliding. From a distance they had the ungainly appearance of three grumpy grandmothers squashed together on a tiny couch, entangled with yarn.

As the deckhands tied up the boats, Mr. Scott and Mr. Buckley greeted each other with the same warmth and good cheer as brothers, although I'd be willing to wager that two, more dissimilar men could scarce be found. Mr. Scott was reserved and squat and frightfully impish; Mr. Buckley towered over him, as boisterous as a beagle, with straw-blonde hair cut in a bowl shape just above his ears.

All of this had transpired very late in the evening. Once the boats were secured and introductions made, I'd collapsed in my cot to sleep the deep, dreamless repose that only travelling can bring. My berth was a cramped broom closet on the lower deck of the *Atropos*, containing nothing but a grey wool cot for sleeping and a travel trunk for personal items, with my entire wardrobe of colourful shawls and dresses hung from lines strung across the ceiling. This gave my room the appearance of a laundry, and normally my clothes swayed with the motion of the waves, but because the boats had been bound to each other, my clothes hung straight and still. When I woke at Honoria's rapid knocking, I was so disoriented that I thought I was living back on land.

Then one hand hit a wall, another tangled in a scarf, and I remembered where I was. Immediately I cast about for some clue as to what had disturbed my sleep.

Another pounding at my door made that clear.

"Rosie? Are you here?"

I held my tongue. During last night's tumultuous crossing, Gertie had made plans to take a streetcar to visit a lovely Japanese tea garden nearby, and it was reasonable to assume I was with her. If I stayed quiet and said nothing, Honoria would never know I was here.

But my curiosity is a powerful force. Once ignited, nothing can stifle it, and it sweeps away all my good reason.

"What is it, Honoria?"

"Can I... can I speak with you?"

I stumbled from my cot, pushed a few silk robes aside, and reached for the doorknob. The narrow door swung open a crack.

Honoria wore a timid smile. She and her sister both had long glossy tresses of honey-blonde hair, eyes as blue as the Aegean Sea, and flawless skin as pale and luminous as porcelain, but Honoria was the older sister, and her chin was a little stronger, her features a little more pronounced. Calliope often wore filmy skirts and seductive chiffon dresses, but Honoria dressed in wool trousers and vest, taking a masculine fashion and making it feminine with her charm and grace. The Gibson sisters were the epitome of classical beauty, but if Calliope was Aphrodite, Honoria was Artemis.

And how must have I looked to them? It's no wonder they shunned me. With my close-cropped hair the colour of cinnamon, whip-thin scars crisscrossing my limbs, and vibrant tattoos across arms, legs and torso, I must have seemed like some strange savage little wild-woman, eccentric and frightful, only a step up from the Geek.

"I'd invite you in, but...." I waved my hand around the cramped room.

She clasped her hands at her waist and tried not to wrinkle her nose in disgust. "Our room on the *Nona* is quite lovely," she said, "We have a particularly fine view of the water."

I scowled and narrowed my eyes. Had she really come all this way to brag?

Then, with a start, I realized she was inviting me -- in her own stilted way -- to join her in her berth.

Honoria glanced over her shoulder to see if anyone was in the corridor. She looked relieved that no one was there. "I need to speak with you in private, Rose," she explained. "Calliope has a... well, we both have... a problem. Will you join me?"

I'd never seen her look so meek!

I grabbed my blue silk robe and followed after her. We left the *Atropos* and climbed the gangplank to the *Nona*, and Honoria's eyes flitted back often, as if she didn't quite believe I'd follow her along the outer deck to her own stateroom door. She gave a small knock to announce our presence then opened the door. Perhaps afraid that I might bolt, she grasped my wrist and practically yanked me inside after her.

When Honoria said her room was lovely, she hadn't exaggerated. I whistled low; the Gibson sisters shared very comfortable lodgings.

The layout was a broad square with three portholes that looked out along the outer deck, a feature that my own below-deck room lacked, and the presence of natural light flooding in from outside reminded me of my old life, when I lived in a normal house on a normal street on normal dry land like a normal person. I had to shake myself out of my nostalgia. Two brass beds sat on either side of the room with a stout oaken chest-of-drawers between them and a couple of cupboards flanking the main door. Not a single item was hung from the ceiling. Nothing was stashed in nets and strung from the corners. The only objects on the walls were two oil paintings: one was the portrait of a young woman, and the other, a portrait of a man with a handlebar moustache. From their features, it was obvious that these were Honoria and Calliope's parents.

Calliope sat on the edge of one bed, her eyes red-rimmed. She dabbed at her nose with a linen handkerchief embroidered with little red flowers.

"Oh, thank heavens, you found her!" she sniffled.

"Please sit down, Miss Rose," Honoria said as she dragged me over to her own bed and offered me a seat there. The mattress squeaked when I sat; it wasn't made of hay, but of springs! Lord almighty! What other treasures did they have hidden here!?

"Oh, Rosie, I'm so glad you've come," Calliope said, "I desperately need your help!"

Still in shock at the luxury and richness of their accommodations, I said nothing. My mind had only enough wits to stare at the books on the sideboard (books!), the fringed lamp on the dresser (an electric lamp!), the thick blue rug on the floor (a real Persian rug!) as I catalogued each facet of opulence and the floor space it took to house it...

"I'm sorry, what?"

The sisters shared a poignant glance at each other. Then both sets of piercing blue eyes fixated on me, and they might have told me then what they needed, except there came a heavy knock at the door.

Without waiting for an invitation, the door opened and Magda stepped inside. Seeing the owner's wife here, in this private room, well! My jaw dropped fully open.

Let me explain. Yes, Magda Scott is Grover's wife, but it's misleading to describe her in such a simplistic way. We're close in age but she possesses a strength and bearing to which I can never aspire; she is, in all ways but legal, the co-owner of our circus and the mighty queen to Grover's king. Magda is tall and broad with an eagle's nest of black braids wound around the top of her head, so tall and ornate that they're almost a headdress instead of a style. Under thick black brows, her eyes are sharp and brown with flecks of gold that flash in the sunlight. She wears flowing gowns made of homespun wool, embroidered with symbols and sigils beyond my interpretation, and she often wraps fringed scarves around her shoulders and dangles silver rings from her earlobes to match the silver rings on her fingers. When Magda speaks, she displays a slight accent; some said she is Irish, while others said she is Polish, but no one is quite certain of her origins and it seems poor form to inquire, like asking a magician to explain a trick.

She had bountiful curves as the result of four children with another one on the way, and when she swanned into the room, Magda moved with the grace of a galleon crossing a calm sea. She saw me sitting on the bed and nodded her approval. "Ah, good, you are here, Rose," she purred, "I was worried you might have gone for a walk into the city and that we would be unable to benefit from your good counsel."

"My what?"

Magda settled herself down next to Calliope, opposite me. She wore a scarlet dress trimmed with gold thread and covered with a black apron, and she smoothed the fabric across her generous lap before laying her strong, sun-browned hands flat upon her thighs.

"You know a little about medicine, yes?"

I looked directly at Magda. The woman had found me and offered me a place on the boats, a position in her circus, a job and a home. She already knew my history; this question was meant to inform the sisters of my background.

"I do."

"I heard a rumour that you were a nurse," said Honoria.

"I had some medical training, a long time ago," I corrected, hiding my surprise at this revelation laid so baldly before me. "What other rumours have you heard?"

"Only that you left your life as a nurse because all of your scars made it difficult. You were in an accident of some sort, I don't know what." Honoria replied, "And your husband abandoned you because of your injuries."

Magda said, in a firm way that demanded no following questions, "Rose's husband died of the Spanish Flu in 1918."

"Then you *were* a nurse," Calliope replied. That was all she really cared about. If they felt any pity for me, they didn't show it.

"Yes," said Magda. "And Rose will know what to do."

Oh dear. What sort of trouble had Calliope gotten herself into?

Honoria sat down beside me. "My sister is... is..." She stumbled over the words, ashamed.

"I missed my blood," Calliope admitted. Her fingers drifted to the flat plain of her stomach. Her chin started to tremble. "I can't be more than a month or two along."

I tried to stifle my surprise. "Oh!"

"There's still time, isn't there?" Honoria pressed, "To get rid of a baby?"

"Yes, there is time," Magda assured her, "You girls were wise to come to us so quickly. At this point, there are methods we can use to reinvigorate your blood, isn't that right, Rose?"

"Yes, of course," I said, "A few different ways."

"But you mustn't tell a soul!" Honoria commanded. She grabbed my hand and squeezed it until my knuckles stung.

"Girls, girls," said Magda, "Most women experience such a trial some point in their lives. Rose will not say a word, nor will I. Your innocence is not imperilled."

"Of course, I wouldn't say a thing," I replied, "But what about the father? Does he know?"

Instantly my mind went to the men who lived on board the *SS Nona*. There weren't many culprits from which to choose. The doctor and taxidermist, Hector Kane, was much too surly and cynical for such an affair; the animal trainer, Orville Mann, had a pungent body odour worse than his pet bear Cosmo. Bill Peacock was happily married to Wanda and I couldn't imagine his devotion wavering. There was Virgil Stonehouse, the captain of the ship, but he was forty years her elder! Of course, there was also --

I gasped. "Is it Alexander McGee? The ringmaster? Has he put you in a family way?!"

Magda cackled out a laugh as Calliope cried, "Oh, goodness, no!"

With a half-shrug, Honoria said to her sister, "Would that be so terrible?"

Alex had the roguish good-looks of Rudolph Valentino and the smouldering intensity of Bert Lytell, along with the swaggering confidence of Zeus and the fidelity to match. After every performance, he enjoyed a parade of admirers following after him and I couldn't imagine he'd make a dutiful father or faithful lover. "It's probably for the best that it's not Alex," I replied. "But if not him, then who, Calliope?"

A blush brought colour to her cheeks. "Morris."

Morris Cave, the roustabout? The horse-faced fellow who strummed on his ukulele to earn a few pennies? I'd never have guessed him! A taciturn and pensive artist, the man kept mostly to himself. He preferred the company of his sketch books and charcoal pencils to drinking and carousing. It didn't matter how big or small of a town we were visiting: while the rest of the men were playing poker or chasing pretty girls, he'd be off to the nearest museum, library or art gallery with his sketch book in hand, perpetually seeking inspiration.

But at the mention of his name, Calliope's eyes filled with stars. "We picked up together at the end of August," she replied, "And we haven't done much together, we've been really careful! We always made sure to stand up against a wall when we did it!"

Honoria nodded. "You can't get pregnant, standing up."

Silly, young, flighty fools, the both of them.

"I'm afraid, girls, you are quite mistaken," Magda replied, patting her stomach. "I'm fairly certain this one was conceived with a similar arrangement."

Honoria cringed but Calliope blushed. For a moment, the tension lifted and she even managed a giggle.

"If you're only a month or two along, Calliope, then you won't have to risk a criminal operation," Magda continued, "Not that I know anyone in this city who provides such a service, but we should be able to find you some herbal teas that will help ease your troubles more naturally."

"So, I won't need a doctor?"

"Not at this point," I said. "Does Morris know about your situation?"

"I told him right after I told Honoria. I was happy to marry him and we could start a family, but he said he'd rather take me back to England and marry in the presence of his father, and if Morris returned already married, his father would be quite cross. If there was already a child, too? No, it's out of the question."

"The time is not right," said Honoria.

"I do love him, and he loves me, but he's of no mind to be a father yet, and this little tin-pot circus is no place to raise a family."

Magda's shoulders visibly tensed and her dark brows arched severely. After all, Grover and Magda were raising their family on our ships, and none of their children seemed worse for it.

Luckily, Calliope was not so clueless or self-centred as Gertie. She realized almost instantly that she'd misspoke. She grasped Magda's hands and her tone softened as she said, "Please don't think me ungrateful. The Circus Salmagundi has been very good to us, Miss Magda, but

I'm in no fit state to be a mother." She turned to me. "Miss Rose, you must believe me: Morris is a very caring soul and he will not stand in my way. He wants to do all he can to make sure I'm comfortable."

Then we'd have no trouble with the father -- that was a bit of a blessing.

"Magda and I can put you back right," I promised, "Give us a bit of time to find what you need, and you'll be done the whole ordeal by the end of the week."

The young woman looked like she might cry with joy. She pressed kisses to our hands and thanked us profusely, but as Magda and I left, Honoria flashed me an expression that was stony and guarded. She put no stock in my promise. She'd only be happy once the deed was done.

Magda and I left the *Nona* without a word shared, yet I felt a silent pact pass between us: this situation required a certain amount of discretion, and the secret that had been shared with us in the Gibson's room was not to be discussed in the open. However, it required planning, and that meant conversation, which demanded a place of privacy and quietude. When we climbed the gangplank onto the *Atropos*, Magda gestured for me to follow her to the galley.

Located at the front of the main deck, the galley was the heart of our ship. It was more than just a kitchen or dining area. Under normal circumstances, people gathered here to eat and converse, to play cards or share stories, to renew those bonds of fellowship that life in a small troupe inevitably forges. On any other day, the galley would be the worst spot for a delicate conversation, but today our circus had fractured into independent fragments and cast themselves out to admire the sights, choosing to spend their free day abroad, and so we found the galley almost empty. Only thirteen-year-old Martha stood there, daydreaming at the big cast-iron stove as she absently stirred a cauldron of fragrant mutton stew. Nicknamed 'Matty', Magda's oldest daughter was a very capable girl with a steady constitution. Sometimes her brother teased her because she was small and slight, but it was common knowledge that the girl had inherited the best combination of her mother's bewitching looks and her father's stubborn disposition. Matty wasn't flustered easily. She walked with her head held high, her straight rope of glossy black hair cascading down the centre of her back, and she was generous to a fault. She'd set out bowls and spoons upon the table; anyone was welcome to share her lunch if they wished, but there was almost no one left on board. Circumstances had aligned to give us all the stew we cared to eat and all the privacy we desired.

Matty turned at the sound of our footsteps on the creaking wooden floorboards.

"Hey, Rosie!" she greeted. Without asking, she ladled out a hearty helping of potatoes and mutton and plunked the bowl in front of me.

I thanked her for the food as Magda sat next to me.

"A woman needs her vitality restored, hmm?" said Magda.

"It can be quickly done," I replied. "She's only missed her first blood."

"And that's a great relief," Magda replied, "The more time passes, the more difficult it becomes." She tapped her fingers on the tabletop as she thought. "It won't be the first time I've had a young lady on our ships who has found herself in such a predicament, and this problem can be dealt with cleanly and quickly, but," Magda held up one finger. "We must not enter into it lightly. Here, as you eat your stew, we shall lay out the cards."

From some hidden pocket deep within the valleys and folds of her scarlet dress, Magda withdrew a small pouch sewn from black velvet and tied with an emerald ribbon. She plucked the knot open and slid a deck of cards into her palm. They were old and blunt-edged, and the white paper had long ago faded into a dirty ecru, but the painted images in red-and-black remained vibrant and arresting. The accents of gilded gold shone like molten fire.

"Now," the woman whispered, "Let us see how this shall play out."

Her nimble fingers danced of their own volition. She shuffled lightly, then one, two, three, four cards were flipped onto the tabletop in a line, each one with their face down.

Magda flipped the first card over. It portrayed a youth in a jaunty red hat, skipping along a road with a cup carried high and sloshing liquid everywhere, but the card was upside down. I reached out to turn it around and Magda slapped my hand.

"Leave it as it falls," she said, "It is the Page of Cups, reversed."

"Upside-down changes its meaning?"

"Ah," she said with an impish twinkle, "When upright, the Page of Cups symbolizes a happy idealist, a dreamer. But reversed?" She shook her head. "The young person seeking our aid is not yet mature or wise. She's insecure and flighty and perhaps even a little silly, and she covers over her nonsense with a haughty disposition. She might appear to an outside observer like an arrogant and over-confident snob, but that's only because she does not know her own self-worth or what she desires. She has not yet gained a sense of independence. She does not know her own strength. If you ask my opinion, she's not in a place to make a very good mother."

How frightfully accurate.

"And the second card?"

"Well," Magda said as she flipped over the next card, "Here we see the Seven of Swords. There's deception and trickery. We've not been told all the circumstances behind this affair, I think."

"She assured us, she's already told the father about the baby. There's no secrecy there."

"Yes, yes," came the reply, "But he has not been truthful with the mother."

"He claims to be content to let Cal --" I glanced quickly to Matty, who was listening, enraptured. "I mean, the mother. He's content to let the mother terminate the pregnancy."

"Well, of course he is! He is a man! They run away from such uncomfortable things as fast as their legs can take them," Magda said, throwing one hand in the air. "He will let her deal with this challenge while he retains his freedom and he will feel no guilt at all. But," she tapped the card, "He has not been truthful to her about his circumstances. I think he has lied to her about himself in a much more fundamental way." When she glanced up at me, her eyes held warmth and affection. "Of course, who on these ships has been truthful about their past? We all keep our secrets well-guarded, don't you think, Rose?"

My heart jumped. "A person's life before joining the Circus Salmagundi is their own business. You told me when you hired me: this place gives each of us a fresh start."

"Yes, it can," she agreed as if to placate me, "But in this instance, the card bids you to be careful. The father is not what he seems."

And yet, Morris seemed harmless. He was quiet, almost painfully shy for a man employed by a circus, and he took great delight in playing joyful songs on his ukulele for the children. As hefty as an ox with a little more flesh than muscle on his bones, Morris had an easy laugh and a silly sense of humour, although he often kept that to himself. The other roustabouts were prone to drinking and crude humour, but not Morris. Instead, he enjoyed simple pleasures, like drawing pictures of birds or portraits of people, and he was a talented artist with a discerning eye. Morris didn't seem like the sort of fellow to harbour sinister secrets.

Magda continued to the next card. Flipped over, it portrayed a serious woman holding a scale in one hand and a sword in the other. She looked like an ill-tempered grocer. Woe to the shopper who crossed the likes of her! With that nasty blade, she was just as likely to cut off your legs as measure out your cabbages.

"This is Justice," said Magda, "What a powerful card to fall in this position!"

"What does it mean?"

Magda chose her words carefully. "My dear Rose, you might soon find yourself in the middle of a great upheaval. You will be set upon the scale and measured."

"I don't like the sound of that."

"Nor should you. A dispute is coming. Your honour will be scrutinized, your actions will be tested. But through all that is coming, you must remain truthful and courageous, and willing to act in the best interest of yourself; only then will you be able to act in the best interest of all."

I furrowed my brow. "What does that mean?"

"Your character will be called into question."

"But I haven't done anything!"

"Not yet, no." She drummed her fingers over the card. "But remain committed to the truth, Rose, even as fear and uncertainty appear on your horizon. If you can do this, perhaps you'll be just fine." She smiled as she said this, but then her fingers flipped over the last card. Her smile vanished. In a whisper, she said, "Oh, dear."

The final card showed a castle tower reaching high into a storm-tossed sky. From heaven above, a golden bolt of crooked lightning fell. It struck the pinnacle of the turret, casting out shattered stones and plumes of fire, and on either side, the flailing figures of unwitting victims plunged to their deaths. The foundation of the castle was crumbling. All was in chaos. Divine and inescapable forces pressed down upon the mighty citadel, and it could withstand them no longer. The spire was falling to pieces and destined to take all with it.

Matty peeped over my shoulder and gave a little gasp of fright.

"Oh! The tower!"

"Is it bad?" I said, looking between mother and daughter.

Magda glanced at me. "It's sure not good."

"The tower is the card of destruction," said Matty as she sat next to me. "It means turmoil and sudden upheaval."

Magda held up one finger to silence her oldest daughter. "Ah, yes, it does mean all that, my poppet, but there are deeper forces here at work. Remember as I taught you: we must look at all the cards together and pay attention to where they fall." She looked to me. "The tower represents disaster, but it can also be transformative. It warns of a radical and momentous change. Perhaps we will come to see our world in a new and exciting way. We will be terrified, we will abandon the beliefs to which we cling or hold precious, and through that cathartic process, we will rebuild ourselves into something more resolute and powerful."

To be honest, my heart sank. The last five years had been nothing but chaotic. I'd fled to the Circus Salmagundi looking for a safe place to hide from the terrible past, and this little tin-pot circus -- as Calliope had so cruelly dismissed it -- had become a blessed haven. My life here was free from constant reminders of hardships faced or lives lost, and the thought that it could no longer shelter me from the challenges looming on the horizon? Well, it was almost enough to make me weep.

I slumped in my chair and closed my eyes to block out the dreadful image of the crumbling tower. "Was the Great War not enough?" I said, "Losing my husband? The pandemic, the deaths, the injuries, loss of everyone and everything in my life... wasn't that more than enough to bear?"

I felt skinny arms around me. Matty pressed a kiss to my cheek.

"It'll be okay, Rosie," she comforted me. "You just watch. Everything will turn out dandy."

Magda reached out to pat her palm against my cheek. "The cards hint at our future, they do not set it in stone," she reminded. "All I can tell you is this: trust in intuition, Rose, and never flinch from being true to yourself."

Chapter Two

The reading unnerved me. Normally, I didn't put much stock in Magda's fortune telling and parlour tricks. After all, I work in this circus: I've seen how gullible people can be dazzled by sleight-of-hand and theatre magic. But the thought of being accused for a crime as yet uncommitted, leading to a horrific tragedy? Such a frightful revelation would unbalance anyone, even if they didn't believe in fate, precognition, or mysticism.

Matty returned to her cooking and, after she tucked the cards away, Magda and I fell to discussing what method would work best for Calliope's condition. My skills did not run in this direction: I could set a bone or dress a wound, but I'd never needed to restore a woman's vitality. It seemed Magda had more experience, for she was confident it could be done quickly and without much fuss, if only we could secure the right supplies. As breezily as preparing a grocery list, the woman wrote down a column of items on a scrap of paper. "Fetch these, Rose," she said, "I can brew up a tea to help our patient regain her maidenly charms."

If only there was a tea to restore innocence! Half of this ship would be guzzling it by the bucketful -- still, I held my tongue.

Instead, I took the list in hand and surveyed the ingredients. It read like a passage ripped from Macbeth: ergot of rye, tansy leaves, oil of pennyroyal.

"I don't think a pharmacy will carry these."

But Magda was not flummoxed.

"No, you need no pharmacy. All you will find in that place is man's medicine, the chemists don't know the first thing about a woman's troubles. Here's what I suggest, Rose," she said, tapping her finger to the list, "Head northwest along the road to the little town of Esquimalt, and once you're there, find the largest, fanciest house. Knock upon the kitchen door and tell the housemaid or kitchen girl what you need. Tell them you can pay them well." She pressed an ancient, tarnished coin into my hand, and it felt heavy enough to be solid silver. "If there's a fine lady living in that house, or even a wealthy man with a mistress, then chances are very good that the housemaid has such items already stocked. This is one of those situations in which women of every class and station occasionally find themselves ensnared. It must be dealt with accordingly."

I promised to be back as soon as I could.

From my berth, I grabbed my shawls and bundled myself up like a birthday gift before leaving the wharf. When I'd joined the Circus Salmagundi, I'd made a solemn promise to Mr. Scott to hide my face and tattoos from the public -- after all, who would bother to buy a ticket to the Ten-in-One sideshow if they'd already seen the attractions? Discretion was required and that meant, when I visited a town or village, I became a ghost in an indigo smock with a silken scarf to hide my face. The outfit could be hot and constraining, and it always attracted stares and pointed fingers, but I wasn't too bothered by the attention.

Today, however, I wore my scarves like armour. When I walked off the boats, up the wharf, through the farmyard and out into the world of the curious public, the anonymity given by my mask and sweeping robe brought me great relief.

I'd lived in Victoria during the Great War. I knew well the grand city that curled around the Inner Harbour, its crooked streets and Chinatown, its parliament buildings and gardens. If I turned east and followed this country road all the way to the broad Point Ellice bridge, I could easily cross the Gorge Waterway and find myself in the same downtown core where I once bought dresses and met friends for lunch. As is the way of city-dwellers, I'd rarely bothered to leave town and wasn't familiar with the rural outskirts, but my husband had worked close to Esquimalt during the early years of the war and, on two occasions, I'd accompanied him to formal dinners at the Naval Base. We'd taken the streetcar that linked the dockyards to the city -- ah, yes, there it was, an electric trolley on a small gauge track, bisecting meadows and farms that were quickly turning to suburbs. As the country road met the streetcar line, I glanced east towards the city, where I could throw a stone and hit some building, landmark, or feature that I'd once known intimately; I turned my back to it all. The last thing I wanted was to be recognized by an old acquaintance from the shadows of my former life. How terrible would that be? I didn't care to explain myself or my situation, and I couldn't abide by anyone's pity.

However, as I started walking west towards Esquimalt, the gentle rolling fields sparked a few stray memories. Back in 1914, when I'd attended a dinner for officers and wives, the village had been a humble farming community surrounding an old naval base, but with the advent of the Great War, it had expanded into a military centre with shipyards, barracks, training grounds, and a convalescent hospital. I strolled along the roads expecting the small cottages and hay carts of my memories, but instead, found grand estates and motorcars. What a surprise! Over a few short years, the place had transformed into a bustling economic hub catering to the needs of wealthy industrialists: men who had made a skookum deal of money during the conflict and who sought rural estates where they could now play at being gentleman farmers.

The closer I walked to Esquimalt's centre, the fancier it became. The road surface turned from gravel to asphalt. The iron street lamps were topped with electric lights and flower baskets. I passed a fine hotel, a few general stores, and a busy Chinese laundry. Newly-planted trees marked the boundaries of future neighbourhoods. Sign posts had crisp edges, fish ponds were perfectly circular, hedges were trimmed with military precision. By God, the whole place had an aura that I might describe as *desperately pretty* -- a community of wealthy individuals striving to hide the grim memories of war behind a clean, posh, highly polished facade.

To the north of the shipyards, the post-war businessmen had snapped up property with pleasing ocean views and rolling clement parkland, the lots interspersed between more established manors from an earlier era. The owners of these Victorian estates -- meaning, not the city, but the queen -- had bequeathed fancy titles upon their mansions to reflect to their own elevated status. My husband had thought they were rather stuffy and ridiculous. We'd laughed together at their pompous epithets on our visits, but unspoken between us, we'd admired their beauty, too. 'Mount Adelaide' had been built in 1890 for Henry and Mary Dunsmuir Croft, and the mansion of 'Ashburn' was even older, surrounded by an orchard of mature fruit trees and gardens. Just north of the Dunsmuir property was a new mansion designed by the talented architect Francis Rattenbury for the previous mayor of Esquimalt, a gentleman named Mr. Coles. His sprawling house was stunning, set apart from its dull neighbours by its arched gingerbread along the eaves, tall brick chimneys, and decorative scrollwork along the upper floors.

It all seemed too perfect for my comfort. After a pleasant walk, I circled away from Esquimalt's core and headed once more towards the outskirts of the village where I might find country estates and genteel farms more fitting to my needs.

The day was cool but not cold, sunny but not hot. I was content to wander as far as necessary. I followed the road through cow pastures and forgotten woods to a row of lovely manor homes, each one nestled amongst groves of crooked oaks and swaying maples, the leaves turning with the season.

And then, coming over a knoll, I spied a place that seemed perfect to my eyes: a massive granite construction with ramparts and bay windows, surrounded by ferns and cherry trees, and situated in the middle of a verdant green lawn. The front of the property was bounded by box hedges and an imposing iron gate, but along the side of the lot ran a dirt path suitable for carts, and following it, I found a wooden gate open for deliveries. Through the gate, I hurried down a short drive that passed an orchard of new apple trees and a trellis ensnared in grape vines. Then I passed a walled herb garden and an enormous greenhouse that shared one wall with a chicken coop. The chickens clucked in the herb garden, scratching at the autumn earth for the last few grubs and crawlers, and from the top of the wall, a tabby cat watched them with little interest. The drive terminated at the rear of the mansion where three wide stone steps led down to a pair of wooden doors, and here the savoury smell of bread and roasted ham hung thickly in the air, making my mouth water. Beyond a doubt, this was the kitchen entrance.

I steadied myself, straightened my robes to make myself look as presentable as possible, and rapped on the door.

A young woman opened it. She was long-limbed and lanky, in her early twenties and probably similar in age to the Gibson sisters, but with a braid of glossy ebony hair and brown almond-shaped eyes, a round face and pointed chin, and a mouth that seemed slightly too large for her features. She wore a tan tweed dress with a modest cut that seemed perfectly suited for the autumn weather, protected by a white apron that was smeared with hay and grime. When she saw me at the door, looking like a ghostly figure wrapped up in colourful shawls, she jumped.

"I'm sorry, I don't mean to spook you," I stammered. "I've coming looking for some items to buy and I was hoping your kitchen might stock them." I thrust out the list before she had a chance to slam the door closed on me. "I can pay very well to whomever can share a little of their stock!"

"You -- you are all covered up --"

"My name is Rose Ivy, and I'm one of the performers with the circus that has come to Mr. Buckley's farm," I explained, and I pulled down my scarf to expose my face, showing the green vines that curled up from my torso to the base of my neck and the scars across my cheek. "See? I'm only a tattooed lady."

I hoped this revelation would put her at ease.

Instead, it was like setting a match to a Roman candle. Her expression blossomed into radiant excitement. She gave a girlish gasp followed by clapping hands, then squealed loudly, "Oh! The circus at Mr. Buckley's farm! I saw the posters! Oh, you gotta come in! Come in!"

Like a hapless leaf caught in the flow of the rushing stream, so I found myself sucked into a welcoming kitchen, bustling with hectic activity from all sides. Maids rushed hither and yon with copper pots, baskets of laundry, flats of eggs, brooms and rug beaters. The noise and clatter of rattling pans was like the staccato of gunfire. After my lonely ramble through the fresh countryside air, the heady scent of freshly baked loaves and the warmth of the ovens almost made me swoon.

But there was no time to collect myself. The woman took my hand in hers and shook it with gusto. "I'm May Tanaka, I'm one of the kitchen girls," she said, "Harriet! Harriet, look! It's a real tattooed lady from the circus!"

At the wooden counter on the other side of the room, a woman was bent to her work, her long neck and thin, wispy hair giving her the appearance of an ostrich. She must've been the head cook, for she was much too busy to bother with a stranger at the door. She gave me little more than a cursory glance before returning her attention to the mixing bowl and whatever troublesome sauce she was whisking.

May focused her full attention back on me. "What are you doing here, of all places?!" she laughed. "You said you need something?"

"I do," I replied, holding out the list again.

"Oh, Mrs. Stuckey can help you with that! She's Mr. Godwin's housekeeper and the head of staff, and she'll be able to say if we can share our stock. Stay right where you are and I'll fetch her for ya!"

Before I had time to thank her, the woman whirled away like a dervish, skirts flapping and apron strings snapping, returning a few minutes later with a middle-aged matron in a stiff grey pinstriped dress, buckled tight with a thin leather belt. The housekeeper had curly salt-and-pepper hair pinned close to her crown and a squared jaw set like a brick wall, and as she approached, her hard boot soles made sharp taps on the tile floor like the ping of a metronome. She wore a steely expression but remained unbothered by May's youthful enthusiasm.

"See, Mrs. Stuckey?" said May, breathless with barely-restrained excitement, "A real tattooed lady, here!"

The housekeeper examined me carefully through a pair of small round glasses, and her pinched expression didn't change at all. I felt diminished by her appraisal. Clearly, she was not as impressed by my profession as the young kitchen maid.

"Ah, yes, I see, so it is," she said. She had a soft, rolling accent,

English but not London. "Mr. Collins at the butcher shop told me there was a circus coming to town."

"We arrived last night. It was a terrible crossing from the mainland!"

"October is a wretched time to travel," she said as if I ought not to complain. After all, what did I expect? A pleasure cruise?

Best to get to the point with this prim woman. "I'm looking for provisions and I hoped you might be able to help." I unfolded my list and held the coin out in my palm. "I can pay very well, I'm not here for charity. I only need some medicine for a friend."

This eased her standoffish nature, just a fraction.

"What sort of items do you require, madam?"

Ah, here was where one must be delicate. I glanced at my list. "I'm looking for something to restore a woman's vitality," I said, "Tansy, pennyroyal or rue, perhaps."

She arched one narrow brow. The wrinkles alongside her mouth deepened. "To restore your friend's menstruation? Ah, yes, I understand completely." For a heartbeat, I braced myself for her reaction: would she give me a lecture on virtue and vice? Would she throw me out, accusing me of living a life full of sin and debauchery, and warn me that a woman who seeks pleasure should bear her punishment as it comes? The housekeeper gazed at the list as I waited for her judgment, and her expression betrayed nothing.

Then, with a little nod, she said, "Mr. Godwin lives here with his adult son and we do not have a missus in the house, but I do keep some of these items on hand should one of the girls in my employment require it. Ergot of rye is best, though I do not have much of it."

With relief, I said, "What about oil of pennyroyal?"

"A bad season for it. Perhaps tansy would be more effective?"

"Exactly the sort of thing my friend requires."

"And how far along is your friend?"

"By her own reckoning, a month. Maybe two."

"And has the baby quickened?"

I shook my head. "She didn't mention feeling any movement in her uterus."

"Then the babe has not been given its soul and that's very good news." She turned and beckoned for me to follow. "If she was at the quickening of her pregnancy, your friend would need more than mere herbs and teas to get the job done, and while I might be able to make the appropriate introductions for a criminal procedure, it would cost you a good deal more than your little silver coin. However," she said as she withdrew an iron skeleton key from a pouch on her belt, "I have a few things that will work for her present condition, don't you worry."

In the corner of the kitchen was a locked door made of thick wooden planks. Mrs. Stuckey used the key to open the door, and behind it, a stone staircase descended into an inky basement. "Come along, girls," she said, pulling on a cord. A series of electric light bulbs sizzled into dim illumination.

We went down into a vaulted chamber with a floor of packed earth. The air was cool and dry, and it probably stayed the same temperature and humidity all year long -- a perfect place for food storage. The entire length of the basement held oak barrels arranged in long lines, maybe a hundred of them, maybe more, but Mrs. Stuckey paid no attention to them. Instead, she led us to another door at the end of the vaulted chamber. This one was smaller and unlocked, and it opened on squeaking hinges into a sub-chamber with a floor tiled in slate.

The pantry was tall and narrow with no windows to let in the sun. The long shelves were fully stocked and carefully organized, and made a beautiful sight after the past few years of restrictions and rationing. In neat lines sat cakes of sugar and glass jars of fruits and vegetables, while on the floor sat crates of hay for storing apples, burlap sacks of turnips and carrots, and cotton bags of flour. At the far end of the room was a hardwood cabinet with a locked door, and Mrs. Stuckey used her skeleton key to unlock it. Inside were small jars of spices and herbs. She plucked one jar from a high shelf, rolling it in her hand to examine the contents. "Dried tansy brewed into a tea could work, but I admit, this stock is old and may not pack as much strength as your friend requires." She looked at me askance. "It is your friend, yes? Or is it you?"

"Oh, no, it's not me," I replied with a laugh. "I don't turn men's heads these days."

Mrs. Stuckey smiled at my statement and a little bit of warmth entered her expression. "I suppose not, dressed up in that pretty potato sack."

From behind us, May gave a cute, quick snort. "You've got a beguiling pair of eyes, Miss Rose. There's plenty of fellas that love a mystery!"

"I'm sure you have your share of admirers on the side show," Mrs. Stuckey added as she set the jar back on the shelf. "On closer inspection, this tansy won't do; it's too old to sell to you. All it will do is make your friend feel queasy." Her fingers played across the jars. "Let me see, this might be better." She brought down a vial containing an inch of pale, mercurial liquid. "A bit of quinine left over from last summer. I normally use it to make the lemon bitters that Mr. Godwin likes so much -- he grew accustomed to taking quinine while growing up in India, you see -- but at this time of year, he prefers hot drinks to stave off the cold and damp. He won't miss it." She handed me the jar. "Promise me, madam, you won't administer too much! Three drops in your patient's tea, every evening before bed, until her menstruation returns."

"I will show moderation," I promised as I paid her.

Then she locked up the cabinet again. "You must not rush the dosage and or you'll ruin the girl's liver in the process," she warned, "If I hear a whisper of death or illness, I'll refuse any knowledge of this exchange. We've never met."

"As expected," I replied, tucking the vial into my own pockets. "Thank you."

"You're most welcome. Who will take care of our feminine problems, if we cannot rely on each other?" she replied as she returned the key to her pouch. "Now, if you'll excuse me, I have a great deal of chores to prepare for Mr. Godwin's return this evening. He'll be bringing another crate with him, May, and we shall need to have the display cabinet in the entrance hall swept out and cleaned before the new mask arrives."

"Yes, Mrs. Stuckey."

"Mask?"

I could not keep the question from tumbling out of my lips. It was not my place to ask, but I've never been adept at knowing my place.

Mrs. Stuckey swivelled her gaze to me. Instead of reprimanding me, she gave a sharp, precise nod. "Mr. Godwin purchases tribal artifacts from around the world. His collection rivals any museum."

"Really!"

Seeing my interest, May stepped forward and set her hand on my forearm. Her enthusiasm for the circus shifted to that of sharing the collection. "Can I show Rose some of the masks? No one ever gets to see 'em and it's a crying shame!"

Mrs. Stuckey's pinched face took a second to consider. "Oh, I suppose you may. I see no harm in it... if you stay to the ground floor, and you're quick about it, and you finish your tasks by the time Mr. Godwin gets home." Her coolness melted a fraction and she bowed her head towards me. "Again, Miss Rose, good luck with your friend's difficulties. I wish you both good health." Then she circled on one foot and strode out of the pantry, her hard heels making a rapid tapping that vanished with distance.

Chapter Three

With a growing sense of wonder, I followed May into the labyrinth of a most luxurious house. We left the bustling kitchen and followed a straight gallery that extended along the length of the building, its only light source coming from a bay window at the far end of the hall. Carpets with a sumptuous floral pattern covered the corridor's floor, the walls were panelled with dark walnut, and heavy drapery in burgundy velvet flanked the window but had been tied back with heavy braided ropes of black silk. We passed open doors leading to chambers that contained a wealth of expensive furnishings and lush decorations, and my breath came out in a series of rapturous gasps, marking out the progressively astonishing treasures that we walked right by. May hardly noticed them, she was so accustomed to them. As for me, I was starting to feel dizzy.

But all of these domestic trappings, while luxurious, paled in comparison to the glass display cases that lined the hall. There must have been twenty of them, and each one contained an exotic artifact gathered from a distant land. Some of the larger cases held carved wooden bowls, others were laid out with intricate spoons or chipped stone spear tips, and yet others held fish hooks made of bone; two or three had been covered with canvas tarps to hide their contents from prying eyes.

Of all the cabinets, the most spectacular items were the masks!

"Good Lord!" I whispered as I tried to take it all in.

The masks stared at us as we strolled by, and I tried to examine each one and commit it to memory, aware that I would never see the likes of them again. Oh, but the variety and diversity were almost too much for one mind to absorb! Round, square, oblong, diamond-shaped, austere and plain or decorated with manes of fur and feathers. Some were carved from wood, some crafted out of leather, some were mosaic composites of shells and ivory; each expression held its own character and spirit. A few of the masks had companion items placed next to them in their case, as if they were showing off a prized possession in their care.

"These are remarkable!" I said in awe.

May gave a good-natured scoff. "This is the back corridor where Mr. Godwin puts the old ones. If you think these are amazing, you should see the ones in the front of the house!"

"Where did they all come from?"

"Oh, all over the world!" May said with pride. "Have you heard of Randall Godwin? Maybe not."

"I'm afraid our circles have not overlapped."

She giggled and tittered like a field mouse. "His family made their fortune in shipbuilding and he owns a shipyard here in Esquimalt. When the war broke out, he built a number of vessels for the navy to use." Her nose wrinkled as she added in a low tone, "The Canadian navy found itself woefully unprepared at the start of the war -- Mrs. Stuckey says we had two warships and less than 350 sailors, and hardly any firepower at all on the sea! It was a bit embarrassing. To make up the shortage, the Navy rented vessels from gentlemen like Mr. Godwin, and he's considered a bit of a hero to some folk around here."

I gazed into a circular face made of tight, grey seal hide. "So, what you're saying is, the war was good to him."

"Very good," she replied. "But you mustn't think he's some greedy old miser! Goodness, no! He has a fine reputation for being a patron of the arts." She bent down next to me and, together, we peered at the sealskin mask. "Mr. Godwin has to travel widely for business but, wherever he goes, he likes to purchase masks so that they are never ruined or destroyed. He says his collection ensures that these masks will be protected for future generations." She stood and gestured to the mask in the next glass case. "See this one? It's come all the way from the Congo! It is called Mwana Pwo. It represents a beautiful young woman."

I leaned in to examine it more deeply. Carved from a single block of chocolate-brown wood, the woman's face was triangular with a small nose, generous lips, and gracefully-arched eyebrows. Her hair was made of beaded strings. A fringe of woven grasses encircled her neck. With her eyes closed, she looked as if she was sleeping peacefully. Her cheeks and forehead had been inscribed with strange carvings: lines and whorls that accentuated the contours of her face.

"Why do they make masks of beautiful women?"

"I'm not sure. For some ritual or another, I suppose."

"What do the marks on her face mean?"

"Mr. Godwin said they represent scars," said May. "He said the women purposely cut scars into themselves to commemorate meaningful moments in their lives. Can you imagine!" She did a little double-take. "Oh, I'm so sorry! I didn't mean to insult!"

"None taken," I said, raising my hand to touch the scars on my face. There were only a few there, thankfully. My robes and tattoos hid the majority of the marks on my body, so May had no idea how painfully, intimately familiar I was with the act of scarification. To assure her, I said, "It's nice to hear of scars representing joy, rather than trauma."

Wanting to move our conversation along, May led me to the next cabinet: it was huge, five feet square, and contained a gigantic wooden mask of a bird with a great curved beak and a mane of twisted golden cords sprouting from the back of its head. The mask had been painted in red, black, and white. The lower jaw of the beak was hinged and held in place by a rope of twisted cedar bark: pulling on the rope would close the beak with a powerful clap.

"This one is called 'The Crooked Beak of Heaven'," said May, "It's a mythological creature from people who live north of here; I think Mr. Godwin called them 'Kwakiutl'. They once held massive celebrations where they would wear these masks and dance, but the government doesn't allow such heathen practices anymore. Too wasteful and savage, I suppose. Now, when they're discovered holding their potlatches in secret, the masks are confiscated, and sometimes they're burned, sometimes they're sent to museums." She smiled as she admired the bird mask. "But, lucky for him, Mr. Godwin knows a few Indian agents who give him advance knowledge of when a raid is about to take place, so he buys up the masks just as quick as they're taken. The agents make a bit of extra money and the masks are saved from the fire. It seems like a good deal."

"What about the people who owned the mask? What happens to them?"

"I don't know," she admitted. "They probably go to jail. After all, they're breaking the law."

"It seems like a stupid law, if you ask me."

"Well," she said, uncomfortable, "They're probably Christian now. Why would they need the mask anymore? At least, in Mr. Godwin's collection, it's safe and protected from harm."

Was it? Here in this dark and lonely hall, cut off from all human contact and any foreseeable use, I wasn't so sure. I gestured to the huge curved features. "Why does it have a crooked beak?"

The woman shrugged. "Oh, I don't know anything about the monster, I'm afraid."

"He doesn't collect the story that goes with it? Or why people wear it when they dance? Or how it's made?"

"Mr. Godwin doesn't bother with that sort of superstitious nonsense. He's more interested in the artistry than any practical purpose."

I tipped my head to one side. "But what good is it, without its practical purpose?"

She glanced at me. "What do you mean?"

"If I took a spoon and stuck it in a case, and never used it nor touched it, would it still be a spoon?"

"Of course, it would!" She scoffed. "Besides, your spoon would remain perfectly preserved for future generations to enjoy." She gazed at the mask again, rapturous. "This mask will always remain stunning. Mr. Godwin will make sure of it."

But the whole situation struck me as quietly pathetic. What good was an object if it was never used for its intended purpose? And if that purpose was lost, then what value did any of these items possess, except to be stared at blankly and admired from afar? These items had been lovingly made to use, to dance, to frighten or inspire, to tell stories or ward off ill fortune: they hadn't been created to sit passively in a box. The chill feeling in my gut was akin to visiting a zoo and watching a tiger trapped in a cage: these masks had been stripped of their reason for being. They'd been rendered inert.

I weighed whether I should share my opinion with May.

But she was already strolling to the next display case. It held a rectangular-shaped wooden mask with round eyes of inset abalone, and at its base sat a broad, flat paddle made of flawless, luminous jade. The stone was unmarked and polished smooth, but the mask was carved with ornate lines that ringed the eyes and zigzagged around the mouth, and the mask had its tongue sticking far out, as if it were mocking me. Yes, I thought as I crossed my arms and considered that expression, this one was clearly goading me into a brawl.

"What do you know about this friendly fellow?"

May crossed her arms. "Only a little. He's from New Zealand."

"The paddle next to him is gorgeous: I've never seen such a large slab of jade." "That's a war club called a *mere pounamu*," she replied. "A beautiful weapon, but it's a real pain to move because it's as heavy as a lump of lead. The man that carried it into battle must've had arms like tree trunks." She glanced at me and smiled broadly. "You wouldn't want to see that one put to its original use, I'd bet!"

"Perhaps it's safer in the cabinet," I agreed.

She beckoned me to follow to the end of the corridor. Here, the sunlight from the distant windows could not quite reach, and long shadows made for gloomy corners. The last glass case was a huge construction covered with a canvas tarp, and when she stopped in front of it, May beamed with happiness. "This one is my favourite. I think you'll like him, too."

She whipped back the canvas tarp.

I let out a shriek.

Inside the case was the most frightful mask I'd ever seen! No description could fully capture the demonic grimace with exposed peg-teeth, the toadstool nose, or the bulging eyes that lurked under heavy brows, between which sat a round boss like a giant wart. Its crown was topped with an exotic creature's piebald mane, more like curly wool than flowing hair, and long tufts of white fur like ermine tails framed the sides of its square face. From each temple sprouted massive ebony horns, spanning almost two feet wide, and a scant, bristly red beard covered its chin. Upon closer inspection, the jaw piece was hinged and held in place by leather cords so that, like the Crooked Beak of Heaven, it could open and close to the whims of the wearer.

But most arresting of all were the eyes -- a pair of terrible, all-seeing eyes -- that had been painted bright white with black discs for pupils, and protruded from under the brow as if the demon was choking or strangled. No matter where I stood, the eyes followed. I'd never seen anything so creepy.

"God have mercy!"

"Isn't he terrifying," May laughed. "I just love him!"

I crept closer to study the devil more intently. The wood from which the mask had been carved was scuffed and scratched from long centuries of use: it was ancient, that was easy to determine. Other than the mandible, the whole artifact had been carved from a single round of wood, and from the colour and texture, I guessed it might be white oak. Or, given the patina, maybe walnut? Really, I only know a little about wood from listening to Lou Grady as he fixes the deck boards on the *Atropos*, so I was certainly no expert, but I could see that the mask was meant to cover the entire head of the wearer, not just the face. The tree from which the round had been cut must have been very old, very large. As for the mask itself, it was a robust thing, and whoever wore it would need to possess immense strength and wide shoulders to support it!

"We keep it covered up because it's so scary," May said, still chuckling at my reaction. "Some of the other maids refuse to come down this hall because they're terrified of the demon."

"Where's it from?"

"I don't really know," she admitted, "India, I assume. Mr. Godwin grew up in Bengal and has a lot of connections in Asia, and this is one of the first masks he ever collected; Mrs. Stuckey told me he purchased it just after building this house, back in 1901."

"It looks ancient!"

"Well, he says the horns are from an aurochs, and they've been extinct since the 1600s, so I suppose it must be!"

I whistled low.

The eyes -- huge, monstrous swellings, each as big as a duck's egg -- contained dilated pupils that stared straight into your soul. It didn't matter if you moved left or right, they followed you with a hunger so intense, it could almost be interpreted as lust.

"I don't blame you for covering him up," I replied with a smile and a shudder. "This horrid beast wants to drag me right down to Hell, I'm sure of it!"

May laughed again as she pulled the tarp back into place. "It doesn't help that he sits in the darkest corner, where I haven't yet had a chance to dust away the cobwebs. I'm sure the old fellow would be much more presentable if he was out in the front foyer with the sunshine all around him, and those spectacular horns dusted and oiled."

"You can dust and oil him all day long," I said, "He'd still be fit for nightmares!"

We laughed together as she walked me back to the kitchen door, and continued outside with me as far as the chicken coop. The hens began cackling at the sight of her; she must be the one to feed them.

"Thank you for all your help, Miss Tanaka," I said, shaking her hand. "This has been a visit to remember."

"My pleasure!" she replied. "And I'm looking forward to seeing your sideshow on opening night."

"I'll watch for you," I said, "But please, for goodness sake, don't bring the devil along with you!"

Chapter Four

My walk back to Mr. Buckley's farm was very pleasant. The route took me between sheep fields skirting a tumbled forest of hemlocks, bounded by the ditches of berry-heavy brambles, and rising in a gentle slope to become a series of stony bluffs. Sandwiched between the city and the village, this strip of woodland was not a sinister forest at all but a very pleasing one, as civilized as such a landscape can be without relinquishing its independence, and certainly no wolves nor bears had lurked in its underbrush for many years. The road followed the woods for almost a mile, then dipped into a small valley only to climb again as it crossed the trolley line and revealed the southern shore. At the crest of the hill, I paused for a moment to gaze with weary satisfaction on Mr. Buckley's farmhouse, the low-slung cow barn with its attached grain silo, and the tidy squares of pastures where his cattle grazed. Our boats, still tied to the wharf and lashed to each other, bobbed gently in the narrow tidal bay against a backdrop of blue ocean, sun-dappled strait, and hazy Olympic mountains. If I turned my head to the left, looking eastward, I could see the bridge leading to tiny brick buildings and wooden roofs of Victoria, hazy with coal smoke. We were so close to the city where once I'd lived, and yet it all felt so very far away -- in distance, time, and philosophy.

I returned my attention to the present, to Mr. Buckley's property, which had undergone a magnificent transformation in my absence. The red-and-yellow striped Big Top tent had already been erected in the cornfield nearest the road, and Gertie's two large horses were hauling cargo up from the boats for tomorrow's performance. Off to one side in the middle of a sheep field, the side show tent was going up. With all the ropes and rigging, and a bevy of workmen swarming over the land, and red flags fluttering on the high pinnacles of the tent, the humble field had adopted the appearance of a pirate barge.

The view from the knoll was pleasant but there was no time to loiter. Enough with my lolly-gagging; I had a job to do and a parcel to deliver. I hurried straight to the docks, between the tents and across the yard, down to the wharf and up the *Nona*'s gangplank.

When I knocked on the door of the Gibson's berth, I found Calliope stretched out on her bed, reading. If she was pleased that I'd returned, she didn't show it. As soon as I stepped inside their room, she scowled.

"I've been sitting here for hours, Rose!" she moaned, "I was starting to think that you weren't coming back!"

"Of course, I'd come back, Calliope. It took a bit of time for me to get what you need," I replied.

"But you found the medicine?"

"I did," I assured her, "A woman named Mrs. Stuckey very kindly found some quinine for you. And the house I visited was marvellous!"

Her scowl deepened. "What's this? You were on a jaunt while I was here, sick with worry?"

"You make it sound like I've been gone for days!"

She dropped her book with a huff. "I can't believe you'd let me sit here, worried half to death, while you went sightseeing. Especially now, in my time of need!"

I suddenly found myself longing for those halcyon days when the Gibson sisters ignored me in all regards.

"Well?" she pressed, "Explain yourself! How could you be so heartless! I thought you were a nurse!"

"I wasn't a nurse," I corrected, "And the house contained a

wonderful collection of things, and there was no harm in me taking a quick peek while I was there; after all, you aren't going anywhere, and I may never get another chance to see such treasures again."

"Treasure?" This perked her up. "Like gold and silver?"

"No, more like exotic artwork," I replied. "The man who owned the house, a Mr. Godwin, collects artifacts from around the world."

She sneered. "That all sounds rather grubby and primal."

"Perhaps it's not for everyone," I said between gritted teeth. I pulled the vial from the pocket of my robe with a wizard's flourish. "But see? Voila!" I set it in her palm.

"This is... quinine, did you say?"

"The same as you'll find in any gin and tonic," I replied, "But this is much more concentrated! You must be very careful not to take any more than three drops in your morning tea for the next three days. Do you understand me, Calliope?"

She splashed the liquid around. "Three drops, morning tea."

"Yes, only three drops a day. After a few days, it will bring on your blood -- but once your blood starts, don't take any more! Understood?"

"Alright, fine," she said, peeved. "I heard you the first time." She set the vial down on her bedside table, then folded her hands in her lap and looked at me expectantly. After a pause that was cringe-worthy in its length and crushing silence, she said, "You have to leave, Rose. Morris and I are going to take a stroll. He'll be here any minute to fetch me."

I was being dismissed. Was I surprised to be shunted out of her state room with nary a thank you? Of course not. I rolled my eyes at my own folly.

As I headed off the *Nona* to return to my own ship, I passed Morris standing near the end of the wharf, smoking a cigarette. He wore a pair of canvas overalls and a slope hat on his head, and he must have been exhausted after helping to set up the tents so quickly, but he didn't show it. Instead, he looked composed and fresh-faced, contemplative as he gazed out across the steel-coloured waters to the American shore. He was a tall fellow in his late 20s, and his down-turned eyes and patrician nose gave him an air of haughtiness, but once he started a conversation, the man wasn't nearly as stuffy as he might first appear; he spoke in an easy, rolling West Country accent that was both friendly and, at times, flummoxing. When he saw me descending the gangplank, he held up his hand.

"Where be to, Miss Rose?" he greeted.

"On my way back to my own ship, Mr. Cave," I said kindly, "The tents are up, I see. Well done!"

"Good lord, what a chore," he exclaimed. "But it's all done and ready for tomorrow. A proper job! We were finished early so I had a chance to help Mr. Buckley with storing his September hay in the barn where it can dry out over winter. A good man, he is, though a mite too jolly for my comfort."

"I've only seen him from a distance. I haven't had the pleasure of an introduction yet," I admitted.

Morris gave me a knowing look. "Oh, just you wait, ee's a boot!"

Without exactly understanding this phrase, I laughed. "I look forward to it. And I've just met with Miss Calliope: I hear you're taking her for a stroll before dinner?"

"Ah, yes," he said. His voice dropped in volume. "She told me she was going to speak with you and Mrs. Magda today."

The brittleness in his eyes betrayed his concern.

I lowered my voice as I stepped closer to him. "I found the medicine she needs," I assured him, "But do keep a close eye on her, would you? She'll need a good friend through the next few days, and I don't know if Honoria will be very compassionate. That one strikes me as a demanding sister."

He shuffled his boots, almost sheepish. "That I can do," he said. "I never meant to put Calliope in a problematic way."

"It happens," I assured him. "But you two be careful from now on! Did you not learn the importance of prophylactics when you were a soldier?"

At the mention of it, he blushed. "My commanding officer told us to use them things to keep from getting the French pox, but we're a long way from France here, Miss Rose!" He shifted his weight from foot to foot, chuckling in quiet embarrassment. "I didn't think women talk about such things. That's all a man's problem, it is. My father always told me that a proper lady never has to worry about nasty diseases."

Poor lad. He probably knew more about the physiology of a ewe or a cow than a female of his own species.

"If you have questions, Morris, I'm happy to help," I assured him, "You are always welcome to ask me anything you like. No topic is taboo, understood? I'd rather we have an uncomfortable discussion, and you learn all you need to know, then to brew up tinctures to treat your syphilis or gonorrhoea, understood?"

The mention of medical terms made his pink cheeks flush a deep red.

"I promise I will, Miss Rose."

"Good lad," I said. "But, in some strange way, I must thank you and Calliope, I suppose. The house I visited today was remarkable, and I'd never have had an opportunity to visit it if I hadn't been asked to help."

He took a drag on his cigarette. "Remarkable? How so?"

"The gentleman who owns the estate also collects exotic art," I explained, "And through the generosity of a serving girl, I was given a quick tour of the ground floor. You would not believe the array of remarkable carvings and masks he's assembled! I've never seen anything like it. I'm sure I never will again!"

Morris paused with his cigarette halfway to his lips. "Masks, you say?"

"Yes! Wondrous things! Beautiful things!" I replied, "This gentleman, Mr. Godwin, is an avid collector with a good eye and very deep pockets. The kitchen maid assured me that he's a great patron of the arts and a bit of a war hero in these parts."

"You don't say!" he exclaimed. His face glowed with wonder and fascination; as a bit of an artist himself, he was clearly intrigued by this kindred spirit. He flicked the stub of his cigarette off the side of the dock and the orange ember whirled through the air until it died with a hiss in the water. "By chance, did you meet this Mr. Godwin?"

"No, he wasn't home," I replied. "The housekeeper, Mrs. Stuckey, mentioned that he was returning tonight. Honestly, that's fine by me, I'm no fancy guest and I don't care at all to hobnob with the rich. I'm just pleased to admire their art collections."

"And who'd have thought there'd be such marvels in this part of the world! Here, of all places!" he exclaimed.

"Not me, that's for sure," I agreed. I bid him good-night as he went to fetch Calliope, and I headed off to my own ship's galley to eat a spot of dinner, rest my weary feet, and prepare for tomorrow's performance.

Chapter Five

Nothing compares to an opening night of the Circus Salmagundi! It's almost impossible to describe in stodgy English words how magnificent a lowly cow field becomes under a transformative string of lights. The tents bulge with music and laughter, and the air buzzes with the anticipation of children and performers. What had once been an unassuming dairy farm on the edge of a pastoral bay had, in only a few short hours, been revolutionized to a lively fairground where people could gather for a night of delights and marvels. An enthusiastic band of musicians played a lively march. A trio of clowns in white grease paint -- Lou, Bobby, and our sour Mr. Scott -- capered amongst the knots of amused children, tossing them penny sweets and lucky charms. The twilight gloom hid most of our rough edges. The roustabouts had even strung lights along the eaves of the barn and spiralling all the way to the summit of the grain silo. People could spot the Buckley farm for miles in all directions.

But with a pea-soup fog rolling in off the sea and an icy breeze slithering over the fields from the north, the quality of light had adopted a baleful cast and our circus magic felt somewhat diluted. During the summer, opening nights are friendly and frolicsome, but October possesses a certain gravity that July or August can't match, and with winter prowling closer and closer, a quiver of apprehension filled the frosty air. Parents, terribly afraid of the Spanish flu, bundled their offspring in jackets and scarves. Wound up tight in their heavy woollen clothes, the children were more reserved than their summertime counterparts, who would whoop and cheer at the smallest provocation. No, autumn was not a time for light-hearted tomfoolery. The clowns stamped their feet and rubbed their cold hands together. Our breath made plumes in the crisp air. If this had been a summer performance, the sun would still be shining, but tonight, the tents were cast in purple gloom. The dark came a little earlier each night.

Magda perched upon a stool at the front entrance to the Big Top, selling tickets. Wrapped in a big tartan blanket, she looked like a mountain of green and brown topped by a snow-white knitted cap. I was hurrying from the ships to my place in the Ten-In-One when she whistled across the farmyard to call me over.

"You found what we needed today?" she asked me as she sold tickets to a man and his family.

"Yes, and I've already handed it off to Calliope," I replied from behind my veils. "Morris seemed happy."

"And how did Calliope respond?"

"She's eager to move on."

Magda's eyes squinted when she grinned. She took a bit of money and counted out two tickets for the next couple in line. "Well, you have my gratitude. I'd have gone myself but -- thank you, enjoy the show -- I doubt I could have walked so far." She patted her gravid belly.

The line was longer than I'd expected. It was going to be a busy evening. I excused myself and headed towards the Ten-In-One.

The sideshow had been set up to the right of the Big Top, a little distance away so that we wouldn't be overshadowed by the noise and applause from the main acts, and the Ten-In-One tent had been ingeniously designed for crowd-control and people-moving: it was long and narrow, made of thick dun-coloured canvas, and divided into ten equal cubicles. Visitors bought their ticket and entered at one end, moving down the line to spend five minutes in each section, progressing from cubicle to cubicle until they reached the exit. The Ten-In-One provided a simple, elegant way of retaining our mystery, entertaining the public, and separating money from the wallets of the curious and gullible.

The entire front of the Ten-in-One was decorated with colourful canvas posters that described, in very fanciful and somewhat fictional terms, the oddities to be found inside. Tonight, on this damp and dreary evening, these flapped in the breeze like war-banners on a forgotten battlefield. Compared to the noise and clatter of the Big Top, our little sideshow seemed grim, grey and lonely. It had been erected downhill from the farmhouse and barn, closer to the water and at the edge of a sheep pasture where the dirt was softer and covered in weeds; how cold would my toes be by the end of the night, I wondered.

At least the posters promised wondrous delights within. They were each a work of art in their own right. Morris had painted them all.

First was the banner for Saltchuck Cecil, who could hold his breath for an extraordinary length of time, and he'd been painted up to look like a salamander -- although, to be fair, he was skinny and a bit goggle-eyed, so perhaps that depiction wasn't too exaggerated. Next to him hung a banner for Stella the Bearded Lady, a flattering portrait with a luscious brown beard; how Morris had been able to both exaggerate her beauty AND her beard, all at the same time, was a small creative miracle. Next came a painting of Argos the Blockhead, showing him nailing a spike into his own nose with a horrid grimace of agony, and then a banner for Martin Spindle, our beloved human skeleton, and then a banner for Morris himself, a self-portrait of the young man playing his ukulele. Next came a poster for Fletcher the Talking Raven, wings outstretched and wicked beak parted, and then a portrait of Dr. Hector Kane's Cabinet of the Bizarre, and a poster for Mary Scott the world's tiniest magician, and for me, Rose Ivy the tattooed lady. His depiction made me roll my eyes. There I was in my chemise and bloomers, as bright as a bird-of-paradise, with cherub lips and generous bust and a backside fit to make wolves whistle. Pure fancy, of course. Morris had been very kind.

But the final banner was the most thrilling of all: a long-haired, filthy, rag-garbed wretch known only as the Geek, tearing apart a rooster with his bare hands. Morris had painted the blood in a wide spatter, reaching into the edges of the banner, as if the material itself had been soaked in chicken guts.

It was suitably revolting.

Hugo Scott, Magda's 15-year-old son, sold tickets at the front of the Ten-In-One. I bid him hello as I slid through the front tent flap, then took my place in my own cubicle, removing my robe and sitting upon a folding wooden chair in my under-garments. God have mercy, it was chilly in here! By the time the first crowd of lookie-loos arrived, my fingertips were tingling, not to mention my other pink parts! The group, comprised of mostly middle-aged men, was rowdy but not too drunk. One of the perks of prohibition was a greater percentage in every crowd of sober gents who could talk reason to their frisky peers, and while rumours swirled that prohibition might soon be repealed in British Columbia, it hadn't happened yet. A few individuals were frolicsome but I was able to contain their excitement with a couple of saucy jokes and a shake of my shoulders.

Still, I thought, if this was tonight's caliber of client, it was going to be a long week ahead! The families headed into the Big Top but very few children visited the sideshow. Depending on the community, parents might view us as tawdry or seedy, and rural communities could be more religious, less curious, more insular and withdrawn. It seemed like the fathers and mothers of Esquimalt were a conservative bunch.

Or, I thought suddenly as I swatted away a patron's eager pinch, they might be willing to risk the spacious arena of the Big Top, but prefer to avoid the crowded cubicles of the Ten-in-One where miasmas might linger. That was understandable; no one wanted to risk picking up a sniffle that could swell into another full-blown epidemic. God, how terrifying the last few years had been! We were all much more cautious since the Spanish Flu had swept through the Pacific Northwest, when everyone had lost a family member or two. The last thing any of these fine people wanted was to risk another outbreak, and honestly, I couldn't blame them.

Suddenly, the curtains parted in a flapping and snapping of hems.

"Oh, ho, ho! Look at THIS!"

The man's voice was big and round and resonant like the boom of a kettle drum. I'd seen him from a distance but not close-up, and Mr.

Buckley was a hearty, full-figured giant wearing a grey flannel suit, a red bow tie, and a pair of mud-caked gumboots on his massive feet. With his round, ruddy face and thick thatch of blond hair, he looked like a jolly medieval monk with a tonsure.

He strode directly for me, a torpedo on a collision course.

"By all the saints, you must be Rose Ivy, am I correct? Oh, ho! What a LARK! So lovely to meet you!"

My hand was suddenly engulfed in two sweaty paws and pumped violently up and down. I stammered, my breath in my throat, my heart beginning to hammer in my chest. The man saw the sudden look of fear in my face. He released me instantly.

"My goodness, I didn't mean to FRIGHTEN you, love!" he bellowed, and his grin was a huge Cheshire-cat affair. "I'm Louis Buckley, my dear, and you are simply LOVELY to look at! The colours! Look at 'em!" He stepped back and held out his arms like he was appraising livestock. "That must've taken HOURS!"

"A few weeks, actually," I sputtered in a small voice.

"Aren't you SOMETHING!" he boomed, turning to the rest of his group: a plain-faced woman with a snot-nosed baby balanced on her hip, two young boys who must have been twins, and a bony girl with missing front teeth and thick brown pigtails. "Have you EVER seen anything like it, Iris?"

"No, never," said his wife as she bounced the baby, "Thank you for coming, it's very sweet to meet you."

"And you," I said.

"I apologize, my Louis is a big presence," she said in a tired voice, "But he does love the circus."

He started to guffaw so loudly, I swear the tent walls fluttered with every exhalation. "If I can't run away and JOIN one, I may as well bring one HERE!" he replied. "I hope you'll make yourself comfortable while you're my guest, Rosie! Alex tells me that you've been a quality performer -- he had nothing but glowing endorsements about your talent."

I knew from ship's gossip that Mr. Scott had introduced our ring-master, Alexander Crask McGee, to Mr. Buckley and the two had become fast friends, although to be frank, everyone became fast friends with the charming Scotsman. Alex was so likeable, so convivial, and so delightful, he never gave anyone an opportunity to dismiss him. He was smooth-talking, eager to discuss most topics over a glass of whiskey from his secret stash, and willing to embark on any mischievous adventure, and those qualities made him very popular with the men. Of course, with his dark hair and fine physique, he was also incredibly handsome and a little cocky, which made him very popular with the ladies, too.

"Alex is very kind to say so," I replied.

"When I told Grover that he MUST bring you all here, he leapt at the chance, and we're just so HAPPY to have you all. Folks are DESPERATE for any form of entertainment, as you must know."

I nodded. "The last few years have been a challenge."

His laughter boomed out again. "Challenge! Did you hear that, Iris? We've survived a WAR and a PLAGUE and Miss Rose here only thinks it was a challenge! Like some sort of SACK race, hey?" He leaned in close; his breath smelled of pickled beets and ale. "Remind me to keep you CLOSE when Armageddon comes, Miss Rose! I'll want a woman of your FORTITUDE on hand!"

I nodded my thanks as he moved through to the next act, his wife and children silently trailing after him. I heard Mr. Buckley greet Dr. Kane in the same boisterous way, followed by the exuberant clinking of glass jars and the droll voice of the doctor begging Mr. Buckley to please put the specimens back down. I squeezed my eyes closed. The touch of his hand on mine still burned. My heart still pounded in my chest. I took a series of deep breaths as I tried to steady myself, only to jump again when a gentle voice said, "Are you okay, Rose?"

When my eyes flashed open, May Tanaka's friendly face appeared. She was wearing a thick grey coat and sunflower-yellow scarf, and she looked gravely concerned. Behind her stood Mrs. Stuckey, her lips held stiff and tight, her eyes narrowed. She studied my face like a falcon.

"Miss Tanaka! And Mrs. Stuckey, too! Thank goodness!"

"Are you alright?" said the housekeeper, "You've gone very pale."

The kitchen maid noticed how little I was wearing and asked, "Aren't you terribly cold? You look half frozen!"

"Oh, I'll be fine," I replied. My hands trembled, but not from the cold. I clasped them tightly on my lap. "The canvas cuts the wind well enough, and my oil lamp gives off a little heat. No, I just find some folks to be a bit overwhelming, that's all."

"Mr. Buckley?" said May with a restrained smirk.

"He can be quite a ham, but he's mostly harmless," Mrs. Stuckey added. "He's simply over-excitable."

My heart still pounded, a sheen of sweat cooled the back of my neck, and I knew my reaction was more than a mere aversion to Mr. Buckley's enthusiasm, but I decided not to elaborate. No one wants to hear about my violent past or the uncontrolled panic I feel at the touch of a gentleman's hand; it's better to just change the subject. "How wonderful to see you, May," I said as I turned the conversation, "You should have told me you were coming! I'd have put aside a free ticket for you."

She waved away the offer. "Aw, ain't you lovely! But there's no need. One of your co-workers already put two aside for us."

"It was that plucky young man named Morris who plays the ukulele a few spots before you," said Mrs. Stuckey, "He came by the house this morning, expressing his appreciation for the quinine."

"Oh, no, I'm sorry he bothered you!" I replied to the two women. "Morris has a sweet heart but he doesn't always pay much attention to good sense."

"It's not a problem," said the housekeeper, "Mr. Godwin was away most of the day in the city. Your lad bothered no one."

"I'll remind him to mind his place in future."

May crooked her thumb towards the front of the tent. "Did he paint the banners? He has real talent! He asked very politely if he could see the masks, so I showed him the Crooked Beak of Heaven. He was much impressed and inspired by it."

"I'm sure he was," I replied, "I should have known he'd be fascinated to see Mr. Godwin's collection. When I mentioned my visit yesterday, he was very keen to see the artwork, but I never guessed he'd overstep his bounds." I shook my head at the folly of youth and said, "And how about you? Are you enjoying the sideshow?"

"Oh, it's wonderful, but that fog outside is thick!" she laughed, drawing her coat around her shoulders a little more tightly.

"We should hurry, May," said Mrs. Stuckey, checking her watch,

"The show in the Big Tent starts in a half-an-hour. I dearly hope it will be a little warmer in there!"

"With everyone crammed together in their seats, and the electric lights blazing, and the horses galloping around the edge, and the ponies and dogs -- yes, you'll find it much more comfortable that our Ten-in-One!" I laughed.

"Oh, you poor thing," May crooned. She unwound the yellow scarf from around her neck. "Take this. You need it more than I do." She wrapped it around my bare shoulders. It was very pretty, with pale pink roses and a white fringe, and when I protested, she said, "No, you keep it, I insist! You look like you need any bit of spare warmth you can find!"

"Don't you catch a chill, Miss Rose," Mrs. Stuckey instructed in a most matronly way, "We wouldn't want you to catch your death." She patted her palm against my cheek and together, the two women continued on to Dr. Kane's display of oddities and pickled punks.

By then, the next group was entering; this would be our final side-show audience of the night, the last to visit me before the Big Top show began. Once the main attraction started, the side show performers would be finished for the evening because, honestly, who'd want to see a sideshow when the main tent was full of magic? As for me, I was eager to be done -- I looked forward to a hot cup of tea on the *SS Atropos* to work the blood back into my fingers and toes again!

Alas, it was not to be.

Chapter Six

When the Ten-In-One's night came to a close, I left through Dr. Kane's cubicle, where I found him arranging his jars neatly upon the table, tidying up after a wearying performance. I'm sure Mr. Buckley's wandering hands had left them in complete disarray.

"Good evening, Miss Rose," he said.

"Good evening, Doctor," I replied.

"I hear you've been visiting the finest houses in the area," he said, arching one eyebrow in my direction. "How did someone of your caliber make it through the front door?"

"Ah, there's the trick," I said, "I snuck in through the back."

He smirked, which in combination with the low light cast from his oil lamp, created a ghoulish expression on his gaunt face. Hector Kane was a slim man who stood with a slight stoop, and he had a tendency to dress in dark suits like a funeral director. He had spidery fingers and a hawkish nose, a dry sense of humour that rarely revealed itself, and a broad knowledge of the natural sciences that made him an interesting conversationalist, if he was in the mood for idle chatter. His skills in taxidermy were second-to-none.

I plucked up one pickled punk and admired the grotesque form floating inside the jar: a two-headed turtle.

"This must be your best work," I said, "I can't even see the stitches."

"That is because there are none," he replied as he pulled on his grey overcoat, "That particular beast was an abomination created by the frightful genius of God Himself."

A shiver went through me. "It was born like this? How awful!"

He picked up his lamp. "The turtle is one of my favourite finds," he boasted as he pushed through the curtain into the final cubicle. He glanced towards the wheeled iron cage that had been parked to one side of the room. "Good evening, old chap," he said in its direction.

A shuffle and a grunt were the only reply. Behind the thick bars squatted a humanoid hump under a mangy, matted pelt, curled into a ball with dirty arms wrapped around filthy knees. The head was angled down. Tangled hanks of greasy black hair and a thick beard hid the face. I didn't like being in the cubicle of the Geek; even when he was sitting perfectly still, he had a silent, predatory intensity that made me uneasy, and I never approached his cage. He was as barbarous and unpredictable as a gorilla, and I likened him to a coiled spring, full of potential that would certainly erupt who knows not when. He possessed long, muscular arms and frightful, gnashing teeth, and he never spoke a word to anyone. Nancy, the dog-and-pony lady, warned me that he'd once ripped the head off a passing cat with his bare hands.

But even with my apprehension of the Geek, a bolt of surprise shot through me when Kane blew out the small lamp hanging from the crossbeam, thrusting the cubicle into sudden darkness. Kane held open the tent flap to let me through, but I paused.

I looked to the cage, then back to Kane. "What about him?"

"Who?" Kane said, "The Geek?"

"Of course, the Geek!" I said, "You can't leave him out here all night!"

"Miss Rose, there's no need to be concerned. He's an imbecile. He's like an animal; he feels neither fear nor cold nor shame."

I glanced at the motionless hulk in the cage. "Balderdash! You can't leave the poor man here to suffer in the dark. We must bring him back to the ships."

At that proclamation, Kane gave a bark of a laugh. "How? You've seen the production it takes to hoist the iron cage out of the cargo hold, then use the horses to haul it to the sideshow. I'm afraid Gertie is currently dancing atop her horses in the main tent right now, and neither you nor I have the strength to move that beastly cage, so here the Geek will stay. Don't worry, I'll bring him a hot bowl of porridge to eat in the morning. He'll be perfectly safe until then."

A gust of raw, icy wind cut through the open tent flap.

"He will not!" I said, "You'll come out in the morning and find him frozen solid!"

"I told you," Dr. Kane repeated, exasperated. "He's an imbecile. He's unable to feel the cold." He waved his hand in my general direction. "In my opinion, your foolish female meddling is doing him more harm! He craves solitude, Miss Rose, and you are keeping him from it."

I looked from the doctor to the poor wretch in the cage, and for a single moment, the light of Kane's lamp reflected on one bright grey eye, hidden under knots of black hair, watching me intently.

Maybe it was May's generosity in giving me the scarf, or maybe it was my own reaction to the dreadful chill, that sparked empathy in me. Whatever the reason, a wellspring of pity blossomed in my heart, leading to an unpredictable impulse.

"I'll stay out here and keep a fire going," I decided.

"What?!"

"It's no problem," I said, "The tent is wide enough. I can build a little fire here and it will keep us both warm."

Kane let out a frustrated sigh. "You'll only catch pneumonia."

"I'll be fine," I replied and I retired to my own cubicle to grab my folding wooden chair. When I returned to the Geek, the doctor was gone. Kane hadn't bothered to wish me good night; if I was going to be a fool, he'd rather waste no more of his precious time arguing.

But he'd left a box of matches on his table of pickled punks. I rekindled the oil lamp that the doctor had extinguished, then hurried out to collect a bit of kindling and cordwood from Mr. Buckley's shed. It was simple enough to build a merry little bonfire. I tied open the top corner of the tent flap to give us ventilation, and the smoke made its way out as a bit of fresh air made its way in, and a few moments later, the space felt very warm and cozy. Outside, I heard the muted sounds of the main show: the gasps of awe from the audience, the whinnying of ponies, the swell of musical interludes. I'd seen the acts practiced so many times, I knew every minute of it by heart, so I sank back on my chair and closed my eyes to imagine the show that was unfolding, using only the sounds to guide my imagination. At last, the rising murmur of a hundred voices chatting about their evening indicated that the townsfolk were leaving together, a mass of satisfied customers sounding like a distant flock of geese or the hush of the waves washing over gravel. The show was finished. Crowds moved homeward along the roads, hurrying back to their own comfortable houses in carts or on horseback or by foot across the fields, and not long after that, the performers made their way down to the waiting ships, where they'd eat dinner and drink ale and tuck themselves into bed, feeling satisfied.

Without the music to distract me, I felt cold and hungry. That blossom of pity in my heart wilted, just a bit, to be replaced by the sly weed of jealousy.

"It's dreadful how Kane treats you so callously," I said to the Geek. "You should have a room of your own, don't you think? I can't imagine living in that cage is very good for your health, physical or mental."

That single glittering eye appeared over the filthy arm, under the curtain of greasy hair.

"When did you last bathe?" I asked. "Or speak? Or even stand upright on solid ground?"

The eye closed. The matted pelt rose up like a shield as he curled his bare feet under him, covered himself a little more, turned one shoulder and shunned me.

"Fine, we don't need to talk," I replied.

Just then, I heard Morris' voice through the tent flap, "Miss Rose? Are you here?" He opened it up and poked his head through. "The doctor said you were staying in the tent tonight? I didn't believe it! You must really enjoy camping, to be out here with no provisions and only the fire to cheer you."

"Come in, Morris, you're letting out all the warmth," I invited, and I heard a low growl rumble through the Geek's chest but I ignored it. "I've stoked a fire and we're very comfortable for the moment."

"I brought you a few blankets and a bowl of stew and a book to read," he said as he handed each item to me, "It's 'My Man Jeeves'. I found it quite funny. And if you want to swap places, I'd be happy to come back and check on you in a bit."

"That's very kind."

"Ere, no trouble at all," he smiled as he backed out the door, keeping watch of the Geek the whole time; he'd heard the stories, too. I wrapped myself in the blanket, pushed and snuggled another chunk of dry wood on our camp fire, and settled in with food and book to while away the quiet hours.

I snorted awake in darkness, my head on the weedy ground, as the empty bowl thumped into the soft dirt near my head.

Disoriented, I rose to my elbows, then remembered I'd been reading and, with the warmth and the full belly, I must have dozed off and slipped from the chair. Mercy, the fire was almost out! The air had grown brutally cold.

"Oh, damn it all," I muttered to myself as I grabbed a couple of sticks of kindling. My hands were too stiff to work without effort; it felt like ice had formed between my knuckles, and I had to rub my fingers vigorously before they'd open and close again. Then it took a few minutes to get the fire burning, stoking up the embers until they crackled and flamed. Once that was done, I plucked up the bowl -- licked clean, I noticed -- and glanced towards the Geek. He must have reached his hand out and stretched his arm to its full length to grab my bowl from where it had fallen, then tossed it near enough to rouse me. Or maybe he was aiming for my head.

Whatever his target, the Geek sat in the opposite corner of the cage now, nearest to the door, with his head up and one hand exposed, the waves of black hair tumbling down over his rag-covered shoulders and his bearded face wreathed in flickering shadow. He stared towards the tent flap. I found his expression impossible to read: he was as calm and placid as a fathomless lake.

"So, you were cold and figured you'd wake me?" I asked, peevish. My hips ached, my spine cramped. I felt wrung out and old. "God, it must be early. Morris never came back... ah, I don't blame him. You are dull company."

That comment earned me a grunt and nothing more. Now that I'd re-built the fire, the Geek had what he needed. He turned his back to me.

But I needed to stretch my legs and my shoulders, so I wrapped the blanket around my torso and stepped out into the October night. The fog from earlier this evening had lifted; it seemed as if a wide black bowl of obsidian glass stretched over my head, containing an infinite number of glittering stars. I took a restorative breath of fresh air, so crisp that it burned my throat and stabbed at the deepest lobes of my lungs, and I snuggled the blanket tightly around my neck as I stepped out into the yard. No moon, no street lamps, nor lights in the farm house interrupted the perfect velvety darkness. The only source of illumination was the weak line of golden firelight cast through the edge of the tent flap and a single lantern hanging from the stern of the *Atropos*, reflecting in a series of crescent shapes off the choppy surface of the bay. My eyes detected a faint glow to the east where the first hint of the rising day gave hope that night would end.

A hush of movement in the grass, a footstep in the soft earth. I turned towards the sheep field that neighboured the Ten-In-One tent, expecting to see a forgotten ewe grazing along the rock wall.

Instead, I saw horns.

A deer? A stag! The shape moved slowly, with great purpose, as it lumbered along the wall, but then it raised its head, and I saw immediately that the great horns upon its brow were not branched, but singular. A bull?

It emitted a soft sound like the moan of a lover in the throes of ecstasy. The beast was moving away from me and hadn't spotted me and, if I stayed perfectly still, maybe it would pass by without notice. My breath caught in my throat. A chill travelled through my core. The sound was like no cattle I'd ever heard before. It was almost a song, but softly sung, like a lullaby whispered to the grasses and clover. Another moan. Another soft sweet cry. The shoulders rocked back and forth like a raft on a rising tide as it moved up the hillock, away from the yard.

And then, as it reached the highest point of land, it pulled itself up.

On two feet it stood, twelve feet tall, rising like a giant from an earthen tomb, with those sweeping horns creating a crescent moon in the pitch-black sky. Two naked arms lifted as if reaching to embrace the heavens. It swayed and swung, circling to the north and the south as the sound of its lament rose a little louder. The song grew more ecstatic and the sound drew a fresh volley of gooseflesh to my arms, not the result of the cold but of occult dread.

I stood in mute awe. This was no animal -- but it was no man, either. Its presence was old and preternatural. The beast's quiet call resonated with a frequency that was too strange and eldritch to be made by a tongue of human flesh. My brain struggled to understand what my eyes were witnessing as the terrible creature strode back and forth across the highest crest of land, holding out its palms, diving its head down low only to thrust itself upwards again, shaking its mane and tossing its scimitar horns.

'I am dreaming,' I thought in a sudden panic, finding comfort in the revelation, 'This is a dream and I have nothing to fear.'

But if I had nothing to fear, then what made my heart hammer in my chest? Why was my mouth dry? How could this moment feel so very, very real? My body remained frozen in place by the bizarre pageantry that played out before me, and I wanted to run or call out for help, but who would hear me? The only two creatures that existed in this mirror-world were myself and the minotaur on the green. A trembling fit came over me and I clung to the blanket in an effort to stay standing, but mercifully, the beast hadn't noticed my presence. It wove a purposeful path through the pasture, bowing down and rising up, and the demon was too engrossed in its uncanny rites to pay any attention to me, a mere mortal, who'd been struck silent and impotent with terror.

I watched and waited and prayed to God that it would pass me by. How long I stood in the yard I'll never know, but isn't that the way with dreams? Time has no meaning there. A century might flash by in the blink of an eye, while a second can stretch out across the length of forever. I no longer breathed. I no longer blinked. The cold burned my eyes but I'd turned to stone. I had become a lady-in-waiting on the outskirts of a faerie court, watching a crucial rite of which I could not hope to decipher, so ancient and convoluted were its movements and meanings. The wordless song went on. It was rarely louder than the grunt of a rooting boar, rising and falling in the same patterns as the devil's careful steps.

Eventually the monster lowered itself down to all fours again. It crawled over the rock wall like a monkey, then shambled towards the barn, crossing the far side of the open yard with a rolling, shuffling gait like a tumbleweed, then followed the base of the silo to the barn doors. Its bipedal footsteps were silent on the packed, frozen earth. One door swung gently open. The gigantic figure, as featureless as the shadows that swallowed it, slipped inside the barn.

I did not call out. Had it seen me, outlined against the gentle glow of the fire, muted by the tent's canvas? For a few heartbeats I was terrified it might come back, but when I realized it had vanished for good, my breath came out in a strangled sob. This was a dream, I reminded myself. This was nothing but a horrible dream, brought on by the combination of poor sleep, long days, the stress of treating Calliope's condition and the fright of seeing the mask in Mr. Godwin's collection. I have too active an imagination.

As my fear and bewilderment drained away, the cold temperature returned and prickled across my exposed flesh like nettles. I'd been in awe of the minotaur but, now that it was gone, the night felt more desolate and the dreary countryside, forsaken. I crept back into the tent, preferring the companionship of a mute simpleton to standing so exposed, so alone, in the gloaming of the dawn. Whatever I had seen -- or thought I'd seen, or dreamt in some altered waking state -- had abandoned this earthly plane, and we were the poorer for it.

Chapter Seven

In the morning I woke slowly, aching and half-starved, to find the Geek snoring lustily on the far side of his cage and looking as comfortable as he could be, all things considered. The fire contained hot but harmless embers. The cubicle's atmosphere was warm and cozy, as peaceful as a country cottage, but I was sore from sleeping in my wooden chair, and I swore at my own generous impulses as I kicked dirt over the ashes and left. What did I hope to prove, sleeping in discomfort and bitterly freezing temperature? I ought to have known I'd suffer for it! It was Sunday morning, which meant that Mr. Scott would lead a prayer group in the Big Top, and while I was never much of a devoted follower, I did enjoy the companionship and fellowship that his church services brought -- but, before then, I needed to get back to my own berth on the boat, change my clothes and wash my face to make myself presentable, and quickly eat a bite of breakfast. After all, I'd endured a strange sleep, full of dreadful and demonic visions. I craved a cup of hot tea and friendly faces around me.

But when Magda saw me approaching the *Atropos*, she flew from the ship, arms outstretched. Her face was ashen, her eyes brimming with alarm.

"There you are! Dear God, Rose, you must come immediately!" She seized up my wrist and dragged me after her, across the wharf to the *SS Nona*, straight to the Gibson sisters' stateroom. Through the door, I heard a horrid sound: halfway between the mewling of a drowned cat and the whimpering of a beaten dog. A few people waited on the deck, drawn to the harrowing noises but too afraid to enter. Hugo stood by the stairs leading to the upper deck, his arms wrapped around a pillar. Lou Grady still had white greasepaint on his neck from last night's clowning, and Nancy cowered on the threshold of her own stateroom next door, wearing only her frilly pink night gown.

"What's happening, Magda?" she called out in her nasal soprano.

"Never you mind," came the curt reply. Magda opened the door and pulled me in.

Honoria sat on her bed, clinging to her blankets like a frightened child. Morris sat on a wooden footstool between the beds, gripping Calliope's hand. As for younger Gibson sister, she lay stretched out on her own mattress with her skin the colour of putty. Pearls of sweat rolled off her brow, soaking into the sheets and filling the room with a sour, sickly stench.

Magda rounded on me. "What did you give her?"

I rushed forward to snatch up the vial from the bedside table -- a vial which had contained enough for three days, yet now was empty.

"Did she drink it all at once?" I asked Morris, horrified.

He shook his head, speechless and overwhelmed, but Honoria answered.

"She figured we didn't have time to wait. Better to get rid of the thing right away than drag it out over three days."

"Stupid girl!" I snapped, "She's gone and poisoned herself!"

Calliope mewled again and clutched at her stomach.

As if an echo, Honoria gave a strangled cry. "She's going to die?"

I leaned over the younger sister and pried up one plum-coloured eyelid, then another. Her dilated pupils were blurred and unfocused. "Can you hear me, Calliope?" I yelled in her face, then slapped my hand against her cheeks to get her attention, but nothing roused her. She was addled and confused. When she attempted to speak, the syllables that came out were slurred into a muddle, and a line of gossamer spit dripped from the corner of her lips. Her eyes were two large black buttons that whirled wildly in their sockets.

"How long has it been since she took the dose?"

Honoria had begun to weep, her face covered with her hands.

"Hey!" I shouted and she snapped to attention. "When, Honoria?"

"Maybe an hour?" she stammered, "I don't know! I think she took it after breakfast."

"Did she eat a light breakfast? Or heavy?"

"I don't know! What does it matter?" Honoria whimpered, "Why are you yelling at me?!" Then she crumbled into sobbing as her sister groaned again.

Morris turned his attention to me. "She ate a bowl of porridge. I brought it to her myself."

"Then we may still have time," I said to Magda, "The porridge is thick and it will have slowed down her digestion, and the quinine may still be in her stomach rather than her intestines. Do you have charcoal biscuits on board? The kind used for flatulence and indigestion?"

Magda shook her head but Morris spoke. "There's a pharmacy in the village. I saw it yesterday when I went to the Godwin mansion."

At that moment, Calliope gritted her teeth and let out a clenched groan, her fingers tightening around Morris' hand as if she were clinging to a lifeline. Her wide eyes stared at a distant point on the ceiling and her fair hair was plastered to her brow with sweat.

Magda opened the door. "Hugo, get over here!"

The boy came reluctantly to his mother's call. He looked stricken and afraid.

"We need charcoal biscuits. There's a pharmacy nearby --" She glanced to Morris for more information.

"Turn left and head along the road towards the village," he explained, "Follow the main road until you reach the military convalescent hospital. It's a large, red brick building with a lawn and a fence, you can't miss it. The pharmacist is next door."

"But on a Sunday, it'll be closed," said Hugo.

Morris nodded. "Yes, but if we're lucky, the chemist may live upstairs."

"Make a fuss, Hugo, and demand that he helps you," said his mother. "Now, go!"

The boy sprinted from the room as if Satan himself was nipping at his heels. I returned my attention to Calliope; she'd started to wretch as her body rejected the quinine in her gut, and Morris helped her to sit upright, propping her up against his body. Magda scrambled to grab a chamber pot. The girl heaved, moaned, and began to vomit. Most of the cascade of porridge and curdled milk made it into the pot, but some splattered across the blankets and rug. It smelled awful, as bitter as apple seeds, as sour as vinegar.

Her convulsions went on and on. How much porridge could a young woman eat? The smell and the sight and the sound was almost enough to make me lose my own stomach contents, but at last her body was fully wrung out. She whimpered again as a fresh wave of perspiration appeared on her cheeks and neck, but Magda brought a bowl of cool water sprinkled with crushed peppermint leaves, and Morris -- who looked as grey as a sheet -- began to wipe her waxen face with a damp cloth.

Magda leaned close to me. "Her blood has begun," she said.

On the bed, a flow of crimson spread out from between her legs and soaked the blankets, spurred by the retching and the poison.

"That's the least of her concerns," I replied, "I told her -- I told her! -- to space out her doses over three mornings! I should have doled them out, one by one. I thought I could trust her to be careful."

Magda crooned over the poor patient. "Desperation makes us do foolish things," she said, "No one blames you, Rose. This is not your fault."

Honoria had sat silent through the whole ordeal but, at this comment, she sat upright and jabbed her finger at me. "But it IS her fault! She almost murdered Calliope!" she sobbed to Magda, "If Rose hadn't given my sister something so terribly dangerous to eat --"

Morris looked scandalized. He opened his mouth to speak but it was Magda who replied, her voice as deep and arresting as thunder rolling over the open ocean.

"Did you think there was no risk involved in getting rid of an unwanted pregnancy, Honoria? If you thought this would be a simple task, without risk or danger to life and limb, then you're a bigger fool than your impatient sister." Magda dropped her gaze to the patient, and stroked her hand over Calliope's forehead. "For a woman, every aspect of pregnancy is like going to war: it will change you, it will wound you, it may certainly kill you, and there is never an easy path to take. Whether a woman decides to keep the child or to get rid of it, both options require a stout heart and the very real possibility of injury or death." When Magda lifted her gaze to Honoria, her dark brown eyes were full of pain. "Have you never sat with a mother who has lost her infant to measles? Have you never known a woman who bled to death in childbirth?" She looked again to the crumpled form of Calliope. "If your sister did not realize the gravity of her situation, then she has lived a blessed life."

A belch, a moan. "Here we go again," Morris said as the woman hitched and convulsed. Another volley of undigested food appeared.

"Better in than out," I said, holding the chamber pot beneath her chin to catch this round.

Finally, after long minutes of retching, Calliope collapsed back into her pillows, exhausted. Her eyelids parted and she glanced at Magda with recognition.

"...I am dying?"

"No," came Magda's terse reply, "Not on my boats, you will not."

"...no performance tonight."

"And not for any time soon," Magda agreed, "Your throat will be in no shape for singing."

"...baby?"

"It appears your bleeding has returned," I said.

She gave a sigh of gratitude and closed her eyes again.

With the worst of it passed, Morris retreated to the outer deck to smoke a cigarette and calm his nerves. Calliope barely noticed as Magda and I cleaned her up, changed her sweat-stained bedclothes, and carted away the bloodied sheets; certainly, Honoria didn't lift a finger to help, being far too occupied with wailing and fretting to assist us. By the time Hugo returned with a box of charcoal biscuits, Calliope was resting easier and a little colour had returned to her cheeks. We fed her the dry, blackened crackers; to her credit, she choked them down with no complaints until her belly was bloated and full.

Morris returned from the outer deck and settled into his seat again. He stroked her hair as she slept.

"She needs time for the charcoal to absorb the quinine in her gut," I said to him, "It will help neutralize any poison left in her system, but she may suffer through another round of vomiting."

"I'll stay with her," he said, "No one will miss me in the Ten-in-One, and Honoria needs to be able to sing on the main stage tonight."

Honoria howled. "How am I expected to perform?" she cried, hands clenched at her throat.

But with her patience long gone, Magda would have none of it.

"Your sister is the one on death's door, not you," she replied, "Frankly, I have very little patience for your antics, both of you -- oh, I know all about your dallying, Miss Gibson, in every port of call and with all the handsome boys, and not a lick of sense to share between the two of you! Your sister may need time to rest and recover, but I expect you to perform because it is your job to do so, and you are not the one who has gone and poisoned herself."

Calliope roused herself just enough to say, "The show must go on," to her distraught sister. Then she slid her fingers into Morris' palm again and slipped back into heavy slumber.

"If anything happens, I'll come and fetch you," said the man to me, his continence reserved by the gravity of the situation. In his eyes I recognized the determined grit of a soldier settling in for a long night, and in his words, there existed a fortitude that I admired. This was not Morris the artist or Morris the roustabout, but Morris of the battlefield, a young British recruit who had survived the war in the trenches and feared neither blood nor guts nor grief. He viewed himself as an integral part of this drama and he genuinely wanted to make all better. Another, younger man might flee from his responsibilities, but not Morris; for his part in this drama, he needed to atone.

"You know where I'll be," I nodded. "Don't you hesitate. If her condition worsens, you fetch me immediately."

"I'll leave her for no other reason than you," he promised, and by God, I believed him.

Chapter Eight

I fretted over Calliope's health all afternoon as I sat in the Ten-In-One. My mood was made worse by the wretched sleep I'd had, but the hours turned by without interruption and, when I returned to the boat for a bit of supper, I took a detour onto the *Nona* to check on the girl. She was fast asleep in bed, breathing easily. Morris sat by her side reading a dog-eared copy of 'The Mayor of Casterbridge'.

"I need to bring your Jeeves novel back to you," I said.

"Oh, I'm in no hurry," he said. His good-natured reply eased my concerns. He wouldn't be so blithe if there had been trouble.

"Is Calliope feeling better?"

"She slept for the most of the afternoon," he replied, closing the book and setting it aside. "We had a few visitors drop by to give well-wishes -- Nancy and Wanda, and Lou in his clown make-up to give her a little laugh -- but it tired her out, too." He dabbed at her dry lips with the damp cloth. "She's bleeding quite a lot, but Magda says it's to be expected. Still, she's no longer wet with perspiration or clutching at her belly, and I take those as good signs."

"Then we caught the poison in time, thank goodness," I replied. I held a hand to her forehead and felt her cool skin.

"It was a spot of good luck that I saw the pharmacy when I went for my walk yesterday morning," he said.

I sat on the edge of Calliope's bed. "Was that when you went to see the masks?"

A blush crossed his face. "Ere, now, I couldn't help myself. But how did you know?" A dawning look crossed his expression. "Of course, the housekeeper and kitchen maid both came last night to the sideshow."

"May told me that you put tickets aside for them, in appreciation for allowing you to sneak a peek at Mr. Godwin's collection." I shook my head. "Mr. Scott would be furious if he knew you were knocking on doors, asking to look at wealthy people's private belongings!"

"How could I not be curious?" he teased in reply, "There are so many wonders to see in this world and I want to drink them all in! Why shouldn't I visit such a collection and enjoy it, if I can?"

"Because it's not our place," I said.

He scoffed. "An artist's place is anywhere he wishes to be!" he said, "And in any case, we're part of a circus, Miss Rose, and that gives us the enviable opportunity to go wherever we wish! We are unbound to any caste or station."

"That might be pushing it a bit," I replied.

"But it's true! Too many young fellows went marching to their deaths because of tradition while their betters stayed at home, safe and sound, but now the war is over and we are free to make our own future. Ere now, we have only to strike out on a grand adventure to find ourselves surrounded by possibility." He pressed his hand to his heart. "I fully believe, the universe wants us to explore it! Why else would God have given us a creative, questioning soul?"

"Those are very lofty ideals, Mr. Cave," I said.

"I am an artist, Miss Rose," he replied. "I'm not content with ideals that are tedious or easy to obtain."

This made me laugh. Morris had always struck me as young and capricious, but I wondered if he was a little older than I'd assumed; there were a few faint wrinkles around his eyes and a certain wisdom to his words. "Ah, so you think your ukulele and your paintbrush gives you free license to go wherever you wish!"

"Aye, I think they do," he replied cheekily. "We travel the world and go where the wind takes us because our hearts are free."

Oh, he could be quiet and reserved, but when he started talking, Morris was an optimist and a poet, and a charming one to boot! And that energetic sparkle in his eye made him captivating, indeed! I could see why a flighty, silly girl like Calliope might tumble head-over-heels for the free-spirited philosophies of Mr. Morris Cave.

"Well," I said as I stood, "I'm afraid I'm not quite so liberated. I have an obligation to the Ten-in-One, and Magda will have my head on a pike if I'm not back to my chair by the time the next crowd funnels through. We're already down one performer," I crooked one eyebrow towards him. "It's been a busy afternoon and it looks like tonight's performance will be packed."

"Word is out that the circus at Mr. Buckley's farm is worth the price of admission."

"I suppose so," I replied, and I once more studied Calliope's relaxed and slumbering face, and touched my fingers to her cheek. "I think she'll pull through with no more than a dreadful stomach ache, and for that, we are very fortunate. It could have been a tragic end. Will you be so good as to stay with her until morning?"

"Of course," he said. His eyes softened as he looked at her. "I know Calliope was a foolish ninny to take it all in one gulp, but please don't let that colour your opinion of her. She was eager to get this whole nasty business finished. I never wished her or Honoria any harm." He held her pale hand tenderly and stroked his fingers along her forearm. "In fact, I considered asking her to come home with me to England, when I was done my adventuring in Canada."

"You're leaving us?"

He startled a little, realizing he'd revealed more than intended.

"Please don't mention it to Mr. Scott or to Magda," Morris replied. "I hadn't yet decided my course of action. I only get a little homesick, sometimes, and the thought of returning to England makes me feel better."

"I won't breathe a word," I promised.

"Who would've thought I'd miss sleepy old Dorset so much?" he said as he leaned back on his stool, resting his spine against the chest-of-drawers and folding his hands behind his head. "Before the war, it seemed like such a boring, stifling place. I couldn't wait to leave and travel the world, but now that I'm halfway around the globe, all I can think is how much I miss my family's house and estate, and how much I miss my grandmother's cookies, and the nightingales singing in the gorse bushes, and all those silly simple things that feel so normal and useless when you're surrounded by them, day and night." He gazed at Calliope's sleeping face. "Isn't it ridiculous?"

I remembered what Magda's cards foretold: that Morris had secrets hidden within him. "Here I was all this time, thinking you were a wandering minstrel, but you're actually a farmer."

He laughed and laughed. He laughed more than my sorry little comment was worth, but I wager his mirth was accentuated by the great relief he felt that Calliope was going to be well. When he finally caught his breath, he said, "I suppose I am, in a manner of speaking... My father is a doctor in Bath and wants me to join his practice, but I don't think medicine is the right career for me. I get queasy at the sight of blood." He stroked Calliope's cheek. "My Uncle Tom owns the family mill house and estate, and when I came back from the war, I moved in and started to care for the land. It was a good life, a pleasant and rewarding life. In any case, he works in town and had little time for the old family home, and so he has agreed that I should take ownership of the fields and the mill when I'm ready. I promised to strike out for a year to see as much of the world as I could before the estate becomes my full responsibility."

"Which brought you to the Circus Salmagundi."

"What better way to travel than with a circus?" he said, "It's every school boy's dream."

"And the ukulele?"

"Easy to learn, difficult to master," he replied. "I picked up the instrument in San Francisco when I passed through last winter. During the Pan Pacific International Exposition back in 1915, Henry Kailimai played a musical revue in the Hawaiian pavilion, and the crowds went wild for his songs, and ever since, the ukulele has quite the following in that city." He picked up his novel. "But I don't suppose I'll have much of a need for a ukulele when I get back to Dorset. Folks back home aren't nearly as cheerful as they are here."

"You'll just have to bring them a little bit of cheer when you return," I said.

The ukulele sat on the ground at his feet; he picked it up and held it out to me. "Here, you give it a try."

"Me?" I said with a dismissive laugh. "I've never been very musical --"

"Ere, now, you've got a fine singing voice. I've heard you when you're scrubbing clean the galley." Morris put the instrument into my hands. "That's right, hold 'er with the neck to the left, and use your right index finger to strum. See? Not difficult at all!"

I strummed a note and he guided me through a few chords. The notes were bright and gay, and the instrument rang with such zest for life!

"Now," he said as I sat down on the edge of Calliope's bed, "Let's see if we can teach you a simple song."

He walked me through a chord progression: G, Eb, E7, A7 and D7. My fingers felt like they were twisted in knots, but he urged me to strum a slow tempo, and as I did, he sang:

> Hone kaua wiki wiki, sweet brown maiden said to me
> As she gave me language lessons on the beach at Waikiki
> Hone kaua wiki wiki, she then said and smiled with glee
> But she would not translate for me on the beach at
> Waikiki
> Hone kaua wiki wiki, she repeated playfully
> Oh, those lips were so inviting on the beach at Waikiki
> Hone kaua wiki wiki, she was surely teasing me
> So I caught that maid and kissed her on the beach at
> Waikiki
> Hone kaua wiki wiki, you have learned it perfectly
> Don't forget what I have taught you said the maid from
> Waikiki

"Ho! See? You're a natural!" he laughed as we finished the song.

"But what do the lyrics mean?" I asked.

"I think, 'Kiss me quickly'," he replied, "But honestly, everything sounds like a jaunty love song when it's accompanied by a ukulele, so I could be mistaken. Maybe she's saying, '*kick off, ya rube.*'"

We both laughed at that, and almost immediately, Calliope shifted under her blankets and gave a little mutter in her sleep. Morris and I swapped mischievous glances, having forgotten that there was a woman sleeping in the same room as our musical interlude. I handed the instrument back to him.

"Thanks, Morris. That was quite fun."

"Thank you for all your help, Rose," he replied. "I'll stay the night with Calliope. She'll be happy to have a friendly face at her bedside when she finally wakes."

"If she needs anything in the night, you come and find me."

He nodded. "Will you be camping again tonight?"

I shuddered at the thought. "No, not again. I made an arrangement with Mr. Buckley to haul the Geek's cage into the barn for the night after the sideshow closes up. The Geek should be more comfortable there, with the cows and the sheep to keep him company."

"And you'll be able to get a good night's rest, too."

"I am very much looking forward to it," I replied with a grin.

He wished me a good night and started to play, gently and softly, as he sang a lullaby to sleeping Calliope. I left, secure that all would be well.

Chapter Nine

The blast of a shotgun obliterated the morning peace. I tumbled out of my cot and scrambled to my feet as my heart leapt into my throat, instantly wide awake. The explosion echoed up and down the rocky shores of the waterway as if a battalion of infantrymen was returning fire, bouncing from cliff to cliff and fading with each volley, but I was under no illusions about the origin of the sound: the first shot had come from very close. I pressed my ear to my door and heard the immediate stampede of footsteps, the clamour of slamming doors, and curses in a range of voices.

The clock on my wall read a half past six. With abundant caution, I opened my door, just a crack. Outside, the sky was dark but the sun was a faint peachy glow in the east. It gilded the underbellies of fleecy clouds that skirted the tops of the trees, and the fresh air smelled savoury with seaweed and spicy with pine.

"By God, what's happened!?" Alex called as I climbed to the top deck of the *Atropos*. After a quick survey, I spotted him by the prow of the *Decimo* in his striped pyjamas and nightcap, looking uncharacteristically dishevelled. Other men were joining him: Bill Peacock, his round face taut with worry, and stout Orville Mann, from all appearances nursing a wicked hangover. Fletcher the raven perched on his shoulder.

The ragged black wings, outstretched for balance, made Orville look gothic and imposing, but the effect was ruined by his pained wince and drool-encrusted chin.

A porthole on the *Nona* slapped open. "Mercy! Are we at war again?!" cried Nancy's shrill, disembodied voice.

From the stern of my own ship, Grover Scott was hurrying from his stateroom, fumbling with suspenders and pulling on a jacket, half-dressed in his business suit.

"What the hell!" said the dwarf as he drew up alongside me, running his hands through his hair to make himself more presentable. "What's going on out there, Rosie?"

"We have a visitor," I said, pointing towards the man standing on the wharf.

The gentleman was in his late 20s, dressed in a black suit and a grey fedora that had been garnished with a feather in its band. A thin black moustache neatly trimmed his upper lip, and his face was narrow, chiselled, and tarnished with a smattering of liver spots. He cut a formidable figure, but he was in such a state of agitation that his finery did nothing to make him look professional or gentlemanly. Instead, he trembled all over with rage. The rifle he held in his hands still exhaled a wisp of smoke from the blast.

"You damnable thieves!" the man shouted. His voice cracked with emotion. "Get out here and face me, you murderous dogs!"

By now, most of our troupe had appeared on deck or through porthole windows, fearful but curious. I saw Honoria in her mauve silk robe leave her stateroom, followed immediately after by Morris; his hair was a mess, his clothes were crumpled, and he'd obviously slept on the floor between the sisters' beds. They both leaned against the railing of the *Nona* and watched as the ringmaster strode down the gangplank of the *Decimo* and Mr. Scott descended from the *Atropos*.

"Murderous?!" Alex replied, "By God, man, what are you going on about?!"

"You deny it?" the man replied as they approached. He raised the rifle barrel to the sky and let out another explosion of fire and smoke. Everybody flinched, a few ladies screamed. Up in the fields, the ponies squealed in terror and, from the hold of the *Nona*, Nancy's dogs let out a chorus of muffled howls.

Alex gave another shout of angry surprise but Mr. Scott didn't even blink. He growled, "Put that damned thing down before someone gets killed, you idiot."

But the stranger only roared back, "Someone already has! Our housemaid, Mrs. Stuckey, had been bludgeoned to death!"

My heart plunged to the pit of my stomach.

"Mrs. Stuckey!?" I called out as I rushed down the gangplank to face him.

The man who stood before me was very tall and fit. He wiped away his tears with the sleeve of his suit jacket, and I could see that his anger was dwindling while his grief remained. He smelled of cigarettes and floral perfumes and sour beer, a combination that brought memories of speak-easies and social gatherings to mind.

"You're the younger Mr. Godwin?" I presumed.

"I am," he assured me. His voice quivered. "Francis Godwin."

"And poor Mrs. Stuckey has been murdered?"

"I found her body this morning in my father's house. She was struck down and killed by one of your reprobates in the course of stealing our property!" He raised the rifle again. "By God, I will have it back, and Lady Justice will hang you all for your crimes, and you will burn in Hell where you belong!"

Alex dropped his voice to a soothing purr. "Come now, put down the gun and let us talk about this in a civilized way, man! There's been no crime committed by us."

A figure galloped towards us from the farmhouse: Mr. Buckley had been woken and he was jogging down to his wharf, his housecoat flapping and his slippers slapping in the dirt. In the distance I spotted horses and riders, along with a clattering motorcar, coming up the road from the direction of the village. The farmhouse must have a phone and Mrs. Buckley had called for help.

I turned to the gentleman. "What was taken?"

"One of my father's masks is gone," he snarled at me, spittle flying from his lips. "Someone stole it in the night!"

"It can't have been us," said Alex, "We can all account for one another! The performance, then dinner together, here on the boats -- "

"Of course, you'll cover for each other! But I know it was one of you," the younger Mr. Godwin insisted. "I heard about your snooping around the house, speaking with Mrs. Stuckey, plying her with tickets to your heathen show... and then you plotted against her and took advantage of her good nature!"

"I spoke with Mrs. Stuckey only two days ago --" I tried to explain but was quickly cut off.

"So, you admit it!" he snapped, and he aimed the rifle at my head.

I heard an overlapping series of gasps coming from the boats but I dared not move to see who had reacted. Instead, I held up my hands. "I only admit to speaking with her. I did not touch your father's property or steal anything from your household. She was very kind to allow me to see a few of the masks on the bottom floor, all of which are very impressive pieces, but I never laid a finger upon them, I swear."

But he was too angry to listen to reason. "You stole the devil mask!" he insisted. "It must have been you!"

"The large one with the aurochs horns?" I asked, still very aware of the rifle's barrel pointing directly at my head. Foreshortened, the gun looked like nothing more than a small round hole in the air, attached to a scope and hardwood stock, and held by an over-emotional and senseless lout. "That's the mask that's gone missing? Good Lord, man, how could I have carried such a thing? It was huge! It must weigh a hundred pounds!"

Mr. Scott did not move except to gesture in my direction, as if to make an example of me. "Miss Rose would never have trespassed against you," he said, "She's a respectable woman."

"Thank you, Mr. Scott," I replied.

"And she's a very weak one, too," he added, "Look at her arms, man! She's a scrawny bit of fluff and hardly much help at all when we're setting up our gear."

"Thank you again," I said with a frown.

Alex nodded in agreement. "I think you're right, Grover: if the mask weighs a hundred pounds, Rosie couldn't lift it, not even if her life depended on it! She has the muscle tone of a limp noodle."

"It's quite pathetic," Mr. Scott nodded.

I know they were trying to save me, but there was still a pang of insult at such an honest assessment of my fitness.

At this point, Mr. Buckley had reached the wharf. His slippers slapped upon the wharf as he stepped up behind the gentleman and snatched the rifle away in one fluid gesture. "For the LOVE of all things HOLY, what ARE you doing, Francis!? What has POSSESSED you?! Threatening to kill a GUEST on my property? Disgusting!"

Relieved of his weapon, the young man cast about for purpose but, finding none, deflated before our eyes.

I let out my breath, which I hadn't even noticed I'd been holding tight in my chest.

"I did not steal anything, and I certainly wouldn't kill Mrs. Stuckey," I said to the man. "I was performing in the Ten-in-One all last evening until very late. Ask any of the audience who came to visit me last night, and they'll tell you I was in my tent, showing off my tattoos. After that, I came on board the *Nona* to check on Calliope, and then ate dinner on the *Atropos* with a few of the other performers. Then, it was off to bed, where I have been until just this moment, when your gunshot woke me from a very pleasant sleep. No, Mr. Godwin, I am not your culprit. I can't be. As Mr. Scott and Mr. McGee have made clear, it's quite impossible."

"Then who could have committed such a horrible act?" he said. Fresh anger appeared in his eyes as he stared at the inky surface of the water, trying to calm his whirlwind thoughts and catch his ragged breath.

If he planned to say more, he was interrupted by the toot of a whistle. The horses drew to a stop in a clattering of hooves and clouds of dust, and a couple of young policemen in blue uniforms sprung from their saddles and sprinted down to the docks, their boots thumping across the wharf boards. A brawny constable, his whistle on a cord around his neck, climbed out of the motorcar to join them as a younger officer, sitting behind the steering wheel, threw the brake lever. "Now then, what's all this?" the constable barked. He jumped at the sight of the person standing at the centre of the wharf. "Heavens to Betsy!

Francis Godwin! What are you doing down here, my boy, threatening folks with a gun?!"

In the easy manner of his reply, it was clear that Francis knew the constable well. "Matilda's dead."

"Dear God!"

"She was murdered in the night during a robbery."

The constable stifled his surprise and shifted his attention to me. "This is your murderer?"

"Hey!" I snapped.

"How dare you make such an accusation! She did no such thing!" Alex said as he stepped to my side and put one arm around me in protection; I cringed at his touch but he held me too tightly to pull away. "Throwing about empty threats -- is that what accounts for good police work here?"

"You will not lay a finger on my performers," said Grover, "If you do, you'll be hearing from our attorneys." Unlike Alex, he'd refrained from flying out in his sleep-ware; instead, he'd taken the time to smooth back his hair and adjust his collar, and as a result, he was the only reasonable, rational, professional-looking fellow amongst us. Grover didn't need height to demand respect: he knew there was authority in one's presentation. He stared directly at the constable with piercing eyes. "What is your name, sir?"

The forcefulness of the question caused a moment's hesitation.

"Robert Turnpike," he said at last.

"Well, Constable Turnpike, you must be aware that this man --" he pointed one stocky finger at Francis Godwin, "-- trespassed on private land and threatened Miss Rose with a gun, and thus could have ended her life with his careless and baseless accusation. I will be pressing charges."

"Hey, now!" Francis barked. Grover paid him no heed.

"What kind of lawless frontier are you running, Constable Turnpike?" he continued, "Is it common for women in your town to be threatened and murdered in their homes? Are you so incompetent that you must rely on hair-triggered vigilantes to portion out justice?"

Turnpike's face turned beet red. "Of course not." He took a step back, looking between Alex and me. "But this woman had been accused of murder. She must come with me to the station immediately to answer questions. "

I felt Alex's arm tighten around me, sparking another flutter of panic. "No, she will not," he said, "Rose is staying right here with me."

"It's okay, Alex," I assured him, shrugging off his arm, trying to keep my heart rate steady and calm, "I can go with the constable and account for myself. I have nothing to hide."

Turnpike held out one arm to usher me to the motorcar, but I was only wearing a cotton nightgown, so Grover shrugged off his suit jacket. "Take this," he said, handing it to me. He didn't let it go immediately. Instead, he yanked until I'd dropped my head to his level. "Be careful, Rosie," he whispered in my ear. "Tell them as little as you can. I'll follow after you and provide representation, if you need it. "

"Thank you, sir," I replied. Then I stood with my chin held high and pulled on Mr. Scott's jacket to keep myself warm. His limbs were shorter than average but his torso was a standard size, so the jacket fit me surprisingly well, even if the cuffs of the sleeves reached just below my elbows. Constable Turnpike passed the young Mr. Godwin but felt no need to arrest him for his threats of violence; I suppose he was a man of quality, and that would be poor form. As I walked up the shore towards the waiting vehicle, Mr. Buckley looked stricken by the whole affair. He clutched his hands to his throat as if I were being led to my execution. The engine grumbled, the wheels groaned. As we clattered towards the village, I looked back towards the boats.

In that momentary glance, three faces snagged my attention. Magda looked very stern, as if to remind me to tell the truth since my character had been called into question. Morris huddled on the upper deck of the *Nona*, taking it all in with bewildered eyes. Next to him stood Honoria, her expression pinched and sour, and looking like she'd known I was evil all along.

The paddy wagon was an old Packard open-top, a rickety contraption with worn leather seats and no suspension; clearly, the British Columbia Provincial Police had little need for motorcars in their rural locations, and the organization wasn't prepared to spend money on luxuries. Turnpike sat in the back seat with me. He still held Godwin's rifle in one hand. As I settled into my seat, he stuck his other hand over the door and slapped the side of the car with a bang.

"To the station, Mitch!" he barked at the driver.

We rumbled down the road, bouncing over every pothole and stone. The sun was starting to rise and a golden autumn light poured across the landscape.

I took the opportunity to look the man up and down. Constable Turnpike was soft around the middle. He wore shiny boots and neatly-pressed pants, and the twin rows of brass buttons on his black jacket had recently been polished. The only creases on his trousers were around the tops of his thighs, no doubt from sitting too long at a desk. His hands were soft, his nails trimmed. Most telling of all, he held the gun awkwardly as if he didn't know what to do with it; he hadn't even removed the bullets. This wasn't a man accustomed to chasing criminals.

"You might wish to put the safety on," I pointed out, dipping my chin towards the weapon.

"Oh, yes, of course," he said, fumbling with the rifle until he was certain it had been rendered harmless, then he muttered into his moustache, "By God, that damned dwarf got me all riled up!"

"Mr. Scott is an excellent businessman with a long list of contacts and some familiarity with the legal system," I replied, "I'm sure you'll be hearing from his attorney."

Turnpike scoffed at that. He wanted to give the impression that he didn't believe me, but his eyes glittered with apprehension and a bit of perspiration had dampened his collar. It was a poor bluff.

"Did you say we're heading to the station?" I asked as fields and farms rolled by.

"That's right."

"Surely you mean to go first to the Godwin residence."

He faltered. "Why would we head there?"

"Well, if there has been a murder and a robbery, you should document the scene before the evidence is cleaned up by the staff, don't you think?" I asked. "After all, I'm not going anywhere. My answers aren't going to change. You can wait to question me, but it would be best for your investigation to examine the scene of the crime as soon as possible."

"They would never --"

"If one of the staff is the culprit, then you can bet dollars to donuts, they'll be eager to clean up their own mess."

He paused. I could almost see his brain churning thoughts like butter.

Then, slapping one palm against the side of the motorcar again, he called out, "Mitch! Take us to Randall's house."

The car turned at the next crossroads, the motorcar trundled west. When we reached the mansion, the driver turned a hard right to sway through the open gate and the boxwood hedge, then followed the narrow drive between slender pairs of elms and arrived in the front yard. The young Mr. Godwin had returned from the Buckley farm, having ridden his horse at a hard gallop directly overland. He was tying the frothy animal to a fence post in the front yard, looking dejected.

An older man hurried through the main doors and strode down the stairs, onto the front lawn. He wore a white shirt and blue waistcoat but no jacket nor tie. The two men shared a similar profile, but the older gentleman was more meticulous in his grooming, more precise in his actions and movements. His clothes were of a higher quality, and his silver hair gave him an aristocratic air. This must be Randall Godwin, the owner of the collection.

At the sight of his father, Francis wore the peevish scowl of a child being punished, but any argument between them was interrupted by the approach of our motorcar. Randall's expression shifted from anger to surprise as we parked near the steps leading up to the front veranda.

Turnpike climbed out of the motorcar.

I stepped out of the car, too, intent on following the constable, but he held up his hand to me.

"No, no, no, you must stay here, miss!"

"If you aim to question me, it's best you keep me in your sights," I replied. "After all, you wouldn't want to risk me running off."

The poor man squinted in confusion. "Mitchell will keep an eye on you," he said, throwing a pointed look to the driver.

But by this time, Francis Godwin was striding towards us, and he looked like a jolt of electricity ran through him. "What in the devil is she doing here?!"

"You accused me of murder, sir," I replied, "I need to clear my name." I strode passed him, directly to the older gentleman, and thrust out my hand to him. "We have not had a chance to meet properly. My name is Rose Ivy, and I'm the tattooed lady with the Circus Salmagundi."

The elder Mr. Godwin took the offered hand cautiously and shook it. "I apologize for my son's rash actions this morning, madam," he said, "He discovered the body and it has left him in a raw, emotional state." To the constable, he said, "Is that my son's rifle in your hand, Robert?"

The constable only nodded.

"I understand this must have all come as a shock to you and your household," I continued, undaunted. "I only met your housekeeper twice, yet she struck me as generous and efficient woman with a good head on her shoulders."

"She will be dearly missed." Randall Godwin said, looking genuinely stricken.

"May we come in?" I said, "It's quite cold out this morning, and if we are to speak further, I'd rather be inside, out of the wind."

Randall stepped back and held out one hand in invitation. "Please, do come in."

Francis looked from his father to me, measuring this cordial conversation, stunned by the welcome his father had offered me. "You can't invite her in!" he railed, "This woman is clearly a criminal!"

"I need to take her to the station for questioning," said Turnpike.

But, instead of protesting, I replied directly to Mr. Godwin. "You son is obviously in shock; I mean, anyone struck by such a vision would lash out thoughtlessly, that's perfectly understandable. Let us forget all about his outburst and I'll refrain from pressing charges." I gave him a warm smile.

The man nodded in agreement, watching me with soft grey eyes under bushy white brows. It was easy to see that Randall had once been athletic and active, much like his son, but those days were vanishing behind him. His hands had a slight tremble and his shoulders had begun to sloop. Under his vest, the chest which had once been broad and strong was now hunched and shallow. "That is very charitable of you, madam. My son does not know what he's saying," the father dismissed. Then to the younger man, Randall gruffly ordered, "Go on, take care of your horse and collect yourself before you do anything more to harm my reputation!" We watched as Francis, wings clipped, stumbled away towards the stable leading the poor exhausted creature and grumbling curses to himself. Randall then turned to me. "I'd heard there were circus folk visiting the house. It was a surprise to me that you'd have any interest in my art collection."

"We're bound together by a love of performance and art," I said, "And certainly, the few masks I had the pleasure of admiring were quite inspirational."

This assessment pleased him. "How fortunate, then, that you found us! I do not mind the imposition, madam, but my son leapt to an unfortunate conclusion when May told us of your visit."

Together we strolled towards the main entrance, a pair of oak doors at the top of a flight of stone steps, flanked by cedar trees in terracotta pots. Alerted by the sound of conversations in the front yard, May opened the door to us. She looked dreadful, her eyes puffy and bloodshot from crying, and when she saw the elder Mr. Godwin, she flew into his arms and began to sob. The gentleman kindly soothed her with soft-spoken words, but he looked unnerved by her sudden show of familiarity. Clearly, he preferred the more traditional relationship of employer and staff.

"There, there, Miss Tanaka," he said in a grandfatherly way, "The constable is here now and we must do our best to answer his questions." He held her at arm's length. "Has anyone disturbed Matilda where she lay?"

"No, sir! No one!" She released him and, spotting me, said, "Miss Rose, what are you doing here?!"

"There was an altercation," I said delicately, "However, we have agreed to forget such indiscretions on the condition that Mr. Godwin gives Constable Turnpike free access to examine the scene."

Of course, I knew Randall had done no such thing, but once spoken aloud, the idea could not be rescinded. Turnpike gaped at me, trespassing so blatantly against a man who was a million times my better.

"It would be unthinkable for Mr. Godwin to refuse such a simple request," I continued, "After all, a man is presumed innocent instead of guilty -- that's for a jury of his peers to decide -- but nor does he want to be seen as standing in the way of Justice, either."

"Let us in, Randall," said Turnpike. I detected a note of satisfaction in his voice. He'd anticipated resistance from the gentleman but my presence had shifted all that distrust away from the law and on to me. He may even have been thankful for the distraction I provided. He looked about and said, "Where will we find the body?"

"This way, Robert," replied the elder Mr. Godwin.

In through the main doors we went, Turnpike walking alongside Godwin, May and me following a few steps behind. I'd only seen the rear of the house but, confronted with the splendour of an entrance that had been designed to impress guests, I was almost struck mute by its opulence. The ship-building industry must be very lucrative, indeed, if Mr. Godwin's home was any indication! Every aspect of the front had been crafted from the highest quality of materials, from the white Italian marble tiles to the crystal chandelier to the sweeping dual staircase and gigantic gilded mirrors on the upper landing. Most arresting of all, the open eye sockets of a hundred exotic masks hanging from the walls stared down at us. This voiceless crowd watched us stroll through the entryway, down a wide corridor past a salon and a library and an office. A maze of connected rooms led to the back of the house, and I found myself in a corridor where the masks looked much more familiar. Here were the specimens I'd seen myself: the Crooked Beak of Heaven, the Mwana Pwo, and the war mask from New Zealand, but the final display case was conspicuously vacant. The devil mask was gone.

In front of the case lay the corpse of Mrs. Stuckey, dressed in her prim grey dress, the thin leather belt cinched around her waist. Such a brutal tableau! The poor woman lay face-down on the red carpet, and her head was a mash of bone and hair, so violently destroyed that Constable Turnpike made a horrible mewl of disgust. He crossed himself.

"Lord have mercy," he muttered.

"She's always the last at night to check the doors and windows -- the thief must have forced his way in before she had a chance to close up."

Mr. Godwin stared down at the body, grief-stricken. "She's exactly as my son found her this morning."

May had already retreated towards the kitchens, hiding her weeping face behind her hands.

"Poor May," he said softly as she retreated, "The girl and Matilda were close. Excuse me, please." The gentleman followed her, one hand pressed against his brow, fighting to retain his own composure.

The scent of cold tobacco smoke hung in the air. Someone had opened the far windows and the smell was starting to dissipate, but I saw a little bowl of ash in the corner of the glass cabinet, most likely the source. A square of grey broadcloth had been bundled under the woman's shoulders. Next to the shattered ruins of her skull lay the jade war club, spattered with bits of pinkish brain and wads of hair; it was no longer a beautiful and luminous piece of art, but a deadly weapon reclaiming its forgotten purpose. She lay with her legs outstretched behind her and the tops of her feet flat to the ground, so that the scuffed soles of her shoes were clearly visible. Her hands were positioned in much the same way: palms up alongside her thighs, stiffening fingers slightly curled. The tips of her fingers were stained dark brown.

I stepped forward and crouched down beside her to study this further.

The stain released a sour, vinegar-like, sharply chemical smell. There was no blood or wounds on her hands. There was very little blood on the back of her dress, too. The carpet below her face had a few speckles of blood upon it, but nowhere near the amount that a brutal wound of this depth and violence would create.

But I had no time to puzzle over it. Turnpike seized the collar of Mr. Scott's jacket and hauled me back to my feet.

"What is wrong with you?" he said. "Accosting poor Mr. Godwin, inviting yourself inside, and now pawing over the body?! Have some decency, woman!"

"Why should I?" I replied mildly, "Whoever has done this terrible thing had none. And if you hope to catch them, you must put aside your own decency, too." I was aware that the younger Mr. Godwin had returned; I could hear him arguing in the kitchen, while the elder Mr. Godwin stood at the far end of the corridor, closest to the kitchens and alongside the case that held Crooked Beak. He was talking in a low whisper to May, and she was comforting him again, her wrists crossed and her head bowed. Harriet the cook had joined them, too, as well as a few of the maids and a young man who, from the dirt on his clothes, must've been the gardener. If the murder had been done by a staff member, I wanted none of them to hear my suspicions, so I dropped my voice and leaned closer to Turnpike. "I don't think Mrs. Stuckey was killed here. She was murdered somewhere else."

"How do you know that?"

"Look at the placement of her hands and feet," I replied, but without a gesture to betray my suspicions to those standing farther down the hallway. "If she was struck here, they would not have fallen so neatly. She was dragged into position, and the killer didn't bother to pose her in a more natural way."

Constable Turnpike recoiled from my explanation, panting as if I'd punched him, then he gathered up his courage and swivelled his attention to the corpse to measure out my suspicions. As he peered closer, his skin turned grey. I felt pity for him; he must have known the woman, and it can't have been easy to examine the murder scene of a friend. His fingers clutched at his collar and his eyes were damp with tears. "Please explain," he said through a tight throat, "What exactly do you mean?"

"I'll try to be delicate, constable. Look how her arms are straight at her sides, how her legs are straight behind her. That is not the body of a woman who was struck down while fighting her attacker."

He turned away from the scene to compose himself.

When he faced the body again, his back was held straight and his shoulders, firm. "Then why leave the club?" he said, pointing to the jade weapon on the ground at her side. "If they killed her elsewhere, why bring her here, too?"

"That's a very good question," I said. "It begs consideration."

I crouched again over the club and, this time, he didn't pull me back. Bits of hair and flesh and bone stuck to its sea-green surface. I wondered if it had ever been used in a gruesome South Pacific conflict, or if this was the first time it had ever tasted human gore.

"What do you see upon it, constable?"

He gulped. "Fragments of bone, and brain, and hair."

"But very little blood."

He peered a little closer. "There is some."

"But not enough. Have you ever seen a head wound, Constable Turnpike? They bleed most gruesomely. If Mrs. Stuckey had been struck with this weapon while alive, the whole area would be a crimson mess."

I clasped my hands before me, studying all with clinical detachment.

"No, I believe Mrs. Stuckey was killed elsewhere," I whispered for the constable's ears alone, "Her body was left for a while, long enough for her blood to coagulate. Then, she was brought here and her skull bashed in." I nodded. "Yes, yes, I think that's what's happened here. Perhaps the murderer hoped that such a horrible sight would keep you from looking too closely."

"So... how was Matilda killed, then?"

I leaned down and touched her neck and torso, rolling the corpse carefully to one side. The head did not lift easily; its contents had been too far incorporated into the carpet for the skull to have retained its own integrity. Still, as the torso rolled up, I saw peonies of crimson across her neat grey pinstripe dress. The fabric was slashed. The skin underneath was puckered and bloodied.

"Ah! Here we are. She was certainly stabbed. Three times, at first glance."

"By God!" Turnpike exclaimed.

Randall Godwin, made curious by the constable's sudden surprise, shouted down the corridor, "What's happened?"

"Matilda was viciously stabbed," said Turnpike, "The bludgeoning has been staged!"

My disappointment at Turnpike's lack of tact could not be measured, but there was nothing to be done: he'd shared the grisly method and everyone in the hall knew it. May let out a fresh wail of grief and clasped her hands over her face. From the kitchen, Francis stormed towards us and sputtered in rage as he rounded on me, his grief still overwhelmed by his anger. "You'd make a sport of how Matilda was killed? What sort of monster pokes and prods at a body? Callous, cold-hearted hag!" Then, confronted again with the sight of her battered body, he sank to his knees, the heels of his hands pressed to his head and knocking his hat crooked. Emotion overwhelmed him as a series of shuddering sobs burst from his chest. "Oh, God! Who could have done this! Who?!"

Turnpike turned to me. "Take the young women to the kitchen, away from all this horror," he said. "Ask one of the help to call the hospital; the coroner will need to come and collect the body. Randall and I will deal with Francis." He glanced at the young man prostrate on the floor, crying and raving uncontrollably. "The poor fellow is crazy with grief and he doesn't need a woman watching. I'll make sure this is all taken care of."

May and I retreated into the kitchen, our arms still around one another, but she had gained back her composure once the body was out of sight. She wiped away tears with the sleeve of her blouse. "Oh, this is dreadful!" she said, sitting heavily at the wooden table in the corner. "Who would do such a thing to Mrs. Stuckey? She was a lovely, upstanding woman!"

The cook and her assistant had returned to their tasks, scrubbing the kitchen and stoking the fires, and when I asked for someone to call the hospital, the assistant obliged. She was a hearty lady with mottled cheeks, a plump face and a tiny round mouth like a rose-hip, and she wore a brown, flour-dusted skirt. She trotted out of the kitchen and towards the front foyer, where a phone had doubtlessly been installed for the homeowner's ease of use.

A pot of tea had been made for the Godwin breakfast. It sat steaming on the sideboard. I poured a cup for May and pressed it into her hands. Wrung out with emotion, she sat down at the kitchen table.

When Harriet the cook spotted me pouring tea, she strode over to the sideboard in a straight line, clucking her disapproval.

"That's not been made for the likes of you," she scolded, but I nipped any further complaint in the bud with a sharp glance.

"Francis Godwin already threatened to kill me today, Constable Turnpike wanted to interrogate me for murder, and by God, it's not even 8 o'clock! I need this cup of tea more than anyone." Then I turned to May as I sat across from her and said, "I am sorry for your loss. You and Mrs. Stuckey seemed very close."

May nodded, her face drawn.

"Tell me, May, when did you last see her?"

"Yesterday, late in the afternoon," she replied. "Normally she took time on Sundays to spend in prayer and reflection, but she was very busy. She had an errand to run in the village just before lunchtime, and when she came back, she had a number of packages with her. Mrs. Stuckey asked me to run a box up to her room and place it on her desk. That's the last I saw her." May wiped more tears away. "After that, I was busy in the herb garden all through the evening, and when I was done feeding the chickens, I took a bath and retired early."

"And what about you?" I asked the cook.

Harriet's manners at first were stiff and formal, proud of her domain and her cooking, but as she spoke, she grew more amenable. "Mrs. Stuckey was here at suppertime to oversee the meal, just as she did every night, then she took the platters out to the gentlemen in the dining room. Then she came back to the kitchen, collected a small plate of food for herself, and retired to her room. But that wasn't out of the ordinary; Mrs. Stuckey often ate alone."

"And that's the last you saw her?"

"It was," said the cook as the assistant returned from the office.

"She did not come down to close up the windows or doors?"

The cook shook her head. "I close and lock the kitchen door."

"And I look after the main doors and windows," said May.

I took a sip of tea as I puzzled over this discrepancy. "The elder Mr. Godwin said it was Mrs. Stuckey who locks up each night."

But the women shook their heads. "What would he know about it?" the cook said, "He's the first to bed, every evening."

"With a wee nip of brandy to sail him off to dreamland," said the assistant slyly.

"Was there any evidence of forced entry on Monday morning?"

"None that I could find," said May, "All the windows are still locked."

"The kitchen door was open but the lock wasn't broken," said the cook. "It's the closest exit to the devil's display case; the burglar must have taken it out that way."

By now, the men were speaking in low tones in the hall.

"The constable and Mr. Godwin seem to know each other well."

"It may be a quick trip across the Gorge Inlet to the city, but Esquimalt is still a small village at heart," said the cook. "We know each other well, even if we don't want to."

May leaned forward and lowered her voice. "The constable's wife and Mr. Randall are second cousins."

"Is that so," I mused, then I circled back to Mrs. Stuckey. "What errands did your housekeeper run yesterday?"

Harriet shrugged one shoulder but the young assistant piped up. "There aren't many spots to go on a Sunday, ma'am. Maybe to see a friend? All the stores are closed," said the girl with the mottled cheeks.

May added, "She never said a word to any of us where she went."

I glanced between the three of them. "Here's a question that needs to be asked, though it's an uncomfortable one: is there anyone that might wish Mrs. Stuckey dead?"

They all looked scandalized. I wasn't surprised. Such a question often provokes that particular response as no one dares speak ill of the dead.

"She was killed during the robbery," said the cook, as if it were the simplest answer in the world and I was daft for not noticing.

"Find the burglar and you'll have your killer," the assistant agreed.

But I had my doubts. There were too many discrepancies in the story for me to let it slide, and a part of the puzzle stubbornly resisted fitting neatly in place. I turned to May. "The last time anyone saw Mrs. Stuckey, she was heading to her room to eat her dinner alone. Could you take me there? I'd like to see --"

Further explanation was interrupted by a gruff cough as the constable strolled into the kitchen. "Come along, Miss Rose, that's enough of your meddling," he said, much as one might collect a wayward puppy, "I'm not about to let you out of my sight again. Leave these poor people to their mourning. The coroner has come to collect the body, and he's shunted everyone out of the hall while he works."

"And where is Francis now?" I said, standing up. Dear God, the last thing I wanted was that lout, sneaking up behind me with his rifle and his baseless accusations!

Turnpike seemed to understand my hesitation. "There's no further need for alarm, madam, he's quite contained. He's soothing himself with a glass of scotch in the library."

"Good, good," I said, "And his father is with him?"

But Turnpike shook his head. "No, the insurance agent arrived with the coroner, to discuss the value of the stolen mask. Randall and the agent are conferring in the front office... but enough of your prying, madam!" The constable blustered as he held out one hand to urge me to move. "We're no longer needed here. If its questions you want, I have plenty to ask you when we arrive at the station, and a comfortable cell to stick you in until we're certain of your innocence."

May slammed her cup of tea down on the table with a slosh and a bang.

"It's no trouble to take you and Miss Rose to Mrs. Stuckey's room, constable. It won't take but a minute of your time," she said. I heard the indignation in her voice; she didn't feel I deserved to be stuck in a jail cell, but she felt it unwise to protest openly. After all, Constable Turnpike was a man of law. He could have easily hauled her along with me for obstruction and stick us in a cell together to commiserate. Instead of defying him, she would oblige me.

Turnpike huffed at this unexpected invitation. "I can see no need to delve any further in that direction --"

"But of course, you'll want to inspect the last place Mrs. Stuckey was seen alive," I suggested.

He glared at me.

"Are you telling me how to do my job, madam?"

"I wouldn't dare," I replied, feigning horror at the thought, "And if this were only a robbery, I'd say you were correct, there's no need to pry in the housekeeper's private affairs! However, this is a murder, constable, and we both know the woman didn't die in that corridor. She was stabbed somewhere else, so we must harry and chase down the clues that will lead us to her place of death, and only there will we find any justice for Matilda Stuckey."

His eyes narrowed, his moustache twitched in agitation.

Then, standing a little straighter and sounding very much as if it were his idea, the constable commanded, "Take us to Matilda's room, Miss Tanaka."

Chapter Ten

In respectful silence we climbed the cramped staff staircase to the top floor of the house, the weight of our combined passage causing the wooden steps to creak and pop. May led us along a narrow corridor that must have followed the line of the roof, for the left side was sloped and the only windows were gabled, and when we reached the last door on the right, she turned the knob. It swung easily open.

"Did Mrs. Stuckey normally leave her door unlocked?"

"There are no locks on the interior doors of the house," she said to me. "We've never felt any need."

The apartment was comprised of a large room and a small bathroom, with a wide window that looked over the garden, the henhouse, and the greenhouse, providing a clear view of the distant forests and fields. A mist had risen in the past hour, and a pretty silvery sheen covered the lowest points in the land; humps and hills rose like tiny islands amid an ocean of gossamer fog. It was a serene view. Directly in front of the window sat a brass bed. I imagined Mrs. Stuckey had woken in the mornings and opened her eyes to this fine vista, the first thing she'd see each day.

The chamber had been tidied with military precision. The maple floorboards had recently been swept, the bed sheets and quilt were tightly tucked into their corners. A chair sat by the fireplace with a basket of knitting alongside it, and a small bookshelf held religious volumes and a few books of poetry, but none of the titles were popular or too thrilling -- clearly for Mrs. Stuckey, reading provided an opportunity for pensive self-reflection, not for cheap entertainment. Two pairs of stockings hung neatly on a wooden rack near the hearth to dry. On the opposite side of the room was a rattan wardrobe for her clothes. All of these items were modest and utilitarian, but I couldn't say the same for the final piece of furniture: a formidable writing desk of dark oak and brass trimmings that dominated the room. It possessed three large drawers, a blotter and a leather top, as well as a tidy system of slots and shelves for holding receipts, papers, notes and envelopes. The mighty behemoth was as imposing as a bison, scratched and scarred from years of constant use, and it provided a clear indication of where the woman's pride lay. The desk had been placed against the wall next to the bathroom door, and there it squatted as if daring anyone to disturb it.

In all directions, the bedroom appeared to be clean and orderly, but there was a scent in the air that seemed out of place: a fragrance like pennies dropped in a pot of boiling water. Mrs. Stuckey had been a woman of precision who took great pride in her neat quarters. I would've expected the smell of dried lavender or mothballs. The scent was odd.

When I glanced at May, she surveyed the room as if she were in a dream.

"What's wrong?"

She gave her head a little shake. "I'm not sure."

Constable Turnpike waited in the hall as I circumnavigated the space. The desk had been well-stocked for correspondence: one drawer contained fine stationery and stamps, another contained a neat line of pens, pen-knife and letter opener, and the third drawer contained little bundles of letters, tied with string. On the corner of the desk sat a pottery bowl containing coins and a small wallet of kid-leather, on the opposite side was a bottle of ink. I opened the wardrobe and found four or five respectable dresses, along with a rabbit fur coat. She had no bedside table, which I found very odd, but perhaps the woman had habits that didn't require it; if she was opposed to reading or lounging, she might go directly to sleep and have no need for a lamp.

On the mantle above the fireplace sat a framed photograph of Mrs. Stuckey with a young man, and she looked quite young, too, so the picture must have been taken many years prior. With his prominent jaw, toothy smile, and deep-set eyes under thick bushy brows, he had a feral look about him like a badger. His clothing seemed rustic, too, but Mrs. Stuckey wore a straw bonnet with a light chiffon scarf around her neck, summery and casual. Both of them seemed very pleased to be together, posing in front of a motorcar on a country road.

"You suspect she was murdered here?" said Turnpike through the open door, "I see no evidence of it."

"You aren't looking," I replied.

He grumped at my tone. "Listen here, madam, I've had enough of your tricks and games," he said. "Dragging me here and there, inserting yourself into the situation... you don't know the first thing about police work."

"I beg to differ," I said without looking up.

Like a tiny comet attracted by the immense size of a sun, I returned to the massive desk. I picked up the bottle of ink, rolled it between my hands, and remembered the stain on her fingers. Had she been writing letters? There was no correspondence on the desk, but of course, whatever she'd written might have been placed with the week's packages and already sent away in the morning post.

That smell persisted. It reminded me of a butcher's shop.

Turnpike was frustrated, I heard it in his voice. "And what exactly is that supposed to mean?"

I must have been frustrated, too, because under normal circumstances, I'd be reluctant to share too much of my history. Today, however, was hardly normal. The smell in the air was like a stone in my shoe or a pin left in the hem of a skirt -- a persistent bother that frayed my composure and was starting to impair my better judgment. On the ships, I'd become adept at keeping myself to myself, but with Turnpike's cutting question, the words just tumbled out.

"Only this," I began, "Once upon a time I was married to a police officer. Crime was a constant topic of conversation between us, and I learned a thing or two from him and his cronies. I'm no stranger to the law and the legal process, Constable Turnpike."

A look of dawning recognition swept across Turnpike's face, but it was May who spoke.

"You were married?"

It was an honest, open, curious question, but it shook me back into place. Damn it, the wall I'd carefully constructed around the events of 1919 had suddenly formed a large crack.

"Yes," I said. "My husband died last year."

"I'm sorry."

"Thank you," I replied, "I only mention it to make a point. This is not the first murder I've seen, Constable Turnpike, nor is it the most gruesome."

I entered the bathroom under the pretext of looking for clues, but honestly, I was badly shaken by speaking aloud the truth of my experience. I didn't like to talk about my former life; I didn't even like to think about it. Last year, my world turned upside down, and it was more comfortable to forget everything that came before joining the Circus Salmagundi.

But I couldn't fault the constable for questioning my interest, my experience, and my suggestions, either. He had a job to do, and I was inserting myself into it without any hesitation; it only stood to reason that he'd be suspicious. Hopefully, knowing a few key details about me, he'd listen with a more attentive ear.

Still. The memory of David made my heart hitch in my chest. He hadn't been in the grave long enough for me to feel any sense of peace. Not yet.

I shook off these wretched thoughts and emotions. It was better to focus on the task at hand. The bathroom was just as spotless as the rest of Mrs. Stuckey's quarters. The toilet, the sink, the porcelain bath, the tile floor in black-and-white squares -- all of it was modern and kept impeccably clean. She had only a hand towel next to the bathtub; all others must have been out-of-sight in a linen cupboard. But above the sink, between the small tiles, I saw the first aberration: a few dots of brown liquid that easily transferred to my finger when I touched them.

The liquid smelled strange, like vinegar, solvent, and beeswax. It was the same scent on the housekeeper's fingers.

"What do we have here?" I said to myself, looking down towards the waste bin.

Inside sat a small tin pan, speckled with bits of ash and stained with grimy streaks of brown that smelled identical to the liquid on the wall.

"How curious," I said, more to myself than anyone, as the constable approached.

"There's no evidence of violence here, either," he pointed out.

"What do you make of this?" I said as I held up the tin.

He frowned and shook his head. "The woman had some mess to clean up, and she tossed that into the waste bin in her bathroom, not bothering to go downstairs to clean it. That's my best guess. Why, do you think it has some bearing?"

I dragged my fingertip over the tin and the ink came away, staining my skin. "She had this same mixture on her hands."

"Who's to say?" he replied. "I think we've wasted enough time here, don't you think? Let's get you to the station."

I was about to protest when May gave a shout.

We found her standing by the desk, her hands to her mouth. The constable looked around for any hint of her distress. "What's wrong?"

"I just realized what seemed strange," May replied, "The furniture has been re-arranged! No one ever comes in here but Mrs. Stuckey, but on rare occasions, I've brought her food or laundry. I see it now! That's not where her bed goes! She always kept it against the inside wall, away from the draughty window." She looked back and forth, trying to remember. "Against the window -- that's where the desk used to be. They've been swapped!" May hurried to the desk, and laid her hands upon it as if touch could tell her more. "This is where the bed used to be, and the desk was at the window, so she could look outside while she wrote to her family back in the Old Country."

"We had a hot summer. Perhaps she moved the bed to catch the breeze and hadn't bothered to return it," said the constable.

"I hardly knew the woman, and she doesn't strike me as someone who wouldn't *bother*," I replied, "She'd have moved it back once the weather turned cold."

May looked from corner to corner, seeking any further items out-of-place. "Mrs. Stuckey kept very strict routines. She liked everything in its allotted spot. I can't imagine her moving her bed at all."

I circled the bed and examined it for any hint of purpose.

It sat on casters, so I leaned my shoulder against one bedpost and gave a push. Surprisingly weighty, it rolled with a reluctant squeal across the hardwood floor. The stiff wheels protested so May came to my side and helped, and the two of us managed to push it in a wide arc.

Underneath were scuffs on the floor. A chair had once been placed at this spot, its legs scratching the maple-wood floor as the seated person moved: here was where the heavy oak desk had sat, directly in front of the window, just as May had claimed. And over the damaged floorboards, in a thick gummy film, stretched an impressive patch of blood.

"Dear God!" Turnpike exclaimed.

The scent rising up from the floor filled my head like a cloud, and the blood was the colour of fresh sausages: brownish-red, gooey and thick. Bisecting the puddle were two long scratches where the corners of the desk had been dragged along the floor. The blood had spilled first, been left long enough to coagulate, then the furniture re-arranged to hide the mess. "Here's the location where Mrs. Stuckey was killed," I said, "The murderer moved the bed over the spill to hide the evidence."

May leaned against the bathroom doorframe, staring at the blood on the floor.

"Oh, God, there's so much of it..."

Patterns swirled in the dark red. Wide swaths curved through the edges of the pool, and I crouched down and crossed my arms as I studied them. A fresh gust of smell, like old pennies, wafted up around me. "The killer didn't expect the woman to bleed so much," I mused, "They tried to quickly clean up their mess but found it quite impossible to contain the volume; see, where they tried to sop it up? That's why there's no towels in the bathroom -- there'll be bloodied towels stashed in a forgotten corner of the house, I wager." I glanced around the room, reconstructing the scene in my mind. The desk here, the bed there, and the woman sitting at her window, looking out across the fields... yet the desk had been tidied and everything put back in its place.

"Mrs. Stuckey was sitting at her desk when she was killed, but what was she doing?"

"No one could have watched her movements after she retired to her room, so I doubt we'll ever know for certain," said Turnpike.

God, had he no imagination? I swept my gaze over the desk again. "If she was sitting with her back to the door, and the thief crept up behind her, and stabbed her thusly," and I reached down and around the chair, as if plunging a dagger into a seated figure's chest from behind, "Then why would he come up to her room on the top floor of the house, if all he wanted to steal was the devil mask?"

"Who's to say?" he replied. "I'm no criminal. No one of sound mind or body can possibly predict what a lunatic might do. I think we can all agree," Turnpike swept his hand out over the puddle of dark blood, "A man capable of inflicting this level of violence and hatred on an innocent woman must be mad!"

"You think he found his way here by chance?"

"Driven to inflict injury on any innocent that crossed his path? Yes, I do! He could have chosen any room in the house. Cruel providence selected Mrs. Stuckey as his victim."

May gave a little whimper of fright. "My room is just along the hall..."

"Get a lock on those doors, then," Turnpike said. "Who knows what other treasures this wild-man might come back to steal."

The murderer could have chosen any room, but he didn't. There is a reason for everything, even in madness, though we may not recognize it from our outsider's perspective.

But the mention of locks set my mind churning in a new direction. No lock had been broken, no window had been pried open. The murderer must have had clear access to the house; if so, perhaps they were familiar with the layout of the house, too, and knew the items in the collection. They hadn't used a gun -- too noisy, too abrupt. They'd chosen to stab the housekeeper in the chest, the broadest target a human body could provide, and that wasn't a method that required pre-meditation. It was a sudden option, an act of violence and frenzy. So, I wondered, had they brought a weapon with them? Or had they been forced to improvise?

And why here? What had drawn them to this attic room?

Perhaps they'd come to Mrs. Stuckey's room to steal something of value from her and surprised the poor woman at her desk. It was an interesting possibility, but they can't have been after money. The wallet was on the desk, as well as a bowl of coins and, on top, the skeleton key for the house. If this was theft, they would have taken it.

If I was the murderer, and I'd interrupted a woman sitting at her desk, what could I use to keep her quiet? I scanned the room as Turnpike talked to May about motivation, only listening to him obliquely.

"Randall told me that the devil mask is worth a good deal of money," he said, "He paid £10,000 and it may have increased in value since then, depending on the insurance agent's evaluation. That seems like motive enough for me."

May gave a little gasp. "Ten thousand?!"

I opened the top drawer: fine stationary, expense and cream-coloured, with matching envelopes. "And what would someone do with such a monstrosity?" I said as I sifted through the neat piles of paper, finding nothing in this drawer of any murderous value. "The devil mask was carved from a solid block of wood. They'd have to be frightfully strong to lift it and carry it away."

"They could sell it."

"It's too unique," I replied. "They'd never find a willing buyer. They'd have had more luck with pocketing the wallet on this desk, if it's easy money they wanted."

I opened the bottom drawer: parcels of letters, tied with string. Nothing here to cause an injury bigger than a paper cut. I closed it and turned to the man.

"Constable Turnpike, I'm starting to suspect that the theft of the mask is secondary. Surely you must see that as clearly as I do."

He blinked twice. "I beg your pardon?"

I lowered my gaze to the drawers and slid open the last one. "Mrs. Stuckey was killed here, in private, far away from the display cases on the first floor. She can't have surprised the thief while he was taking the devil mask, because they never would have crossed paths.

"But," I continued, "She did surprise him. He came up here to take something else and stumbled across her while she was at her desk, and he was suddenly confronted with a witness to his crime. He needed to shut her up; he had to improvise."

I scanned the pens and pencils. Suddenly, my breath caught in my throat. I reached into the drawer and pulled out the letter opener: a slender blade of polished steel with a pearl-inlaid handle. It felt deceptively heavy in my grip, as cold as an icicle and solid as pig iron.

"You mistakenly believe the murder was a result of the theft, constable, but I think you may be looking at it the wrong way," I said as I lifted it up to examine it more closely. Sure enough, a thin line of blood clung to the fissure where the handle met blade. Someone had tried to wipe the knife clean but, in their haste, managed only a superficial job.

I held it out to the constable.

"Mrs. Stuckey was murdered first. Only then was the scene staged to make it appear like a robbery. The mask is incidental: whoever did this wanted Matilda Stuckey dead."

Chapter Eleven

I suppose uncovering the method, the scene of the crime, and the bloodied weapon was proof enough for stubborn Mr. Turnpike that I was not, in fact, directly involved in the murder of Mrs. Stuckey, but merely an innocent yet observant bystander who'd been rudely awakened at the crack of dawn and dragged unwillingly from her warm bed by a gun-toting lunatic. He let me go with a stern warning to stay out of trouble. Then he instructed May to accompany me back to the boats just to keep an eye on me. After all, I was only wearing my nightgown and Mr. Scott's jacket -- hardly suitable attire for a woman with a sense of decency.

The autumn air nipped at my bare legs. I was hungry, cold, and eager to get back to the *Atropos*, so we hurried along the gravel road leading away from the village, heading east.

The silence that stretched between us was as heavy as the air before a storm. Tiny creases collected in the corners of May's eyes and mouth. After a half-mile, she opened her mouth to speak. I'd been anticipating her question the whole way, but she took longer to break than expected.

"Was your husband really a police officer?"

"He was," I replied.

"By the way you spoke, you might have well been a detective yourself. You certainly ran circles around Turnpike."

I sighed and shrugged helplessly. "It wasn't my intention."

"Oh, dang it all, the man deserves a good shake-up," she replied. "The worst crime he's ever had to solve was the theft of a few cows. Trying to solve a murder is far, far above his skill level. And thank goodness, too, that you told him about your past, so that he'd listen to you. He should be grateful for your help."

"It's not my place, though."

She shrugged. "I'm glad you spoke up. Hardly anyone does, anymore. The war trained us all to follow orders: we see a uniform and we jump to attention."

"Was Turnpike in the war?"

But May only shook her head. "I don't know. Possibly. Most of the men here worked in the shipyards or joined the navy."

"And you said his wife is Randall Godwin's cousin?"

"Second cousin," she corrected. "Not that they're close, though. Godwin is the one with the fortune, and he keeps his distance from the working-class relations. To be honest, Miss Rose, I don't know if their family connection will influence Turnpike; he's not the best at deduction, I admit, but I don't think he'd try to cover up anything, either."

"He was quick to decide that I should spend a few hours in a cell," I grumbled.

"Goodness, not if I could help it!" She dropped her voice to a whisper, and notes of grief and of pleading snuck into her words. "But why would someone want Mrs. Stuckey dead, Rose? She never did any harm to no one!"

"I don't know," I said, "What sort of woman was she?"

"She was very chaste, very quiet, and kept mostly to herself," May replied. "She always tried to do her Christian duty. She gave clear instructions and she could be fair if there was a dispute. She was a good boss to have."

"How long had she worked for Mr. Godwin?"

"A long time, much longer than me." May gestured to the corner of a field. "Here, there's a short cut across this pasture, let's go this way." We both climbed over the low stone wall, and as we started rambling through the grass, May said, "I've heard she used to travel with Mr. Godwin before he purchased the estate and settled here back in 1901. She was from the south of England, I think. Her family worked for a lord or some such."

"Then she comes from a line of servitude."

"That's only what I've heard," said May. "It's different in Europe, isn't it? People are more likely to follow their family's occupation, unlike here, where people strike out on their own and make do with whatever job they can find." She smiled. "My father's family were fishermen in Japan, and he owned a salmon trawler in Steveston. My mother came from Ukraine to work in the cannery; that's where they met. I guess I was destined to work in the cannery, too, but I'd had enough of the stench of fish by the time I was ten years old! When I got old enough to seek out my own employment, I wasn't going anywhere near a dock!"

"So, you traded in fish for chickens?"

"I suppose I did!" she chuckled. "But you know, chickens can be very clever and loving, once you get to know them. You can train them to do simple things. I have a chicken that can count to ten. She can even do simple addition!"

"Really?!"

"No one ever believes me when I say so," she replied. "I guess most people would rather think of chickens as stupid because it makes it much easier to eat a stupid animal than a smart one." She wrung her hands before her. "But, as for Mrs. Stuckey," May continued, "She hired me in 1914, just after the war started; like I said, Mr. Godwin has a shipyard, and he had a number of military contracts. With the war, he was going to be hosting political events and she knew they'd need extra help around the manor."

"That must have been a lucrative position for him."

"Oh, yes," she agreed, leading me down a trail and across a second pasture, "He made a good deal of money."

"What about his son, Francis? How did he and Mrs. Stuckey get along?"

May pursed her lips with disapproval.

"They didn't always agree, but then again, who does Francis get along with? He's a bit of a hot head."

"Ah, yes, I noticed."

"On paper, he works for his father's company and so he was exempt from the draft, but he isn't very reliable. He comes and goes at all hours; he keeps poor company. He wouldn't show up for work for days at a time! So, Randall treats him like a child. I think it bothers Francis that the only action he saw during the war was making coffee and shaking hands," she said. "And, because Mrs. Stuckey controls the finances for the running of the house, she's the one who doles out Francis' allowance. If he needs money, he must go to her."

"Ouch!"

"I've never seen them argue, though. She never withheld anything from Francis."

"But it would be a matter of pride. He's a young man; he wouldn't be too pleased to ask the housekeeper for his money." We startled a small flock of sheep which scampered out of the way, bleating and snorting, and we altered our direction to give them space. "Did Francis approve of how his father used his fortune? How did he feel about his father's art collection?"

"I don't know," she replied, "As far as I can tell, he doesn't pay it much attention except to grumble about how much space it takes up. But the collection is Randall's obsession. He started collecting masks while on safari as a young man in Africa. Francis wouldn't dare upset his father. He wouldn't want to put his allowance in jeopardy."

"Was there every any strife between the elder Mr. Godwin and Mrs. Stuckey?"

"Oh, no, not at all," May replied, "Her death has struck the old man very hard."

"And what of Francis' mother...?"

"Died in childbirth."

"Ah," I replied, "And Randall never remarried?"

May shook her head. "I suppose Matilda Stuckey was the closest thing to a wife that Mr. Godwin had. He didn't need another woman around."

"I hate to ask again," I started delicately, "But you're quite sure no one had a problem with her? Of course, you wouldn't want to speak ill of the dead, I understand that, but if there's anyone with whom she had a disagreement...?"

May pinched her lips.

"I shouldn't say. It's not proper."

I paused in my step. Even though my legs were covered in goosebumps and I was starting to shiver, I stood still until she turned to face me.

"You absolutely should," I urged. "Who?"

The young woman balked.

"You know how I said Mrs. Stuckey looks after all the household finances? Well, she hasn't paid the staff for a month," she admitted, "All of us are waiting for our money. Old Mr. Godwin assured me it's in the account, but Mrs. Stuckey said she's had a terrible time at the bank, and there's been some sort of mix-up -- please understand, everyone thinks the world of her, and I'm sure this has only been a banking error." May's voice trembled. "But it's made life difficult for some of us. A few of the staff, like the cook, live in the village and support families on their pay, and they've had a difficult time without their money. You can't pay a rent with promises."

"Of course not," I agreed.

"She hasn't paid Francis, either, and that's caused a few nights of yelling and carousing." May shook her head. "He accused his father of holding the money back."

"Why?"

"I don't know, nothing has changed as I can see it," May replied, "Like I said, I think it must be a bank error." We started walking again. "Believe me, Rose, in all other ways Mrs. Stuckey has been a good employer. I can't imagine who would do such a horrible thing to her. There was nothing in her character to foretell such a brutal end; she was a good woman, very modest and conservative. She once told me that she had a nice little nest egg saved up, and she was planning to return to the south of England when she retired in a year or two, and buy a little cottage near the sea to live out the rest of her days." May sighed. "She has family there and she was eager to see them again. I suppose someone will have to send a letter to her cousin and inform him of her murder. He'll be very upset. They were close and wrote to each other almost every week."

I played over the scene in my head. Had one of the staff finally lost their patience and killed her for her meagre savings? I suppose it was plausible. People do strange things in desperate times, and there would have been plenty of opportunity after the household had gone to bed to sneak into the woman's room through her unlocked door, surprise her at her writing desk, and dispatch her in order to steal whatever funds she had hidden away.

But then, why bother with the ruse of a theft? A staff member would never be able to sell the mask. They'd have no connections, no ability to move it. If someone was worried about making their rent, the last thing they'd want is a huge piece of evidence that linked them directly to the crime scene, stashed in their house.

We reached the top of the hill. The broad rolling fields of Mr. Buckley's farm unfurled before us, bumping up against the rocky shore of the bay where our colourful boats were moored. The fog of dawn had lifted. A pretty, peach-coloured sky arched over the meadows of tents and horses, farmers and wagons, creating a pastoral painting of placid perfection. Yet even as May commented on how lovely it all looked, I noticed a flurry of activity around the boats.

"Goodness, there's a lot of commotion at the wharf," said May.

On the shore, a group of men had assembled: even from this distance, I recognized a few of them. There was Bill Peacock, our knife-thrower, and next to him was the animal-trainer Orville Mann, and set a few paces apart stood the bulky blond figure of Mr. Buckley. At his side, Mr. Buckley held a rifle. Bill Peacock was carrying an axe. When the wind shifted, the buzz of angry voices percolated up from below.

Something was wrong.

We rushed down the road, across the pastures, to the edge of the crowd. I pushed through the men with May following in my wake. As we boarded the *Atropos*, Mr. Scott was joining the men on the shore. We found Magda and Alex leaning against the railing of the top deck, watching from above as Mr. Scott began to speak to the crowd.

"What's happened?" I asked as we joined them.

"Morris is gone," Alex replied. He noticed May following behind me and, for a fraction of a second, his dour expression transformed into one of interest and geniality. He doffed his hat to her and bowed his head. "Good morning, miss! This pink sky is a bonny start to the day, don't you think?"

But Magda snarled like a weasel: she had no time for pleasantries or flirting. "Didn't the cards warn us?" she said to me, "Morris is not what he seems."

"You can't think he murdered someone!"

"As soon as he saw that you'd been taken in by the law, he went as pale as a carp. I saw it, so did you," Magda said to Alex.

"I thought he'd taken an ill turn, being such a sensitive lad," Alex replied. "He claimed a need to lie down in his own bunk. He was shocked to hear you'd been tangled up in a murder, Miss Rose, but so were we all! Nancy was crying in fits and bouts, carrying on like a wee bairn, and everyone was in a right state! It wasn't until Honoria went to fetch Mr. Cave for breakfast that she found his room was empty, and we've turned the boats upside-down, but no one can find hide nor hair of him."

"He's left us, the craven bastard! And there's only one good reason I can think," said Magda.

"Morris can't have murdered Mrs. Stuckey," I asked, "It's impossible. He was with Calliope all night."

"Was he?" Magda needled, "She was sleeping heavily."

"Aye," said Alex, "The lad could have slipped away and returned and no one would be the wiser."

"I was with him in the evening and he was very dedicated. I can't believe he'd abandon her while she was recovering. And yes, she was sleeping so heavily that he might have had time to slip away, but," I pointed a finger towards the *Nona*, "Honoria was sleeping in the same room and she would've noticed. By God, she'd never have let him leave, if she thought he was shirking his duty of care!"

"Maybe..." said May in a tentative voice, for she was an outlier here and nervous to speak.

"What is it, miss?" said Alex. My goodness, he could turn on the charm when it fancied him, and he did so right then with Miss Tanaka, taking her hand tenderly and lowering his volume to a velvety hush. "If you can help us in any way, I would be most grateful."

A flush raced over May's cheeks. "This fellow named Morris? He came to visit us, the day before yesterday, and he told Mrs. Stuckey that he was very interested in the masks. She showed them to him."

"He'd met her!" said Alex.

"Yes, and he gave us tickets to come to the show in appreciation," she replied. "You don't think that has something to do with this, do you?"

"Seems like too much of a coincidence to me," Magda growled.

But I was certain Mrs. Stuckey was killed first and the mask taken to cover it up, so I protested this theory. "Morris had no reason to murder a stranger."

"But the cards told us, Morris is not who he claimed to be," Magda reminded me.

"I won't be swayed by superstitions and fortune-telling," I replied. "What reason would Morris have to murder a woman he'd only just met -- a complete stranger! -- and then deflect the guilt on to us by staging a robbery? He's never even been to Esquimalt before! He had no reason to attack the woman."

"But if he did kill Mrs. Stuckey for some reason that we do not yet know, he might have grabbed a mask to make a bit of bob," said Alex.

"But if he only wanted to steal it for a bit of money, why choose the devil mask?" I pressed. "It's huge, unwieldy, dirty --"

"Didn't you hear the constable?" said May, "It's also worth £10,000!"

Alex's mouth dropped open.

"Yes, but it didn't look it," I insisted. "The New Zealand war mask is much smaller and more finely wrought, and the murderer opened that display case to snatch up the jade club to stage Mrs. Stuckey's bludgeoning; if they'd already opened the case, why not just take that mask, instead? It would've been much easier to transport and far easier to sell."

A shiver crossed May's shoulders. "Because... I never thought much about it at the time, Rose, but when I showed Morris the devil mask, he let out a big laugh and looked very interested in its shape and design. Honestly, I thought he was reacting to its frightful grimace, like you did when I cast off the tarp."

Magda threw me a suspicious glance. "There is more to Morris Cave than we know," she insisted.

On the wharf below us, Mr. Scott had portioned the group of roustabouts and performers into two lots: Lou Grady, Bill Peacock, Saltchuck Cecil, the young Hugo Scott and the animal trainer Orville Mann in one group, and in another group was Wilson Ito, Virgil Stonehouse, Hector Kane and Argos the Blockhead, along with the clown Bobbie MacKenzie. Mr. Scott strolled between the two groups like Napoleon rallying the troupes before Waterloo, and in a loud voice, he called out to all of them, "Don't fetch the law just yet, lads. I'd rather we take care of this ourselves. If you find Morris, you bring him back here and we'll have the truth out of him."

May crossed her arms and shivered. "That sounds terribly ominous."

"Grover doesn't mean anything by it, except that the law rarely favours our kind," Magda assured her. "If we want to hear Morris' side of the story, then we're his best chance to make his case. Anyone else will twist his words to pin the guilt on him."

The two groups of men fanned out and followed the roadway, one group heading northeast and the other heading west. As I watched them go, Alex and May began to chat about the dreadful business of the murder and theft. Magda settled next to me against the railing.

"Watch out for your pretty little friend," she said, "Alex is turning on his charms."

"He wouldn't dare," I replied, "We're already entangled in one mess. Alex is too clever to bed the housemaid and make things worse."

Magda laughed. "Oh, you don't know him like I do. A pretty girl in every port."

"May is no dummy," I replied. "She won't be led down the garden path." The comment sparked a question. "How has Calliope reacted to Morris' disappearance?"

"I don't know, I haven't talked to her. She's still recovering in her room."

"Morris didn't run when he'd knocked her up."

"And...?"

I tapped my fingers along the railing, thinking.

"He's been with us for a few months."

"Since June," said Magda.

"And in all that time, he's never dodged any responsibility. Have you ever seen any fault in his character? Has he ever been lazy or dishonest?"

She shook her head. "A bit too quiet for my liking, but artists are like that," she said. "They're a watchful bunch. People think they're flighty with their head in the clouds, but really, they notice everything around them and remember it for later inspiration. Still, he doesn't drink, he doesn't gamble very much, he's first to help when a task needs to be done. Even Mr. Buckley said he was good with the cows, and cheerfully shovelled the manure out the barn. I figured, if his only fault is being an introvert, then I'm happy to hire him."

"He's not the sort of fellow to lose his temper, either," I said, "Whoever stabbed Mrs. Stuckey and then crushed her skull must have held a great deal of anger and resentment. Morris doesn't strike me as so... so... brutal."

Magda shivered. "Crushed her skull? Jesus have mercy! That sounds like something the Geek might do!"

The comment snagged Alex's attention. "You think the Geek did this?"

"No, of course not," she replied, "If -- by some miracle -- the Geek escaped his cage, found his way to town, and broke into a fancy house, he'd grab the first thing to catch his eye, and I can assure you, it wouldn't be some bit of carved wood. No, that bastard would go straight for a roast chicken or a nice baked ham."

"I don't know... The eyes on this mask were arresting," I said with a smile. "The Geek might've recognized his own wildness in it."

"But if it was a matter of impulse, he wouldn't have seen it," May replied. "No one would, if they didn't already know it was there. The case was kept covered because so many of us were afraid of it."

"The case was covered?" said Magda with interest.

"Mrs. Stuckey covers some of the cases with canvas to keep out the damp. Mr. Godwin says our wet, cool climate is hard on the wood and fibres, especially those that have come from hot dry countries. They can crack."

I recalled seeing the twisted length of canvas under Mrs. Stuckey's body, ripped from the cabinet.

"Sometimes," May continued, "If Mr. Godwin thought an artefact might be infested with bugs, he'd ask Mrs. Stuckey to fumigate a mask by burning a bit of smouldering tobacco under the canvas. The smoke drives out any pests, but that particular process requires a few days to work."

"I smelled the tobacco smoke in the hall," I remembered.

"The rest of the staff don't have much to do with the masks. Mrs. Stuckey is the only one who cares for the collection," said May, "But your Geek would never have known the devil mask was there: it was in the darkest part of the hall, covered over, and long forgotten by most everybody."

I chewed on my lip, thinking.

"May, when was the last time you laid eyes on the mask? Think back: the precise time you last saw it."

"Let me think," she said, more to herself than to me. "I showed it to you, I was with Mrs. Stuckey when she showed it to Morris. Then I covered it back up, but I was in a hurry and I left a gap in the tarp... I remember because that evening, before we came to the circus, I had to fetch Mrs. Stuckey's handbag. She'd left in the side hall closet at the end of the corridor, and gosh, I hate walking through that hall in the dark! When I got to the end, I saw those big goggled eyes peering out through the gap, and they almost gave me a heart attack! I grabbed her handbag, and I pulled at the tarp so the devil was hidden again, and then I ran back to the kitchen fast as possible." She shivered at the thought. "The devil mask always makes me feel like a frightened child... yes, that was the last time I saw it."

"What about that night?"

"We came home from the circus, entered through the kitchen door, and went straight up the staff staircase to our bedrooms. Nothing in the corridor had been touched or disturbed."

"Did anyone see it after you?"

"Well, Mrs. Stuckey did," said May, "The next day, she fumigated some of the masks. She scolded me and said I hadn't put the devil's tarp on straight, and she'd had to fix it." Her brow furrowed. "But only Mrs. Stuckey, and she was very clear that the staff members were to leave the corridor empty. She didn't want the fumigation process to be interrupted by someone carelessly opening a window."

I glanced at Magda. "Whoever took the mask must've known it was there. A staff member?"

"Or you," she replied.

I thought of my dream, of the minotaur dancing on the crest of the hill, and suppressed a shudder. "That damnable thing rooted itself in my imagination, but I didn't touch it. I wouldn't dare."

She gave a helpless shrug, as if the ways of the world are beyond our comprehension or influence, and what must be, must be. "If not you, then I can see no other option," Magda replied. "It must've been our mysterious Mr. Morris."

Perhaps the mask played a more crucial role in this murder than I'd originally assumed. I left May with Alex and Magda and went directly to Morris' cabin on the *Decimo*. His disappearance had shaken my certainty of our troupe's innocence, and the more I learned, the more he was upending all my theories.

I found his cabin door unlocked.

The room was slightly larger than mine, or perhaps it only seemed more spacious because, instead of a cot, Morris had slung a wool hammock between the walls. The hammock hung directly over an old, battered travel trunk that had seen better days, its moldy leather speckled with stickers from countless ports-of-call. An oil lamp sat on a small collapsible table in the corner, next to the thumbed copy of Hardy's 'The Mayor of Casterbridge', a straight razor, and an ivory comb, and the ukulele was on the floor in a brown corduroy case, leaning against the table, waiting for its owner to return. A comfortable scent of pencil lead and wood shavings and beef jerky, mingled with old leather and the tang of boot polish, hung in the air.

Morris' boots, coat, and hat were gone.

What did I really know about this reclusive young man? He kept his opinions to himself, he lived with simple contentment, he loved art. His tryst with Calliope had been a surprise but not wholly out-of-character -

- after all, she was pretty and he was energetic, and when people spend time in a common campaign, they naturally attract. These two were stuck on the boats together, both of them part of the circus cast, both of them part of a limited social circle. It was natural that they'd cleave together and find companionship.

The lid of the travel trunk squeaked when it opened. Nothing inside hinted at the young man's intentions. There was a pad of paper, a collection of charcoal sticks and pencils for drawing, and even a battered box of watercolour paints that were spattered and muddied from years of use. A couple of old photographs showed a gentleman in a suit and top hat holding the hand of a small boy in overalls: the child was obviously Morris, and the older man must have been his father, for the shape of their grins and eyes were almost identical. They stood outside a stone mill next to a little bubbling stream, and on the road behind them was a coach with driver, a severe-looking fellow with prominent square jaw and deeply-set eyes, but he was smudged and blurry with distance. When I flipped it over, I read words scrawled across the back: 'Doctor Cave and wee Morris, Holt Farm, 1905."

This must be the family farm.

Why would Morris leave such a personal item? Had he fled in such a panic that he'd abandoned anything of sentimental value?

I ran my hand over the nape of my neck, closed my eyes and thought back to the dark hours before dawn, when we'd all been so rudely wrenched awake by the blast of a gun. Francis Godwin had discovered the body of the housekeeper, then without a moment's pause, rode hard to Mr. Buckley's farm and let nothing stand between himself and vengeance. With the smallest provocation, he'd pointed a rifle at my head. He'd been mad with rage and shock. The young man was explosive, hair-triggered, and itching for a fight.

No wonder Morris left everything behind. He saw the writing on the wall, and it was his own name in blood.

Morris had run for his life.

Chapter Twelve

The two groups of men spent the whole morning searching the shoreline and the woods, peering into every woodshed or pig pen or outhouse they crossed, and Mr. Scott had given instructions to be thorough but he was adamant that our afternoon performance would start precisely at 2. Nothing ruined a reputation like unreliability. Mr. Scott was not willing to disappoint any townsfolk that came looking for quality entertainment, and while the loss of Morris had thrown a wrench in things, there was no good reason to make the situation worse by closing down our stages for the day. This might seem harsh, but Mr. Scott would never permit us to miss our opening call for any reason, up to and including the Rapture, and Calliope's delicate condition had already worn his patience thin. Everyone was given strict orders to be back and assembled by early afternoon, in costume and ready to perform.

Above all, the audience must not know we were missing one of our own.

And yet, even with Mr. Scott's precise instructions to say nothing, the gossip still got out. At half-past noon, Constable Turnpike raced through the gates of Buckley's farm on the back of a chestnut horse, galloping down to the wharf. The poor animal was frothy with lather and steamed in the cool air. Thank goodness Gertie wasn't near, or she'd have torn a strip from him for pushing the beast too hard! The constable was flushed in the face from exertion, too, and looked very much like an irate walrus.

I was sitting on the deck of the *Atropos*, resting briefly after rifling through Morris' room and belongings, when I heard their approach down the driveway. By the time I peeked over the handrail to the wharf, Alex was already half-way down the gangplank with a convivial grin on his face. He'd dressed for the ring in the bright red jacket of a Hungarian Hussar, trimmed with gold cord and epaulets, and he cut a dashing figure with his waxed moustache, fur busby, and a shiny black riding crop dangling from his belt.

"Here, sir, let me help you," he offered. He held the reins to quiet the beast as Turnpike dismounted. "What brings you back out this way?"

"I've heard you're missing a man," came the gruff reply, "You didn't think to inform me?"

"I can't see how it's your concern, sir, especially when you're busy with other, more pressing matters," said Alex, congenial and disarming, "We've just misplaced one of our younger roustabouts. He's a good lad but he's probably off and away with a pretty young thing and he's lost track of the time." His laugh was easy, unconcerned. "Tis a common problem with the boys when we dock in a new town, but no you worry, he'll return before opening curtain."

"I doubt that," sneered Turnpike, throwing a glance to me. "You know as well as I do, he's on the lam with Randall Godwin's stolen property."

"Mr. Turnpike, is it your job to assign guilt?" I said from my perch above them. "I thought that was for a judge to decide."

Turnpike's cheeks reddened more deeply. "Are you about to trot out your knowledge of the Queen's law and policing techniques again?"

"No, only my good sense," I replied. "You have no evidence linking Morris to this crime, plus he has a solid alibi for the night in question."

The walrus moustache twitched, the eye narrowed into mean slits. "You best watch your step, madam, or I'll throw you in jail for insubordination."

"Insubordination?" I gave a sharp laugh. "This isn't the army and we aren't at war. Besides, I've been nothing but helpful to you since we met, and I should think you'd be interested in what I have to say, rather than ignore me or, worse, throw me in the clink like some common pickpocket!"

There was a certain amount of sass to my statement, even I admit it. Alex's eyes bugged out and he stammered an apology for my behaviour, but Turnpike did nothing more frightful than give a harrumph of displeasure. "You've proven to be very observant, Miss Rose, and you've shared your theories with me quite liberally -- whether I've asked for them or not. So? Where do you think your missing man has gone?"

"Honestly? I think our ringmaster here may be right," I replied, "Morris is off with some farmer's daughter and they've lost track of the hour."

"You don't really believe that."

"I believe Morris is more capable of a silly fling than of cold-blooded murder. Doesn't it seem plausible? You know how capricious young men can be. They aren't the most responsible creatures, especially when there's pleasure involved. But I have a question for you, sir. Have you interviewed Mr. Godwin's staff for their alibis? Because certainly, whoever committed the murder hid it as quick as they could, and might have been keen to come back and tidy up their mess when the worst had blown over."

"I've interviewed them all. They seem respectable enough."

"And they told you they were owed money?"

He scowled.

"No one mentioned that, no."

I arched my brows. "They won't speak ill of the dead, but that doesn't mean they aren't thinking it." I left the stern and walked down the plank to the wharf so that we might talk without loudly broadcasting our theories up and down the shoreline. "Did you find anything suspicious in Mrs. Stuckey's apartment? Was she missing any of her belongings, like a stash of money or a jewelry box?"

He huffed. "I'm here to question you, madam! Not the other way around!"

"Fine," I said, softening, "Ask away."

"What brought you to the Godwin estate three days back?"

Alex gave me a look of caution but I knew where discretion was needed; his concern was appreciated but not required. "I was asked to fetch a bit of medication. I thought, in a such a fine house, the head mistress might keep a good pantry stocked and I was willing to pay well for what they might offer me."

"But you did more than just fetch some supplies, hey? You manipulated the poor garden girl to take you on a guided tour?"

I rolled my eyes at that. "Hardly! Miss Tanaka is a kindred spirit and a great supporter of the circus, and I never influenced her in any way. We stayed to the rear of the residence, only on the ground floor, and I was allowed the merest glimpse of Mr. Godwin's collection. There was no manipulation in mind, sir, just good-natured curiosity and fellowship."

He squinted slightly, and when he pursed his lips, his moustache twitched again. "Why didn't you go to the pharmacy for your medicine?"

"I'm not averse to such things. Why, when we needed a remedy yesterday, one of our boys was sent to the pharmacy to fetch it. Ah, there he is now, on the bridge of the *Decimo* -- Hugo, come here, please!" I returned my attention to the constable. "However, on the day in question, I needed something for a woman's malady and I thought it best to leave a pharmacist out of it. They hardly ever know what to prescribe for monthly cramps or excessive bleeding, you know how it can be."

The mention of *a woman's malady* made him swallow in discomfort, much to my wicked delight. Alex struggled to stifle a grin.

"Do you know much about menstruation, constable?" I pressed, "Have you had to deal with a monthly bleed? It's a tricky time for a lady, and the last thing I wanted was some know-it-all in a crisp white doctor's coat telling me what's best for our poor patient. A woman knows best how to help another woman through a difficult time of the month."

He nodded vigorously. "Yes, yes, fine." He consulted his notebook, if only to avoid my gaze. "And the young man who is missing. His name?"

"Morris Cave," said Alex.

"And he also visited the Godwin estate, yes?"

Both Alex and I swapped glances.

"He did," said Alex.

Turnpike made a few pencil scratches in his book. "And now he has vanished. The timing is suspect. You can see this puts me in a bit of a squeeze."

"I just can't believe Morris would murder anyone," Alex insisted. "He's a plum lad, hard-working and good-natured."

By this time, Hugo had climbed down from the rigging of the *Decimo* and joined us on the wharf. He was dressed in patched brown pants and a patched grey shirt, a smear of grease on his chin. Standing next to Alex in his finery, the poor boy looked little better than a street urchin. "What is it, Miss Rose?"

"You went to the pharmacy for charcoal biscuits, yes?"

"I did. The pharmacist had already opened the shop for another emergency, even though it was Sunday."

"And when you came back, Morris was still sitting with Calliope in her bed chambers, nursing her back to health, isn't that correct?"

"Yes, ma'am."

"And you checked in on them through the evening, too, did you not?"

"Once or twice." His dark eyes darted between the constable and myself. "And my mother brought them soup, and Honoria came back quick after her performance, and she spent the night in her own bed, with Morris sleeping in the chair in case Calliope needed him."

"See? Morris was too busy making sure our patient was comfortable during her recovery. He couldn't have been out causing mayhem or murdering the unfortunate Mrs. Stuckey."

Hugo's head snapped back to me. "Did you say... Stuckey?"

Turnpike pivoted his attention to the boy. "Do you know something?"

"Well, no, not really," Hugo stammered, "But maybe? I don't know."

"If it can help clear poor Morris' name, then please share, Hugo," Alex insisted.

Hugo fidgeted his fingers. "When I went to the pharmacy, there was a woman already there. She was in a big flap, looking like the end of the world was a-comin'! The pharmacist was tryin' to calm her down and such, and he called her Mrs. Stuckey."

"Yes, yes, she was out running errands that afternoon, the staff already told me that," Turnpike grumped, checking his notebook.

"It was very odd, though," said Hugo, "She was right flustered. She needed a bunch of items and I've never seen anyone look so upset."

"What, precisely, was she there to buy?"

Hugo closed his eyes, trying to remember.

"Paraffin wax. And onionskin paper. A bag of loose tobacco. Oh, and a disc of shoe polish, of all things."

None of these items were particularly special; why not wait until Monday morning to buy them? I leaned forward but Turnpike spoke first.

"Shoe polish?" he said. "Are you sure, boy?"

"Yes, sir," said Hugo, "Although I don't know how that helps you."

"Nor do I," Turnpike dismissed. He returned his attention to Alex. "I want to know when your missing man is found, and I want to speak with him directly, understood? If any of your people return with the smallest clue, you'll share it with me or I'll have the lot of you brought in on charges of conspiracy, including the Buckley family."

At first Alex bristled, but then he turned up the charm and gave his widest, toothiest, warmest smile. "Of course, sir! We want to do anything to help."

"Good." Turnpike mounted his skittish horse and was away at a fast canter, eager to put a few respectable miles between himself and our lowly horde.

I was angry -- furious, even -- that Turnpike had inserted himself into this matter, and that he'd dare to blame the Buckleys for whatever mischief Morris had done, but as I watched the man disappear over the hill in a flurry of hooves and dust, I tried to sort out the clues that had been made available to me. So, Mrs. Stuckey had visited the pharmacy for a few random supplies, looking upset and fretful -- how did that intersect with what I'd learned at Randall Godwin's home?

I stood quietly thinking and pondering for so long that I naturally assumed Alex and Hugo had left me alone on the dock. It wasn't until the ringmaster spoke that I realized they were still here, standing just behind me. Hugo looked as uncomfortable as only a teenager can be. Alex stood with his arms crossed and a fearsome scowl on his face. He didn't show his anger often; it was an expression that made him look very handsome and self-possessed, and more than a little intimidating.

"Morris has only made the situation worse for himself," he growled.

"What can we do?" said Hugo.

"Not much, as I see it," Alex replied. "If he's smart, then he's already boarded a ship to the Orient, in which case we'll never see hide nor hair of him again."

"But with the mask?" I said, "It was a massive thing, Alex! It would be difficult to move, especially for someone with no money, no horse, and no connections."

He considered this. "Do you think Morris might be hiding? Gone to ground like a wee fox that's waiting for the huntsmen to pass?"

"Maybe."

"If so, then he's put himself at a wicked disadvantage," Alex said. "He's in unfamiliar territory, with no weapons or food, and on the cusp of winter? These nights are terrible cold for anyone unprepared! Even you said as much to Kane when you stayed with the Geek -- aye, I heard about it from the doctor. He was pure raging over the whole affair. I think the man wants you sacked for overstepping your bounds." But his icy tone melted a little; he obviously found it amusing.

"I checked Morris' room for any clue to his intentions," I replied. "He left all of his personal belongings behind."

"If he's run off with a mask worth £10,000, what does he need to pack? He'll have more than enough funds if he manages to sell it."

Hugo gasped. "Ten thousand?!"

"Aye, not a bad take, if Morris can find a buyer."

"You believe he took it?" I said to Alex.

"Maybe he did, maybe he didn't, but I know one thing," he said, "That boy didn't kill anyone. He no has the constitution for murder. He is a wee sook and a good lad, mind, but not a mean bone in his body."

We parted ways, with Alex heading up to the Big Top and Hugo returning to the *Decimo*, and I found myself wishing I knew more about Morris and his side of the story. But how? No one knew his plans, no one knew his ways and habits. He'd kept himself to himself for all these months. Honestly, I'd learned more about the quality of the character since helping Calliope and her unwanted pregnancy, and I'd spoken more to him in the last three days than I had all summer.

Maybe that was the key. Of anyone on the boats, she knew him best. Maybe Calliope could tell me more.

I went straight to the Gibsons' door and knocked upon it gently. When Calliope called out, I entered.

The woman lay bundled under thick layers of blankets, quilts, and woven throws. Only her pallid face peeped out from a plush mountain of satin pillows. "Hello, Rose," she said. "I'm so glad you've come. I'm dreadfully bored."

Her voice was as lacy and frangible as spring ice. The vomiting had left her throat raw; she would not be singing again for some time.

I sat in the chair by the bedside. A sheen of sweat on her exposed skin reflected the lamplight, but her eyes were clear and bright, and her pupils shrank down to pinpricks when they gazed upon the flame. "It's good to hear you talking again," I said, "It looks to me like the effects of the quinine are wearing off."

"I feel much better," she said.

"That's good to hear," I replied, "We were all worried."

"And Morris? Magda told me he'd left, but has he come back?"

The quality of her question caught my attention. She didn't sound concerned at all, nor did she sound surprised.

"He hasn't returned and no one can find him. But, did you know Morris was planning to leave?"

"Of course." She winced with pain as she shifted to sit up a little. "I mean, eventually he planned to leave. Who would want to stay here forever?" she laughed, as if I was daft to think someone could make the Circus Salmagundi into their home. "But he hasn't returned to England, Rosie, not while I'm bedridden. He'll come back to fetch me. I'm sure of it."

"He mentioned that he was feeling homesick."

Her smile was the mischievous grin of a co-conspirator. "We both are: this dreadful wilderness is driving us mad! Morris promised to take me and Honoria home with him when he goes, but I suppose we'll have to wait until I'm strong enough to travel." She coughed. "I don't think I could get any farther than Vancouver, I'm so weak and tired."

"You'll get your strength back, your body has just been through a terrible jolt," I assured her, then asked, "Where, exactly, is home for Morris?"

"His family owns a large estate in Dorset," she said, sounding tired. "I think his grandfather was titled. A baron, maybe? Are there still barons in England? So much has changed with the war, I don't recall."

I remembered the photograph. "Was the estate called Holt Farm?"

She nodded. "That's it, yes. It's near a village called Melbury." She tipped her head to one side and her eyes grew dreamy and soft. "Morris said his family has owned the land since the beginning of time. But Morris' father was ambitious and he became a doctor, and moved to Bath to take a position there. When his grandfather died, the estate was inherited by his father and his Uncle Thomas, but because both men were employed elsewhere -- his uncle had a successful business in London, and now he's an academic, you see -- the land was left in the care of their coachman. He turned out to be an untrustworthy cad." She shifted her weight in the bed and fluffed the pillow behind her shoulder. "Morris was angry that his father hadn't returned to the estate: he said it was wrong to abandon its care to the staff." She gave a sad smile. "His father and uncle have no interest in farming, so the land and the title belong to Morris, and he wants it back."

"What's he doing here, then, halfway around the world?!"

Her smile was dreamy. "Who knows? Playing at being poor, I guess, like a prince pretending to be a pauper."

I felt a shiver cross my arms: Magda's cards had spoken truly. Morris was a farmer, yes, but not impoverished, common or uneducated. He was a titled land-owner, and with that came certain responsibilities and status.

Perhaps his disappearance had nothing to do with the mask or the murder. Perhaps poor Morris simply didn't want his secret life -- his real life, his life before he joined the circus -- to be revealed in the course of a police investigation.

I could relate to that.

When I stood to leave, Calliope reached out her hand. "Could you do me a favour, Rose? Morris was reading a story to me."

I chuckled and said, "You don't want me to read to you, do you?"

"Oh dear, no! I think I have the strength enough to turn my own pages," she said with good humour, "But did he take his book with him?"

"No, in fact, he didn't. He left it in his room," I replied. "Let me fetch it for you."

Out I went, back to Morris' cabin, where I found 'The Mayor of Casterbridge' on the bedside table. I plucked it up and returned it to Calliope, handing it to her as she struggled to prop a few pillows behind her shoulders.

"It's not a book I'd normally read, but it'll stave off the boredom until I'm healthy again," she explained as she removing the bookmark, setting it down on her lap in preparation to read.

There, staring up at me from the slip of plain white paper, was an artful drawing of the devil mask, all frazzled hair and frightful horns.

Chapter Thirteen

My yelp of surprise must have startled Calliope, because she dropped her book and skirted back across the mattress in a burst of adrenaline, looking around wildly.

"What is it?" she cried, "A spider? A rat?!" Then, seeing the direction of my gaze, she scoffed. "God, Rose, it's only a sketch!"

"Did Morris draw this?!"

"Of course, he did! He's a very talented artist," she said.

I plucked up the paper and held it to the light.

Sure enough, the devil mask stared back, its goggled duck-egg eyes pointed directly at me. The rendering had been wonderfully executed, if a little heavy-handed.

"When did he draw this?"

"I don't know," she replied, her nose wrinkling in scorn, "He's had it for ages. I found it spooky and told him to put it upside down on the table when he reads to me."

"So before yesterday, then?"

Calliope looked at me as if I'd grown a second head. "He's been reading the book for more than a week, so yes, I suppose so. Why? Is it important?"

I stared hard at it, thoughts pinging around my mind like sparks off a whetstone.

Morris must've known about the existence of the devil mask before May showed it to him in Randall Godwin's collection. I peered closer: intricate details, cross-hatched shading, every scraggly hair on its brow. The drawing was perfect. This rendering proved he was intimately familiar with the mask, from its hinged jaw and the scruffy chin to its woolly piebald mane and ebonized crescent horns.

A single word was written in small, neat letters across the bottom.

"Ooser," I read, then glanced back at the girl, "What does that mean?"

Calliope was clearly losing patience. "I don't know. Why would I know? It's Morris' frightful imagination, not mine!"

I still had a million questions but there were no answers here, so I left without another word, taking the bookmark with me, and ignoring Calliope's disgruntled call to bring it back when I was done.

I went straight to the *Atropos* and knocked upon the largest stateroom at the stern of the ship.

The door flew open. Grover Scott blocked the threshold, looking sour at being disturbed, a pipe clenched in his teeth. He wore his trousers and undershirt with a towel draped over his shoulders. Half his hair was trimmed neatly while the other half was shaggy and damp. The man was more than a head shorter than me but he still managed to look down on me with disdain.

"You've come to return my jacket, hey?"

I was still wearing it. The day had been so strange and full, I'd forgotten to get dressed. Shrugging it off my shoulders, and said, "I need to talk to Magda."

"She's busy."

"Oh, my love, it's no bother," said Magda's voice from inside the stateroom, "We still have an hour or so until the curtain opens, and I can cut your hair and visit with company at the same time. Come in, Rosie dear."

He stepped aside to let me enter.

The owner's stateroom was cozy and cluttered, with a gigantic bed covered over with blankets and throws, and at its foot, a wooden crib carved with runes and symbols. A wooden chair sat in the centre of the room, behind which stood Magda with a pair of silver scissors in hand, and around her, toys lay scattered across the rag rugs: tin soldiers, dolls sewn from scraps, and a set of jacks that looked like caltrops spread out to injure unwary visitors. I skirted around them and set the suit jacket on the end of the mattress.

"Thank you for lending it to me this morning," I said as he returned to his chair. "I didn't have time to dress, what with the gunfire and all."

Mr. Scott waved the comment away with a rough snort as he sat down awkwardly, his boots sticking straight ahead: his legs were too short and he could not bend his knees.

Magda was more sympathetic. "How terrifying!" she said, "Are you alright, Rose?"

I gave a weary sigh. "It's not the first time I've had a rifle aimed at me."

"That damn copper, dragging you off at an early hour, and without a scrap of evidence against you... and barely a scrap of decent clothes on you!" he muttered, jabbing the air with his pipe stem to accentuate his points, "You can't trust the law, Rose. They always try to pin their bullshit claims on us if they're given the opportunity. Turn around twice and they've have charged you with prostitution for being so scantily dressed."

"Hush," said Magda as she bowed to her work and started snipping at her husband's hair. "Don't move your head."

"That little Godwin bastard ought to face justice for pulling a gun on Rosie here, but do you think he will? Of course not! *Too much money, not enough sense*, as my ma used to say."

"Don't move."

"And who's reputation is ruined at the end of it? Ours. If we aren't working our asses off to entertain the rubes, God forbid we have our own lives and needs that might happen to inconvenience them! Mark my words, Rosie: they'll love you as long as you twirl around for them, but they'll resent you the rest of the time -- gah!"

A garnet of blood appeared on the upper curve of his cheek.

"I told you, my love, don't move," Magda said as she dabbed it away with her sleeve. "Rosie didn't come here to listen to you rant about the rubes."

He settled in the chair, scowling, and returned his pipe to his clenched teeth. "What *do* you want, Rose?"

I sat on the edge of their bed next to the jacket, moving a rag doll out of my way. "The cards were right, Magda: Morris isn't who he claimed to be."

Grover snorted. "I got a cut on my face for that?"

Magda gave a waggish smile. "No, you got a cut on your face because you can't sit still when you're feeling self-righteous, and I love you for it." Magda always matched her husband's cantankerous nature with abundant good cheer. She planted a kiss on his tousled crown, then said to me, "Of course Morris isn't who he said he was, Rose. The cards never lie."

"*The cards never lie*? Jesus Christ, Magda, is that what your blessed cards told you?" Grover said to his wife, "That's just low-hanging fruit! I mean, look at yourself, Rosie: none of you lot are who you claim to be!" He started to laugh, a low rumbling sound full of dismissal, "A bunch of criminals, run-aways and tricksters, the whole lot of ya! Is it any surprise that Morris is, too?"

"I'm no criminal."

"Aw, don't get your panties twisted, Rosie," he chuckled as he wiped away the blood on his cheek. "I don't know your past and I don't want to. You got yourself a fresh start here and I know you're a good egg. Most of the time." He glanced up at his wife. "But Morris not being who he said? You might as well have predicted he takes a piss in the morning."

"He's a baron," I said.

They both paused at that.

"Where'd you hear such horseshit?"

"Calliope told me," I said to Grover.

He rolled his eyes. "Aw, c'mon now, Rose, you can't be that naive! A young man will claim to be just about anything to get under a pretty gal's skirt."

I pulled out the drawing and held it up to show them. "He also knew about the mask before we arrived at Buckley's farm."

Grover snapped the paper out of my fingers and looked at the devil's face.

"By God, it's like looking in a mirror," he said, brows arched. "Why, Morris just drew a portrait of yours truly!" He tipped his chin back and howled with glee.

Magda pushed his head forward again to avoid stabbing him in the eye. "Oh, my love, it doesn't have half your fire. And what does it say at the bottom?" She peered over the curls of Grover's hair. "*Ooser*? What does that mean?"

"I have no idea," I replied.

"I heard the term 'hoosier' plenty of times when I was traveling with the Frank Bros. Wild West Revue, doing the Midwest circuit," said Grover, "It's what the folks from Indiana call themselves. Just ask Lou Grady, he was born in Muncie."

Magda returned to snipping Grover's hair and said, "I sincerely doubt the mask is from Indiana, my love."

He handed the slip of paper back to me. "I'll ask around and see if anyone has a clue what the word 'ooser' means."

"Thank you, Mr. Scott."

I was about to leave when I heard him say, "You got an hour 'till showtime. Get yourself a quick nap, Rosie: you look exhausted, and no one wants to pay a penny to see a tattooed lady asleep in her chair."

That afternoon, the Ten-in-One was down a performer, but no one complained that we were only nine acts; as much as I enjoyed his jaunty tunes, Morris' ukulele recital had been the least interesting part of our retinue. He was neither a talented singer nor an engaging comedian, he had no compelling deformities, and he was too soft-spoken to be memorable, especially compared to the Geek, who happened to be in a frightful mood. His yowling was far more entertaining to the locals than anything Morris could've played.

I sat in my own cubical, answering questions about my tattoos, and cringing every time a bone-shuddering scream erupted from behind the canvas walls. God damn it, the cries of despair that man made were heart-wrenching! He bellowed like a bull in a slaughterhouse. How he must have suffered! The wretched idiot never used human language, yet through the medium of wailing and roaring and punching at his own skull, he was able to convey to us how much his head pounded. Dr. Kane turned down the oil lamp in the Geek's cubical until the cage was cast in flickering shadow, and the audience responded with delight to the dramatic, spooky atmosphere; the doctor claimed he was trying to ease the wretch's suffering, but I had my doubts.

However, I could not bear to be close to the Geek when he was like this. I cowered in my folding wooden chair and tried to muster courage as I chatted with my visitors, but I could feel my nerves slowly fraying, like the hem of the tent canvas or the ropes that held the poles up. The crowds thinned and the hour grew late, and eventually the Geek's noises ceased and the evening calm returned. I heard the Big Top music playing out a closing tune as the audience roared its approval, and I knew our sideshow performance was almost finished. I let out a great shuddering breath that I'd been unintentionally holding tight in my chest.

Stella the Bearded Lady poked her head through the curtains.

"Dammit, Rosie, how can you stand it?" she exclaimed, her voice pitching high and squeaking out the last syllables. She didn't wait for my reply. Instead, she strode across my cubicle and threw open the tent flap that separated me from the Cabinet of the Bizarre. "Kane, you god damned bastard, you ought to put that poor fella back on board the ship where he'll find a bit of peace and privacy!"

A weak, inhuman moan rose up in reply at the sound her voice: a plea from the Geek for clemency. His pain had not diminished, only left him wrung out fully. The mournful sound drew gooseflesh to my bare arms.

But Kane remained unsympathetic. He was straightening the jars on his table and he didn't look up when we entered. "Why bother, Miss Stella? It won't stop the old chap from making a racket. At least his pain brings in a decent income."

She straightened the pink ribbon tied in her beard as her eyes threw daggers. "May the sweet Lord have mercy on us," she said, "I've got the shakes from having to listen to that racket, and I'm not even next to him! Kane, you must have nerves of steel."

"No, ladies," said Kane, standing back to admire his tidying, adjusting one last jar, "I'm merely heartless." The doctor gave a shallow bow when he saw me. "Miss Rose, how are you this evening?"

"Rattled, frankly," I said. "Is there nothing you can do for him?"

"The Geek is beyond all medical assistance," he replied. "But I'm sure ticket sales were brisk tonight. Didn't it seem busier to you? The howling of that poor man attracts the curious like moths to flame." He rubbed his hands together to bring warmth to his fingers but there was a greediness to it that was unsettling. "Shall we return to the ships? It's a cold night out and we'll have frost in the morning."

Stella turned to me. "Are you planning to stay out here again?"

But the doctor replied. "No, Miss Rose has made it very clear to me, the Geek must have his own private lodging with a staff to attend him." His sarcasm was cutting; he clearly thought I'd gone soft. "I've arranged for Lou and Hugo to stay the night in the barn with him and keep a fire going. They'll happily play cards until dawn." He led the way through the last room, speaking to the lump in the cage as we passed. "Good night, old chap. Your entourage will be here within the hour to attend you."

He and Stella both laughed, but I did not.

Instead, I lagged behind and waited until they'd left the tent before I dared to creep close to the cage.

The poor pathetic wretch. He lay curled in a tight ball under the matted pelt, hiding his face from view with his arms. Tangled ropes of black hair cascaded from under one edge of the pelt, and from under the other, his bare feet appeared waxy in the flickering lamp light. It was impossible to get a clear view of him: even though he lay exposed in an iron cage, he remained a master at keeping himself hidden.

"I'm so sorry," I said.

But the Geek didn't move a muscle. Maybe he was sleeping, or maybe unconscious. For a second, I feared he might be dead. I stepped forward and peered close at his torso, examining the shapeless lump for any signs of life, and only letting out a sigh of relief when I saw his ribs rise and fall. I laid my hand on one bar. I'd never dared to step so close to the cage -- it felt solid and immovable under my fingers, as welcoming as a gibbet. How long had this man been trapped here? How had Kane come to be his care-taker, and would the Geek eventually die here, without friends or family ever knowing his fate? I must have been very tired, for I found myself lost in thought without paying attention to my surroundings and, consequently, I almost leapt out of my skin when a gentle hand set itself to the crook of my arm.

"Christ!" I shouted as I skittered back into the cage with a bang.

"Oh! Rosie! It's only me!" said Alex. "Dear me, I didna mean to scare you!"

My heart hammered in my chest. I heard the Geek grumble behind me and, realizing I was well within the range of his arms too, I fled into the centre of the room, away from both men.

Alex took a step forward, arms out. "Are you alright?"

I stepped back. "Yes, yes, I'm fine."

He noticed my avoidance and dropped his arms to his side, the gold fringe of his epaulets shimmering in the low light. "I didna mean to sneak up on you, but you were verra deep in contemplation."

I still trembled, so I pulled my robe more tightly around my shoulders as if I was shivering from the cold. "I just wondered how the Geek came to be, that's all."

Alex gave the lump a cursory glance. "Grover found him stumbling through an alley in Seattle," he said, "The doctor thinks he suffers from syphilitic madness, but I know little more."

"Poor fellow."

"Aye, but it's charitable of you to want him warm in the night."

"The doctor can be a callous fellow, I've noticed."

Alex shrugged as a way of agreement. "We all have our quirks, don't we?" He smiled kindly, but his eyes were curious and prying. "You didna seem to care when a gun was aimed at your head, and you certainly had no qualms about talking to yon constable like an equal, but I've noticed you are not overly fond of standing too close to me. You go all peely wally if I dare get too near."

I crossed my arms. "Yes, that's true."

"Why?" he asked, "What have I done to offend you?"

The question seemed so innocent and aggrieved it brought a chuckle to my lips which I quickly hid behind my fingers. It occurred to me that Alex, with his alluring smile and dashing constitution, was entirely unaccustomed to members of the fair sex flinching at his touch or withdrawing from his presence, and the only reason he could see for my hesitation was that he'd hurt my feelings.

"You've done nothing wrong, Mr. McGee," I assured him, "You're a gentleman through and through. Over the course of my life, I've been left with an inability to trust men, and I find it... uncomfortable... to be close to them. I hate to be reminded of my own weakness."

A dawning realization crossed his face. "Ah, your scars. I suppose you must have got them from someone's unkindness."

"Precisely," I replied.

"I'll ask no more, then," he assured me, "But please know, Miss Rose, that I have only your best interest at heart. I've never raised a hand to a woman, nor would I ever. You're perfectly safe in my company."

I'd heard those sorts of promises before.

But I only bowed my head and thanked him for his assurance, and we left the tent together to begin our slow return to the ships.

"I came to find you," he said, "Grover told me about the drawing made by young Mr. Cave. It contained the word 'ooser'?"

"Ah yes!"

Alex gave me a particularly impish smile. "That is an ancient term that I've not heard since I was a wee laddie!"

"What does it mean?"

"A good question but not one with an easy answer," he replied. "I've heard the name said a million ways, depending on the county -- hooset, wooset, ooser, gruigach. Up in Aberdeen, my gran called him 'Auld Clootie'. All of them refer to a mythical figure oft portrayed in kirks and churches as a devil, but that's just a Christian interpretation of his true, primordial, pagan identity: the Horned Man."

"You say that like I ought to know who that is," I replied. "Is he a god?"

"Yes and no. The Horned Man is a figure who pops up all across the British Isles and Europe. He's sometimes known as the Green Man, and sometimes Old Horny, but no matter what name he wears, he brings the springtime and cares for the crops, he makes the world fertile and growing, and he keeps the community safe and strong. I wouldn't say he's a god, as such -- not like our saviour Jesus Christ -- but he's a spirit that the common folk still recognize, even if they don't know exactly where their traditions hail from."

"And the church calls him a demon?"

"Aye. To a good Christian priest, the Horned Man must seem like a bit of a pervert and a savage," Alex grinned. "He's the wild man of the wood who lays with all the pretty girls under the hedgerows, wearing a crown of antlers and greenery upon his head."

Those lustful eyes, the blackened horns, the greedy and lascivious grin. Yes, I could see it. "So, the mask is English?"

"Now, I don't know of any masks, exactly," Alex continued, "But in some towns, they'd make a figure out of a horse's skull topped with a pair of stag antlers, set on atop a pike of yew wood and garbed in cow hide, and the townsfolk would parade it around the town with noisy music and pans clattered behind it. They called the figure a 'wooset' and the ritual was called a skimmity-ride. The crowd would stop at the house where someone has been unfaithful, and they'd rattle the chains and sing their bawdy songs, and the offender would be brought out and beaten with sticks, then sent for a ride backwards on a donkey." He shook his head slowly at the ridiculous image. "The whole demonstration is done to bring shame to those caught cheating on their wife or husband. It's done very rarely now, and I've never seen it with my own eyes, but my gran warned me of it; she'd seen it happen as a lassie."

I looked at him askance, suspicious. "I thought you said the Horned Man lay with all the pretty girls under the hedgerows."

"Aye, but none of them betrothed. Once a promise is given, it ought not to be broken, for that's truly the devil's work."

"I wonder if this ooser might have been used for such a frightful punishment."

"Did it look like a grotesque monster that might be trotted out to terrify cuckolds and whores?"

I laughed. "Staring down that ugly mug would certainly scare me into behaving!"

He gave a gruff chuckle. "Aye, then, this ooser might be an old pagan god hiding in a bit of folk magic and wicked fun, used to dispense justice." Alex lost his levity. "And you say this was the mask that was stolen?"

"The very same."

"Then Morris must've known it was here, and it must've been him who took it," he replied and shook his head with disappointment. "That ridiculous fool! Who'd have thought him capable of murder? If he drags us into his troubles, I wager Grover will leave him behind and let him hang."

Chapter Fourteen

I tumbled into my bed clothed in my chemise and bloomers, and my bones were so weary that the thin mattress seemed to swallow me up in one gulp, allowing a depthless, restful slumber to wash over me. Sleep became an inescapable current. As if caught in a rip tide and pulled out to sea, I had not the strength nor inclination to fight it. I may have dreamt of gods and demons and skimmity-rides, but any visions vanished like candle smoke, too weak and distant to disturb my exhausted mind.

I woke, feeling wholly refreshed. The thumping of waves against the hull was like a balm to my soul. No gun blasts, no yelling voices, no knocking on my door. My consciousness returned naturally and without any outside influence, and it was glorious.

But my comfort was short-lived. On my trip to the galley for breakfast, I was intercepted by Hugo.

"Miss Rose?"

He stood on the top deck of the *Atropos*, leaning against the bow railing. The boy looked sheepish. I went to him and, as I drew close, he glanced over his shoulder as if afraid to be seen with me.

"What is it, Hugo?'

"I have a note for you." From the pocket of his grey flannel shirt, he pulled a scrap of paper all marked with penciled letters, and he pressed it into my hand as if it burned his fingers.

It had been crushed into a wad. Fifteen-year-old boys are not renowned for their delicate nature, and folding it neatly probably never occurred to him. It was just as simple to crumple it up and cram it in his pocket.

I took the note and smoothed it out. In a looped script, it read, 'Come to the house as soon as you can.'

"What's this, Hugo?"

"I think her name is May?" he said cautiously, "Late last night, after the show was over and everyone was finished, she came to the barn. Me and Lou were playing poker out there --"

"Ah, yes, I heard you were on Geek duty," I said, "Thank you for that."

"It's no problem. Lou was teaching me how to bluff, and I'm getting pretty good at it, too, and he says we're gonna have a public game at the next town we visit, and he's gonna let me sit in -- that's if my ma lets me, of course, but I think my pa would be perfectly fine with me doing a bit of gambling if I'm good at it -- and so I figured I might make a bit of money on the side, which would be real helpful because pa says things aren't nearly as lucrative as they were before the war --"

"Hugo," I said firmly, "Tell me about May."

"Oh! Yeah!" His eyes brightened. "She said she can't get away from the house on account of it being so chaotic there with no housekeeper no more, but she needs to talk with you, and I told her you'd gone back to the ships but she said she didn't want to bother you, so she wrote you a note. And there it is."

I glanced at it again.

"If anyone needs me," I said, "I'll be back as soon as I can."

The sun was bright and bonny, the road was dry under my boots, the groves of oak trees were merry and welcoming. Half the leaves still clung to their branches and these blazed out in stunning hues of orange, red and gold against a bold blue sky. A chill in the air spoke of winter, and I wore the shawl that May had given me along with my regular robe and head-scarf, so that I was a perfect temperature and colour palette to match the weather, all garbed in deep cerulean and bright yellow. I stayed to the roads and enjoyed a pleasant walk to Mr. Godwin estate, but I admit, it was not my most inspired idea -- I should have gone overland to avoid meeting anyone on my way. As soon as I spotted Constable Turnpike's horse trotting up the roadway, my stomach sank and my disappointment rose. I briefly considered hiding in a copse of trees but it was too late: he'd already seen me and was heading straight for me.

"You should be on your boats or staying to Mr. Buckley's farm if you know what's good for you," he said as he approached.

I chose to ignore his opening statement, and instead, greeted him with a chipper voice. "Isn't it a lovely day? I hope you're enjoying it as much as I am!"

The man dismounted with a heavy hop. "Where do you think you're going?"

I was already hungry, having missed breakfast. The lie was on my lips before I knew it. "We need eggs," I said, "Our troupe goes through an awful lot of them, so I thought I'd see if May had any to spare. And how are things with you? Have you had any luck with the investigation?"

We began to stroll along the road towards the Godwin property. I noticed his uniform looked a little more worn than when we first met, and the creases of his trousers didn't bunch around his thighs from sitting at a desk. He was working hard, trying to sort this whole mess out, and I warmed a little to him.

"Once I started asking about pay, the staff clammed up," he said to me, "I think you may have been on to something there."

"Now you believe our circus is innocent?"

"I wouldn't go so far as that," he replied, "I still have my eye on you, Miss Rose."

"That's fine with me. I have nothing to hide."

Something in my comment emboldened him.

"May I ask you a question?"

I glanced towards Turnpike. "What is it?"

He gestured towards his face. "What's with this costume of yours, all wrapped up in robes and scarves, like some restless phantom haunting the roads? Doesn't it bother you?"

"Covering my face? Oh, I don't mind at all. It's part of my agreement with Mr. Scott. I can come and go as I wish without diminishing the sideshow's mystery." I pulled the scarf down to expose my mouth and chin. "It's part of my uniform, no more or less bothersome that your hat or your belt."

Turnpike shook his head. "Aw, I don't know about that. I hated wearing the cotton masks we were given when Spanish Flu came 'round."

"They were hot and bulky," I agreed.

"Of course, we were lucky here; we only lost three men in the Esquimalt department, but the whole provincial service was already down from the losses of the war and even a single death hit the force hard. A lot of good young fellows never came home."

He opened his mouth as if he were about to comment further, then reconsidered. After a pause, he said, "I was sorry to hear you'd lost your husband."

I swallowed. "His death set off a chain of events that has led me here, and my life with the Circus Salmagundi is a comfortable one. Present difficulties, notwithstanding."

"Still. It can't have been easy."

"The past few years haven't been easy for anyone," I replied. "I'm not special in that regard. But I have a home and a job to feed me, and that gives me hope that the future will bring happier days. May we all be so fortunate in these uncertain times."

"Agreed," he said.

By now, we'd reached the front drive and the gate at the boxwood hedge, and I spotted a motorcar parked by the house, as well as a group of young men dressed in hunting flannels. They had with them horses and gear, and the whole shifting, stamping, restless lot of them clustered to one side of the lawn, churning up the grass with hoof and boot.

Unsteady and noisy, they were not waiting patiently. Prohibition had not yet been repealed but the word on the wind said there might soon be a referendum, and if the public wished it, the law could change by the end of the year; by the looks of them, these fellows had jumped the gun by a few months and were already drunk.

"What's this?"

"Ah," said Turnpike, "You didn't know? The elder Mr. Godwin has offered a reward to find the man missing from your boats. It's a bounty of $500 to the first fellow who hauls Morris in."

"What?" I scowled. "Does Mr. Scott know about this?"

"No one's kept it from him."

"But no one's informed him, either, that a posse is after one of his employees," I snapped. "You didn't think this might be dangerous?"

"Mr. Godwin is trying to be helpful. He wants this whole thing resolved and he feels awful about his son's actions yesterday morning."

I rounded on Turnpike. "You don't believe that."

"Why wouldn't I?" he replied. "The man is very charitable. He's well-loved by the community."

"He's also your wife's cousin."

"You think I'd be influenced by that?" Turnpike scowled. "I am not, I assure you. Mr. Godwin has honourable intentions."

"Intentions be damned, this mob will drag poor Morris to jail, if they don't shoot him first!"

At that moment, a flustered gentleman in suit and bowtie strode out of the mansion to the motorcar without hesitation or goodbyes. He cranked his car, the engine sputtered and roared, and he slipped into the driver's seat. The noisy contraption squealed out of the drive in a shower of gravel and dirt, spooking half the horses, and as the car zoomed passed us, Turnpike's chestnut mare hopped and reared, squealing in fright. I stared at the driver as he went by: a rat-faced man with thinning black hair and round glasses, looking sour.

"God!" said Turnpike in exasperation, settling his horse. "Infernal contraptions!"

"Who was that?"

"Mr. Benjamin Sully, the insurance agent," Turnpike replied.

I looked to the house. Francis was striding down the front steps in his riding attire, adjusting a sloped cap upon his head, and Randall followed closely afterwards, crowing after him and looking disappointed, gesturing to his son to return to the house immediately. Francis was frowning. His eyes were black with fury. I wouldn't dare cross a man wearing that expression! He demanded a wide detour.

"It doesn't look like Randall's meeting with the insurance agent went well," I pointed out.

"No, it does not," Turnpike agreed.

"How much of a reward did you say he's offered? Five hundred?"

"I believe so."

"Then Francis is hoping to make a bit of money off his old man," I guessed as we watched the scene unfold before us like a Greek tragedy. Their voices were tightly restrained and too quiet to hear clearly from this distance, but their conversation played across their features: Randall did not want his son involved, Francis was too distraught to follow his father's wishes, and the chorus of huntsmen and horses created a semicircle of watchful faces. I glanced to Turnpike. "You know Francis gets an allowance from his father, and must ask for it from Mrs. Stuckey."

"No!" Turnpike looked scandalized.

"Finding Morris and claiming the reward would give him a bit of financial freedom, at least for a while."

"Freedom to pay off his prohibition debts," Turnpike replied. He arched one hoary eyebrow in my direction, looking self-satisfied. "You see, Miss Rose? I'm not completely useless. I know a few facts." He tipped his head towards the arguing gentlemen. "Francis financed a speakeasy in Victoria but he's a terrible businessman: he's more interested in drinking his product than selling it. He was using the old man's money and making none of his own."

I was impressed by this show of sleuthing. "So how badly in debt is Francis?"

"I'm sure $500 would hold off the wolves, but not for long."

The two men had graduated from a heated conversation to open shouting. I heard Randall say, "Keep it up and you're going to get hurt, you pathetic worm! Get back in the house!"

I glanced at Turnpike. "How does Randall hope to pay the reward, if he can't pay his staff and his insurance claim is rejected?"

"A good question," he replied, and might have said more, except that there was a great shout of rage as Francis pointed his rifle to the sky and let off a blast of fire and black smoke, and everyone standing on the lawn jumped at the suddenness of it.

"See here!" shouted Turnpike, striding towards them, but we were too far for his reprimand to be effective. He was no more than half-way across the wide sweep of lawn when Francis and the young men mounted up, turning their backs to the officer in a most disrespectful manner. The group galloped into the hills, disappearing among the trees and bushes, but the sounds of their passage lingered long after they were gone. Hoots, shouts of encouragement, the nickering of horses, toasts and jests and good-natured insults. Clouds of crows rose from the highest bowers, startled from their roosts. Stealth was not part of their agenda. I found it encouraging that the nature of this hunting party leaned more towards the 'party' and less towards the 'hunting'.

As their noises faded with distance, Turnpike left me behind to join Randall in conversation. The elder Mr. Godwin jabbed his finger in the direction of the young men, and I could hear him pleading for patience from the constable. They were good boys, all of them, just a little high-strung with recent events.

'High-strung' was hardly the adjective I'd use for firing rifles willy-nilly, but I didn't care to get pulled into this drama. I had another purpose here. To avoid any further interactions with the policeman and the gentleman, I returned to the end of the drive and made as if to leave, then followed the hedge and the service path, circling around to the rear of the mansion.

As I came through the apple orchard, I heard May's voice call out my name from the herb garden. She stood in the centre of that little patch of earth, a hoe in one hand and a canvas apron covering her dress and blouse. Most of her hair was tied up and tucked under a white kerchief, but a few dark wisps had broken free and brushed her shoulders.

"Are you putting the garden to bed?"

"Tidying up before the bad weather hits. We still have chives and onions, and potatoes under those mounds there," she pointed out with pride as I joined her. "I'm glad Hugo gave you my message. I need to speak with you but I couldn't leave the gardens, and the cook has us all working doubly hard. The house is in an uproar! Mrs. Stuckey was the glue that held everything together, and without her, we are in fits and starts."

She looked more haggard than I remembered. Her collar was unbuttoned and her apron smeared with flour and grime.

"Did you see the group on the front lawn?" she continued. Her eyes flitted from side to side, as if she were afraid of being heard. "The younger Mr. Godwin has arranged for his friends to search for your missing man."

"And the elder is offering a generous reward, too," I replied.

"They're both quite certain your fellow is the murderer. I don't know what will happen if they find him." She leaned heavily against the hoe. "Francis has been a shameful mess -- sleeping a little and drinking a lot -- and I'm afraid he's going to kill someone, if he doesn't hurt himself in the process first!"

"I think Randall shares your fears," I said, "From the look of their conversation, he didn't want Francis involved."

"Oh, those two," she said. "It's a constant battle between them. The only thing they seem to agree on is Morris' guilt."

"Well," I began, "Morris may not know the area well but those overbearing goons in the posse weren't exactly quiet. He'll hear them coming from a mile away."

"But they're very determined," she replied. "And Francis doesn't like to lose."

I leaned against the stone wall that circled the garden. "He wants that reward to pay his debts, that's what Turnpike told me. Five hundred dollars to locate Morris?! Who'd have known the boy was worth so much." I shook my head. "And have you been paid for your labor, yet?"

Her frustrated scowl was all the answer I needed.

"I don't think any of us will see our money," she grumbled as she drew close and leaned against the wall next to me. "The gardener has already quit and Harriet's looking for new household staff. The old man has always been a kind employer but we can only last so long without money."

"Of course."

"And the insurance agent was here all of yesterday, examining the collection and going through bills of sale. What a circus! Oh, no insult intended," she stammered quickly. "I only mean, old Mr. Godwin pulled apart the whole office while looking through his accounts, and the place is a real mess, and there's no maid left to tidy up after him, so I suppose that's going to fall to me, but I already have a list of chores as long as my arm..." She shook her head. "The insurance agent wanted my side of the story, too, and when I told Mr. Sully that Morris was the last visitor to see the devil mask, I only made the situation worse. I didn't intend to convince the senior Mr. Godwin that Morris is the culprit, but the next thing I knew, he was offering a reward and organizing a manhunt." She covered her face with her hands and started to weep.

I put my arm around her for support. "This is not your fault, May. Morris has only made it worse for himself by running," I said, "He's a foolish lad but no murderer at heart."

"But he was so interested in the devil mask when he came to visit the house...." she said, her meek voice trailing away, and I realized she was wracked with guilt for unintentionally turning the hounds on him.

"I don't know where he is. I wish I did, May, but he's evaded us all." I weighed my next statement carefully; information is a kind of currency, and one must be careful where one spends it. "Morris knew about the mask before I ever set foot in Mr. Godwin's house."

"He did? But how?!"

"I hoped you might know," I replied as we walked towards the greenhouse and garden shed. The building was almost as long as one of our boats, with a low construction of glass at one end attached to a squat house made of red bricks and timber beams, used as the chicken coop. Before following her through the greenhouse door, I raised my eyes to the rear facade of the mansion. The windows were dark. On the top floor, I saw Mrs. Stuckey's window, the very spot where she had sat at her desk and died in her chair. Was her ghost still locked there, forever staring out at the living world until Judgment Day? I try not to be superstitious, but still, the thought caused a shiver to skitter down my spine, so to May I said, "I wondered if there might be some connection between Morris and Mrs. Stuckey that I've missed."

She paused momentarily to consider this. "I don't think she's ever mentioned him. Her life was her work in this house, and she's been employed by Randall for thirty years or more."

"But she had family still living in England?"

"Only a cousin, Artie. But he's quite old, too, and never had any children of his own." She shook her head. "The math of it doesn't work. The devil mask has been in Mr. Godwin's collection since long before the war, so how would a man like Morris know about it? Why would he bother to come so far for something he's never seen?"

"I don't know," I admitted, "I only wish I could find Morris and ask him myself."

The air in the greenhouse was moist and warmed by the morning sun, and the walls were lined with clay pots containing the last of the season's herbs and vegetables. The scent of fresh loam and leaf litter made a very pleasing perfume. Where the greenhouse met the chicken coop, the wall was made of red brick interspersed with iron hooks from which hung shovels, forks and rakes. In the centre was a small wooden door. May hung her hoe on the wall next to the shovel, then opened the door.

"Come in, come in, but don't let the girls out," she said, ushering me through quickly. "They love nothing more than to get into the greenhouse and cause mischief."

Inside, the coop was aflutter with wings and golden feathers as the birds converged upon us, cackling and pecking at our shoes. There must have been twenty of them, at least! They scurried over our feet, taking short flights up and down off roof beams, and hopping up onto the five big wooden barrels that sat here-and-there along the edges of the room -- the same sort of barrels that filled the basement by the pantry door. May threw me a sunny smile and, patting her hand on the top of the barrel, said, "Here, I want to show you something."

"What?"

She tapped her finger on the barrel again and one red-gold chicken hopped up on its edge.

"This is Uno," she said, stroking the hen's head, "Isn't she lovely?"

I was no connoisseur of poultry, but I agreed nonetheless.

"Watch," said May, then holding one finger up in front of Uno, she said, "Uno! Five!"

And wouldn't you know it, the blessed thing tapped its beak against the barrel five times!

"It can count?!"

My level of astonishment equaled her level of delight. "Yes!" she laughed, "And... Uno! What is five plus three?"

A moment's pause. Then, the chicken rapped its beak against the barrel eight times.

"What!"

"Isn't that amazing? They're exceedingly clever creatures."

I looked askance at her. "But how come, when you call its name 'Uno', it doesn't count out one?"

May looked at me like I was insane. "Because she doesn't speak Spanish, silly. She's only a chicken."

I couldn't help but laugh as May shooed the hen back to the ground and pulled up the top of the barrel, revealing that it was filled to the brim with pale golden grain. She took out a few handfuls and scattered them across the floor, and the chickens converged on the food with a ferocity that startled me. They were almost lizard-like in their hunger.

"There you go, my sweet ladies," she said in a sing-song voice.

"How much grain does Mr. Godwin keep?" I laughed.

May looked at me like I'd cracked. "What?"

"These barrels," I began, slapping my hand to the side of one. It rang out solid and deep. "There must've been a hundred of them, down in the basement, when Mrs. Stuckey was leading us to the pantry door."

She giggled. "Ah, yes, those."

The realization hit me with the force of a slap, creating an almost physical sensation, and I reached out for the barrel to steady myself. Pulling pieces together, I said, "Francis owns a speak-easy."

"You know about that?" said May brightly.

"I do. Turnpike told me."

She didn't seem all that concerned. A wicker basket hung from one rafter; she took it down, slung it over her arm, and began to search the nests for eggs as she spoke. "Randall likes his scotch. When prohibition went into effect in 1917, he brought in barrels of wheat and barley, and invested in a sill and a speakeasy to distill it. They only keep the grain here. The rest of the process takes place elsewhere." She smiled as she found an egg and put it in the basket. "It's illegal, sure, but no one really minds. Turnpike has always turned a blind eye for the price of a bottle or two."

"But prohibition is going to end."

She looked at me with naive confusion. "What do you mean?"

"There's going to be a referendum soon," I said, "The rumour is, the people of British Columbia want prohibition repealed. If the majority vote against the present law, it'll be changed and restrictions on alcohol will be lifted. It's bound to happen sooner or later -- and my money is on 'sooner', given the present mood. Have you seen the opinion pieces in the newspapers?"

She shook her head. "I don't spend much time with newspapers, except to light the fires in the kitchen. But, what would the repeal of prohibition mean for Randall and Francis?"

"Well, if the government takes over the sale of alcohol, all of their investments may soon be rendered worthless."

"And that's why Randall has no money to pay us?"

"Possibly."

Her face flushed with sudden anger. "And why he so desperately wants the insurance money from the loss of the devil mask."

"Also, possibly."

"Fiddlesticks!" she spat, and the chickens scattered and squawked at the sharp edge of her voice. "So, what you're telling me is: I'll never get my pay!"

"I'm afraid so."

"The insurance agent and Godwin argued all morning about money, and something called 'provenance', and I heard the words 'blanket policy' a few times... but not once did I think their quarrel meant I'd never get what's owed me! The whole staff will quit when they hear this!"

"The agent mustn't have agreed with the mask's evaluation of £10,000."

She snarled. "I can guess from all the shouting and carrying-on that the news was not good."

"If Randall Godwin is having troubles with his finances, he'd be clutching for every penny owed him," I replied as I found one egg, a beautiful speckled green specimen, and laid it gently in the basket. May set another one, a flawless ivory-beige, on top.

One first, and then the other.

"Damn it," I said quietly to myself.

May looked concerned and glanced into the basket. "Did you break an egg?"

"No," I replied, "I'm a fool. I've put all my eggs in the basket in one particular sequence, and I've left them there with the assumption it's the only way things could have happened."

May's anger and confusion shifted to concern. "Are you feeling alright, Rose?"

I took out the two eggs. "We discovered that the murder," I held up the green egg, "Took place in Mrs. Stuckey's apartment. Therefore, she couldn't have surprised the burglar while he was in the middle of stealing the mask." I held up the beige egg to represent the theft. "Her death must've come first, right?"

"Yes. She was murdered, and then the thief carried her body down to the cabinet before opening the case and taking the mask."

"But what if," I said, lifting up the ivory egg, "We reverse the order of events? What if the theft came first, and the murder came second?"

"Why?" she said, "It makes no sense. The thief wouldn't bother to haul the mask all the way up to her room, only to kill her, and then drag both her body and mask downstairs. It would be heavy, and cumbersome, and someone would've heard the racket. It's impossible."

"Yes, it is impossible -- if the thief and the murderer are a single person."

"Hold on," said May, shaking her head, "You think Morris has an accomplice?"

"I think..." I began, then said, "I don't know what I think. But Morris can't have hidden the mask on the *Decimo*. His room is too small, and I searched it for clues after he left and found nothing. If he has an accomplice, maybe they're hiding him and the mask until everything dies down."

She took the precious eggs out of my hands and put them, one at a time, carefully back in the basket. "So why did Morris and his accomplice kill Mrs. Stuckey?"

"Why, indeed," I said, my suspicions swirling, the pieces gently rolling into place like eggs settling into the lowest spot in the basket. "That is an excellent question."

Chapter Fifteen

Francis was out hunting for Morris while Randall and Turnpike still stood in the middle of the lawn, deep in conversation; I heard their raised voices echoing around the building from the front of the house. Confident that no one would stumble across us, May and I returned to the mansion and climbed the staff stairs up to Mrs. Stuckey's room, now armed with fresh eyes and new suspicions.

The hinge creaked, the apartment felt cool and damp. It had been left without an occupant or a fire in the hearth for a day, but none of the furniture had been moved since I'd last been here. The air still smelled of old pennies. The writing desk was still in its place alongside the bathroom door. The bed still sat at an awkward angle from its spot under the window where we'd swung out in a wide arc. The pool of blood on the hardwood floor had dried and become crazed with cracks, but no one had attempted to clean it; I suppose none of the staff dared to undertake such an ugly, emotional job.

The wastepaper basket in the bathroom had not been disturbed, either. In it, I found the tin container stained brown and speckled with ash.

I touched my finger to it, suddenly recognizing the smell.

"This is shoe polish," I said, "Hugo saw Mrs. Stuckey buying shoe polish in the pharmacy. That's what's in this tin, but..." I took another sniff, "There's solvent here too. Mineral spirits, I think. She diluted the polish."

"Why?"

I looked around the room, trying to figure what purpose the diluted shoe polish might have. "Light the lamp, would you, please? We need a better source of illumination than the autumn sun through the window."

As the lamp hissed to life, I bent over and examined the desk.

It was here that Mrs. Stuckey had been killed, so it stood to reason that she had needed the shoe polish for some tasks. The papers and ink on the desk were very neat and orderly. Nothing had been touched or moved. Even the letter opener was still in its place; Turnpike had not taken it with him, even with the knowledge that it was the murder weapon. His incompetence rankled me -- but a smear of brown at the edge of the desk suddenly demanded my attention. I dipped my finger in it.

It was slick, glossy, and gooey.

"She made a witch's concoction and used it here. Let's see -- ah!" Inside the drawer, just behind the pens and pencils, was a metal tin containing a small sponge. Its original use was to dampen the glue on the back of stamps, but when I opened the tin, I discovered the sponge was stained brown and still moist to the touch.

"What is it?"

"The oils of the polish and the mineral spirits don't dry quickly," I said, "The sponge is still wet. I think she must have been using the polish and sponge to age a piece of paper --"

"Whatever she was working on is now gone," May replied.

"True," I replied as I absently pulled open the bottom drawer, full of letters bundled together with string. Most of them were tightly bound and stacked in neat rows, but one bundle seemed a looser than the others, as if the string had been untied and hastily tied again. A smudge of brown shoe polish marred the white string.

I pulled it out.

The date across the stamp was from the summer, and the address on the envelope was to Matilda Stuckey. Then my eyes drifted to the return address at the top corner of the page, and my breath stuck in my throat. In neat script, the address read, "Mr. Arthur Lawrence, Holt Farm, Melbury, Dorset, England."

"Ah!" I exclaimed.

She looked over my shoulder to see what had caused me such a surprise.

"Holt Farm!" I said, "That was Morris' home!"

"Then your fellow Morris *did* know Mrs. Stuckey!"

"This is too much of a coincidence," I said. "Morris must've known the mask was somewhere close by, and he'd been waiting for an opportunity to dig deeper and locate it." I thought back to all of Morris' expeditions to museums and galleries, no matter how big or how small, in every port of call we'd made since he joined us. "All this time, he wasn't seeking inspiration," I said to myself, "He was searching for the long-lost ooser!"

"The *what*?" May asked.

I rooted through a few more letters as I said, "And here I was, stumbling over the ooser quite by accident! And saving him a good deal of trouble! But who is this Mr. Lawrence?"

"Oh, I can answer that question!" May said in sudden excitement. She took the photo off the hearth and brought it to me. "He is Mrs. Stuckey's cousin."

I held the picture of Mrs. Stuckey as a young woman, standing alongside a young man in front of a motorcar. Of course! The man looked the same as the coachman in the background of Morris' photo, the one I'd found in his travel trunk: the face had a prominent jaw and deep-set eyes under thick brows. Of course, this man was youthful and happy and this photo was crisply focused, while in Morris' photo, the same fellow was older, dour, and blurry in the background. Still, I cursed myself for not noticing the resemblance.

"A cousin!" I set the framed photo on the desk and unfolded the letter to glance over it. The writing was loose and rough, and the spelling was atrocious, but I couldn't read it: half the words were missing, having been cut out with a sharp pen-knife.

"What do you make of that!" said May as the light shone through the tattered remains, casting a pattern of squares over the desk like sunlight through a woven rattan screen.

The other letters in the bundle were in the same ragged state. Mrs. Stuckey had pillaged them for words.

"I know what she's done," I said as I scanned the remains, "She forged a document in her cousin's handwriting," I said as I tucked them back in the drawer. I recalled the smear of ash in the tin. "She cut out words to create a letter, traced over the words onto thin onion-paper, then burned the original bits and pieces to rid herself of the evidence."

May was crestfallen. "It'll take ages for us to figure out what words she plucked from these letters, and even longer to determine the order in which she put them."

"True, but we don't have to puzzle over it," I replied. "We know exactly what document she needed to forge."

May followed me downstairs but she refused to join me into Randall Godwin's study; she said it was improper for a woman of her station to trespass against her employer, and she dared not lose the job she'd secured in his fine house, even if her future was uncertain.

No such worries held me back.

A plush carpet muffled my footsteps as I entered the study. The still air was pungent with the scent of the leather chairs and cigar smoke. The crystal chandelier that hung from the middle of the high ceiling cast out shards of light in all directions, glinting off brass doorknobs, cut-crystal glasses, and a bottle of amber liquid sitting on the sideboard. Along the south side of the room, windows obscured with gauzy curtains provided a glimpse of the front lawn, where Turnpike and Randall stood and conversed. In the centre of the room was the hub of Mr. Godwin's office, a desk as long and broad as a coffin, built of red-hued rosewood. Behind the desk was a bookshelf containing leather-bound volumes; many of them had been pulled out and now lay scattered on the floor, the chairs, and the desk. The remaining walls, to the east and north, provided a backdrop for four huge glass-fronted cabinets. From each one, a mask stared out.

These were, without a doubt, his most prized artifacts. Each was stunning in its own unique way. The first mask was the wrathful face of a man, created out of delicate filigree and inlaid with turquoise beads, with baleful eyes and contorted lips. The second was a woman's face carved from a single piece of quartz; it glittered and sparkled as I moved around it, and for a moment, the reflection of my own face in the glass was superimposed over its deathly facade. The third was bronze, peppered with small rivets to create whirls and patterns, and the fourth was polished mahogany, narrow and lean, with graceful lines spiralling over each cheek. Each of the four were a different style and taken from a different culture, yet they complimented each other beautifully, as if the makers over unimaginable boundaries of time and space had managed, somehow, to conspire together.

The masks also made me anxious. My movements were being scrutinized by these unblinking guardians.

Francis had been in a hurry to join his hunting party and Randall had followed quickly after him, distraught and angry. Mr. Sully the insurance agent had also left in a hurry, and from a single glance at his desk, it was obvious that they'd quarrelled here. An ink pot had been left uncapped. Papers were scattered in random piles. In frustration, Randall hadn't bothered to put anything away and he'd left a ledger in the centre of the desk, surrounded by a few scattered notes.

I circled the desk, reading as I went.

The dusty ledger was a financial record of amounts in and out. I could see on the lowest book shelf where it must have sat for many years, never touched, between its brothers. The date at the top of the open page read, "October, 1901': a full nineteen years ago, when the world was a very different place, before the Great War shredded it into pieces and left us to stitch it back together again.

I glanced down the columns of expenses. Halfway down the first column, I discovered the amount for which I had been looking: £10,000 sent by wire to a Mr. Lawrence in Melbury, Dorset.

I sat down in Godwin's desk chair to think.

He'd paid the amount to Mrs. Stuckey's cousin, who no doubt acted as a broker for the piece between Godwin and the original owner. There would be no cause for concern: after all, Mrs. Stuckey had been a trusted housekeeper and she would have vouched for her cousin's reliability. The funds had been transferred by wire without trouble, the mask had doubtlessly been sent, and here on the corner of the desk was the bill of sale, proving its value and transfer of ownership.

I picked up the slip.

The paper felt tacky in my fingers.

Suddenly a great many puzzle pieces fell into place.

The slip was made of thin paper, quite translucent when I held it up to the light cast by the glittering chandelier, and the handwriting was jagged, hesitant, unnatural. The words did not flow easily one into the other. Rather, they read like words clipped from other letters and assembled, not always making the most sense. The letter outlined the cost and certified the mask's authenticity. It had been written and signed in handwriting similar to Mr. Lawrence's, which could be easily verified by examining old letters, and the legal owner of the piece had signed the bottom: 'Dr. Edmund Cave'.

The strange choice of words could be explained by Mr. Lawrence's level of education or affectations in his lexicon, but it was more difficult to dismiss the sticky film that clung to my fingers, a light brown hue that stank faintly of turpentine. The page had been aged, but the method used had been clumsy. If only Mr. Godwin had waited a week or two to claim the mask was stolen, he might have given Mrs. Stuckey's hamfisted attempt at counterfeiting a chance to dry.

What had Mr. Sully said when he'd picked up the bill of sale? Had he realized right away it was fake? Had Mr. Godwin attempted to cover the mistake with some flimsy lie?

'I spilled a bit of bacon grease on it.'

But Mr. Sully couldn't risk such a payout. It was too much. Whether the mask was a fake or stolen, he couldn't approve the claim.

I looked at the ledger again. Maybe Mr. Sully had accused Mr. Godwin of over-insuring. That would explain why Godwin pulled out the ledger, to show the amount transferred and to prove he'd paid the amount in full.

And then what? Did Sully tell him he'd purchased a worthless chunk of old wood? Or a stolen item that Mr. Lawrence had no right to sell? Or worse, that Mr. Godwin himself was the mastermind behind the whole scam, planning and executing the 'theft' in a desperate effort to ease his financial burdens from a changing market?

Execute.

I glanced out the window to the two men on the lawn, and a shiver ran down my spine.

By God, Randall must have suffered a terrible shock to discover that there was no bill of sale received with the shipment -- that in fact, there had never been an evaluation, and no way to prove to Mr. Sully that the mask was worth what he'd paid for it. If the mask was ill-gotten, then the only people who knew were Matilda Stuckey and her cousin, and Arthur Lawrence was safely living over a thousand miles away. Now, this little oversight wouldn't have posed a problem if the mask remained tucked away in the dark corners of Randall Godwin's exotic collection, hidden from the world for his own greedy delight. He'd never need to prove the mask's provenience. Its value would be subjective and no one would be the wiser. Left alone in its glass case, both the mask and its dubious history were safe.

But it hadn't been left alone. The mask had gone missing. And deep in financial troubles, Randall might see the theft as a turn of good luck: he could submit a claim to the insurance company, collect his money, and be done with the whole affair. He'd looked through his records and found nothing but that could've been dismissed as a case of poor filing, so he approached Mrs. Stuckey and demanded that she provide the bill of sale for the insurance claim. Knowing there was no such thing, she'd tried to fix that little oversight as quickly as possible. She'd harried the pharmacist to open his shop, frantically purchased supplies to forge a bill of sale, and spent Sunday crafting a document to fool the eye of the appraiser.

And Randall, desperate to submit his claim as soon as possible and hounding her for the receipt, could have surprised Mrs. Stuckey while she was seated at her desk, forging the document. Perhaps he felt a surge of fury and embarrassment at being duped and robbed. Perhaps he demanded his money back and she'd refused. The particulars of the moment were lost. Of all I could be certain was this: Randall Godwin had snatched up Matilda Stuckey's letter opener and, without hesitation or guilt, stabbed her over and over through the heart.

Chapter Sixteen

I said nothing of this to May; after all, what *could* I say? She'd respected and admired Mrs. Stuckey, and I wasn't ready to shatter her illusions with the revelation that the woman was a con artist and a thief. As I left the office and hurried out the rear door, I told her that I needed to return to the Buckley's farm for my afternoon performance, but in the core of my being, I struggled over my theories. In whom should I confide?

Grover Scott was my first thought, but of course he'd want nothing to do with this, and I was certain he'd tell me to forget it all. I couldn't fault him for it: self-preservation is a powerful motive. If the circus entangled itself in this dreadful affair, we might be stuck here for months and lose every scrap of good reputation we'd earned. The loss of reputation and income, as well as the crippling of our freedom, would kill the Circus Salmagundi.

What about Turnpike? I wasn't sure that was a good idea, either. I still felt he was too friendly with the elder Mr. Godwin to be trusted. He'd never believe my suspicions, even with a wheelbarrow-load of evidence. If I baldly accused Randall of murder, I might push my luck a little too far and find myself in jail as an accessory or a suspect, and if I was too much trouble, the circus would leave me behind.

No. Best not to risk it.

So, do I forget all and leave silently when our engagement finished? That didn't seem right, either. I imagined May, left in the employment of a man who had brutally, viciously stabbed his housekeeper, and whom I couldn't trust to treat her well -- by God, I'd never forgive myself for doing that! I'd spend the rest of my days wondering if she was alright, or if he'd taken out his guilt and frustration on her in the same manner as he had with Mrs. Stuckey.

No, I wouldn't leave May in that sort of danger.

So, what should I do?

Today's performance would be our last and I knew my call-time was getting close. If I wasn't in the tent by 2pm, I'd have to suffer through a dressing-down from Mr. Scott; he expected punctuality, even if the universe was coming to an end and crashing down around our ears. By the time I crested the hill, I saw a line of people stretching out from the ticket booth.

Damn it! I was about to be very, very late.

But as I broke into a run to head towards the farm, I felt a sharp pain on the back of my head, enough to make me stumble forward and raise my hand to my scarves, letting out a grunt of surprise.

I brought my hand down. A few specks of dirt covered my palm.

Something had hit me!

I turned quickly and scanned the field for any sign. A small, sharp granite pebble lay in the long grass. Then I looked to the direction from whence it came, ready to catch the next missile.

The day was a clear, bright, autumnal affair, containing no reason to inspire any fear or hesitation in me, and the edge of the forest stood out crisply against the open meadows and pastures as they sloped upwards away from the sea. There was not a horse or rider in sight, but a movement in the bushes caught my eye, little more than a beast slinking through the woods. At the edge of the trees, a grey figure obscured by grey trunks held up one hand to hail me, then stumbled into the forest.

This wasn't Francis or one of his men. I let my scarves fall away from my face and hair, trying to get a better look.

But the figure didn't return. For a moment I hesitated, knowing I was already late for my engagement with the sideshow, but curiosity is a powerful drive. Before my better judgment could convince me otherwise, I was running full-tilt across the open pastureland towards the point where the man had disappeared through the trees.

A few rocky outcroppings poked through where the soil was thin, covered over with crooked Garry oaks. Higher and exposed to the wind and thus made naked of leaves, they were the hands of dead men reaching up from the hillside, clutching for the sky. I saw the figure far ahead, rustling through the twigs and underbrush, so on and on we ran, with the sky above us and the mossy rocks below us, until we were a good deal away from the Buckley house. When the figure finally slowed to a trot, I was heaving for breath. He stopped amid a copse of crooked oaks that sprouted from the stony highland and turned to face me. The exposed gnarl of granite offered a wide vista of the farms, estates, and nearby town unfurling towards the jagged edge of the sea, and in the distance, the gentle undulations of the Strait of Juan de Fuca were topaz and white and silver. but I was too busy examining Morris to admire the view.

He looked filthy, haggard, exhausted, half-starved. He leaned heavily against a tree, sucking each breath deep into his lungs, dirt-stained hands gripping his thighs. His overalls were ripped at the knees, his shirt was mud-speckled, bits of leaves had matted into his hair.

"Ere now, there's mud on your face! I'm so sorry to have struck you with that pebble, Miss Rose," he said when his breathing slowed, sounding sincerely remorseful. "I didn't know how else to get your attention!"

"By God, Morris, where have you been?!" I asked.

"Everywhere and nowhere, all at the same time," he said, "I've tried to be one with the land like a mouse hiding in the hedgerow, and I had to keep moving or that police fella would find me." He clutched at his chest and his side. "That there Mr. Turnpike, he's like the devil, he is!" He wiped sweat from his brow with the sleeve of his shirt and took one more heaving breath, standing up straight. "They all think I killed the housekeeper, but I didn't, Rose! I swear, I couldn't do that! I could never kill a lady!"

"I know, Morris," I tried to assure him, "But by running, you've made it look like you're guilty. Even Alex thinks you might have done it.

You must come back, Morris, and plead your case! Prove to them you're innocent!"

He shook his head. "I can't do that, Miss Rose. I'm not full innocent: that's the problem."

I gestured for him to sit next to me, and we positioned ourselves to face the fine view so that we could spot any riders coming across the fields. The silo of Mr. Buckley's barn was visible just above the gentle swell of the land, but the waterway and the farm house were hidden by golden grass, stone fences, and trees.

"I took the mask," he said when we were settled, "And if I face the old Mr. Godwin, he'll make me give it back, and I can't do that! It's mine by right!"

"I found your drawing of it... what was the name you gave it? Ooser?"

"Aye, the ooser," he said, hitting the 's' hard so that it sounded more like a 'z', "But I didn't give it that name. It's been called 'ooser' since the beginning of time, so long in the deep past that the reason for the name is lost. No one knows exactly what the name means -- it just *is*." He took another restorative breath and let it out in a sigh, rocking back to lean his shoulders against the base of a tree. "Oh, Miss Rose, I don't think I've sat still for three whole days!" His stomach let out a fearsome growl.

"You must be starving," I said.

"Ere, I've had to make do with what I could find, but it's not much at this time of year," he admitted. "Moldy apples scrounged from under some trees, a bit of seaweed, a loaf of bread nicked from the bakery... oh, a raw egg from the chicken coop would be absolute heaven right now."

"You said the mask is yours by right," I prompted.

"Aye," Morris replied. "It belongs to my family. It's ours to have and protect." He folded his hands over his scuffed knees. "In my earliest memory, the mask is sitting in my uncle's study, and it scared me something awful! When I was growing up, I had nightmares about the ooser staring at me with those ruddy great eyes, like it could peer into my soul and read my worst sins there. If there was lust in my heart, the ooser knew of it!

"But one day, my uncle sat me down and told me that the ooser might look like a frightful old relic, but it's a powerful thing, that mask, and full of venerable magic. He said a man might put it on and feel the spirit of the land flowing through him like a torrent. Uncle Tom used to scare his cousins in the garden with the old thing, thinking it would be no more than a harmless prank, but he told me that when he danced around wearing the ooser, he felt himself overcome with the ancient ties linking farmer and field, and he knew in his blood that every step made the world grow green. And," Morris added, his eyes shining, "If he danced with the ooser on the first of May, then that was when the magic was strongest, because the ooser is a direct connection to the old ways, the ancestors, and the god of woods and wilderness."

"It is a pagan thing!"

"It's old, that's all I really know," Morris replied. "Now, don't you be thinking my uncle was wicked or crazy or none such! He's a pious man, a good teacher, and he's the vice-principal of Wye College, where he's much loved by his students. He's modern in all things and he goes to church every Sunday. He even paid for the chapel renovations in the village, and he was generous when the tithe plate was passed around the congregation. But when he was a young man, for one night every May, he would bring back the old ways and dance with the ooser on his noggin out in the long grasses, just to make sure that everything would grow nice and lush over summer."

I found the idea of a man casting off his teaching robes and capering around the fields to be rather charming.

"But your father did not follow the old ways."

"No, he did not. When my uncle went off to college, he gave the ooser to my father for safe keeping, but my father chose to become a doctor instead of a farmer, and he said we were living in a new century and a modern era. It was time to put away silly heathen superstitions. In 1897, he moved to Bath where he could build a good practice, and he put our coachman, Mr. Lawrence, in charge of the Melbury property. The ooser stayed in the attic of the old farm house." Morris gave a sad, regretful shrug. "I suppose, with him and his practice and my uncle working as a teacher, my father thought the superstitions would melt away and the mask would be forgotten by everyone."

"But you didn't forget."

"Of course not! How could I!?" Morris laughed. "I remembered seeing Mr. Lawrence wearing the mask in a carnival procession when I was a wee tyke, so I figured he would take good care of it, knowing its history and its importance. And I would've reclaimed stewardship over the ooser when I became a man, except as soon as I was finished my schooling, I was sent off to France to fight and, by God, I couldn't return to Dorset until the fighting was finished and I was released from service. But once I came home, it was gone, and I had to find it, didn't I!"

This was said with great purpose. "Why?"

"Just look at the state of things, Miss Rose! What with the war and the plague, the world is in a right muddle. We've forgotten our ties to the land so the land punishes us. We're like a wagon with a crack in one wheel: we're still moving forward but it's all off-kilter, and we can feel something is unbalanced in our flesh and our bones." He rubbed a bit of grime from his chin as he surveyed the farmlands. "We've forgotten our place in the natural order but maybe, if I take the ooser and dance on the first night in May, I can resurrect a few of the old ways to put us back on course."

How bizarre, to hear this young man speak of old gods and arcane rites.

"Morris, you know you sound..."

"A wee bit cracked? Aw, I don't care none about that. Can't you feel the desperation in the air, Miss Rose? Haven't you noticed? We're all so tired of the sadness and the greyness that we've forgotten it's possible to be deliciously, gloriously, deliriously happy."

The wind rustled through the naked branches and, for a heartbeat, I thought I heard a musical rhythm there, like a distant drummer playing a carefree tune.

"You mark my words," he continued, "This modern world only covers up the blessed brilliant magic of the old. The Ancient Gods are still here, all around us, waiting for us to speak to them in a language they understand."

I thought of my dream and the minotaur on the hill, and realized with a start that I had been privy to a holy rite, unfurling before me in that dark and sacred night. I suddenly saw Morris with new eyes: he was not some lonesome, immature man on a capricious holiday, exploring the west before leaving his youth behind to assume his adult responsibilities. No, Morris Cave's path had been stunted by years of war and, resuming the journey of civilian life, he'd chosen to become a knight on a hallowed quest, seeking to restore the equilibrium between humanity and nature. His purpose had been handed down through generations, no longer forgotten or left to fester.

I smiled as I realized, it was not Morris I'd seen dancing on the hill; it was the Ooser itself, once more set free.

Questions filled my mind. In a split second I wrangled them and sorted them, and picked one above all to ask. "What happened when you came home to Holt Farm from the war?"

The sparkle in Morris' eyes dimmed as he remembered.

"When I got back to our old village, I found Holt Farm in a state of damnable disarray. It seems Mr. Lawrence was hoping that my father and uncle would never come back; the old coachman had sold off most of the furniture and pocketed the money. The wheat fields were full of stones and thistles. There were great holes in the roof. The millstone was cracked, the mill wheel missing half its paddles. And as for the ooser?" He tossed a little stone over the side of the hill, and it clattered and clacked as it bounced down the cliff. "A few folks in the village said they'd seen it hanging in a loft in Lawrence's house, but that building had been torn down for a new post office to be built just before the war, and everyone figured it had been destroyed with the building."

"But you didn't believe that."

"Not a whit. Arthur Lawrence was a seedy bastard. If he could sell something to make a bit of bob, he'd do it."

"So how did you discover it was here?"

"A bit of luck, really," he said. "Once he heard I'd survived the war, Lawrence wasn't going to hang about, and he scarpered from the village before I returned. No one knew where he'd gone and I lost hope of ever recovering any of my family's lost possessions. I set my mind to fixing the house and the mill, but I didn't believe the ooser was destroyed -- it's too powerful a thing -- and the fate of it chewed away at me for months. Then, one day, a natty fellow came to the door. He was an accountant and he'd been sent by a gentleman named Mr. Godwin in Canada. It seemed Mr. Godwin had purchased a piece of exotic artwork from Mr.

Lawrence and he wanted a bill of sale, which was supposed to have been sent with the piece but was missing." Morris gave a snort. "He needed the bill of sale to prove the value of the piece, you see. Without it, he couldn't insure it properly. As Holt Farm was the sole address for Mr. Lawrence that Mr. Godwin had on file, the agent had come directly to me."

"What did you say?"

"It was almost impossible to keep a straight face but I managed it! I said I didn't know a thing about any sale of artwork but I'd certainly keep Mr. Godwin informed, should I hear more about Mr. Lawrence's whereabouts. The insurance agent was a very accommodating fellow. He gave me a general post address in Victoria, British Columbia."

"So, you came west."

"As soon as I could raise the funds," Morris replied. "But I'm not a wealthy man: Mr. Lawrence saw to that! I'd need to find a way to feed myself without tying myself down. When my ship arrived in Vancouver, the Circus Salmagundi was looking for extra hands, and it made for a good agreement. And when Alex told me we were heading here, only a stone's throw to Victoria, I knew the ooser was working its magic."

"You think the ooser brought you here?"

"I do!" he said, "It's a mystical object, Miss Rose. It has its own mind, and it works miracles in strange and beautiful ways."

"My belief in magic is tenuous, at best, Mr. Cave."

"That's alright," he laughed, "I believe enough for the both of us."

"And you truly, honestly think that the ooser wants to be reunited with you?"

"Here is what think," he began, "The ooser shouldn't be sitting in a display case for only a select few people to see. It's a living thing and it needs to be out and dancing in the fields where it belongs." His eyes flamed, his words grew deeper and more passionate. "It's the same for all them masks in that man's collection. Each one belongs to a family, and no sum of money can ever match what they represent. All that meaning? The depth of history and connections they hold? They're priceless to the folks who own 'em but worthless to someone like Randall Godwin."

I folded my hands in my lap and gave a nod of agreement. "That's what I was trying to explain to May! Their reasons-for-being are stripped away when they're severed from their past and stuck in a sterile glass box. Now that they're part of Randall's collection, they're dead."

"Oh no, Miss Rose! They're only sleeping," said Morris, "I have faith that they will live again, once they're reunited with the people who love them."

Chapter Seventeen

"So now what?" I asked, "Are you planning to carry the ooser all the way back to England? I'm surprised you could carry it out of the house!"

He let forth a boisterous laugh at that idea. "It is a damned heavy object," he agreed. "My uncle was a skinny man and I don't know how he was able to wear the blessed thing! I hoped Mr. Scott would let me bring it aboard the ships and keep it with us over winter, then next spring when the weather clears, I'd take it by train and ship, back home with me where we belong." He lowered his gaze, sobering. "But I never for a second thought I'd get wrapped up in a murder. That complicates things."

"How did you even manage to steal the ooser?" I asked.

He puffed himself up, feeling clever. "I'd gone that afternoon to the house and, when I explained that I was a friend of yours from the circus, Miss May was very accommodating. She took me in directly to the masks, and seeing those ruddy great frightful eyes again filled me with such excitement, I thought my heart might explode right out of my chest! The ooser was exactly as I remembered it, Rose: I could almost hear my uncle's voice in my head, bellowing out like a bull from between those wooden jaws! But the time wasn't right, so I knew I had to keep calm and plan. I told May I could give the staff tickets to see the opening night, and by God, she was over the moon with delight -- she told me that Randall Godwin went to bed early most nights while Francis went to town to socialize at the speakeasy. With both men otherwise engaged, the staff would be able to come and see the show. I couldn't ask for a more perfect arrangement."

"So, as soon as I saw May and Mrs. Stuckey, I knew the house was safe to visit again. Out I went, right after the sideshow finished and the main show began. When I reached the Godwin estate, the whole house was as still and dark as a tomb. The main doors and side doors were locked, of course, but the kitchen door had been left unlocked for the staff when they returned. It was no trouble at all to slip through kitchen, along the corridor to the main floor, throw back the canvas and open the cabinet, and pull out the ooser. Then off I skulked into the night!"

"And you hid it somewhere safe?"

"Aye," he agreed.

"Where's the ooser now?"

Morris shook his head. "Sorry, Miss Rose, but I'm not prepared to say. It's secure enough where I've stashed it."

"But you couldn't move it very far, otherwise you'd have left for England and never looked back." I grinned. "It was you that I saw in the early morning hours, when I was sitting with the Geek in the sideshow tent: you were dancing with the mask in the field and then you slipped into Mr. Buckley's barn. Is that where the ooser is hidden?"

A twinkle gleamed in his eye but he said, "After I took it from Godwin's collection, I came straight back to the boats. I can't have been gone more than half-an-hour. No one missed me." The twinkle diminished, replaced by confusion. "The next morning, I expected to hear news of the theft but nothing happened. And then, the next day, when I heard about the murder -- good Lord, Miss Rose, I had nothing to do with that! I swear it!"

I nodded at this discrepancy in the timeline. "When Francis came to the boats, gun in hand, he claimed the mask had been stolen the next night but, by in truth, it had been missing for more than 24 hours."

"I was so perplexed why no one noticed!"

"No one noticed because Mrs. Stuckey often kept it covered. It frightened the maids," I explained, "But when the housekeeper discovered the mask was gone on the morning after you stole it, she burned a little bit of tobacco to pretend she was fumigating the items in the rear corridor, then forbid the staff to enter."

He gazed out over the fields, his brow furrowed and his mouth drawn down. "Why would she hide the fact that the ooser was gone?"

"Mrs. Stuckey covered up the theft because she knew the mask had been ill-gained. It had already been stolen, years before." I glanced at Morris to gauge his reaction. "Matilda Stuckey was Arthur Lawrence's cousin."

The sound he made was halfway between a gasp and a whistle; I could have knocked him over with a feather.

"Together, they sold the mask to old Mr. Godwin and pocketed the money: a nice, tidy nest egg for them both to retire on. Mrs. Stuckey and her cousin probably believed, after so many years, that no one from the Cave family would ever come looking for it," I explained.

"How much did they sell it for?"

"Ten thousand pounds."

Morris collapsed back against the tree and pressed one hand to his head. "Ten thousand -- blimey!" he whispered, astonished, "Is that really what Godwin paid Lawrence for the ooser?! No wonder Mr. Godwin sent an agent all the way to Dorset to collect the bill of sale!"

"As I figure it," I began, "If the agent failed to find Lawrence and wrangle the receipt from him -- thereby establishing provenance -- then the mask would have no determined valuation. Randall must've had his entire collection insured under a blanket policy, but if he tried to collect the insurance after the ooser was stolen, they'd never allow it. A lack of legitimate documentation for the mask would render it worthless, and no firm would replace his lost money for a single item that could not be verified."

"Crickey! The old fella must have had a right fit when he saw the mask was gone!"

"He would have been a very desperate man, indeed. With his fortune in tatters, and his investments flimsy, and his son spending money faster than he can make it? Randall saw an opportunity in the mask's disappearance. He must've hounded Mrs. Stuckey for that bill of sale, and in her desperation, she decided to create a counterfeit document to pacify her employer and to cover up her crime from almost twenty years ago." I wrung my hands to keep them warm -- a cold wind had risen and clattered through the branches above us, filling the air with the chatter of wood. "But Randall Godwin was impatient. He went up to her room to badger her and discovered her in the act of forgery."

"Then he murdered the only person in the house who knew the mask was stolen."

"And who'd broken his trust, all those years ago."

Morris whistled low. "So, Randall Godwin is the murderer?"

"I think so. And he might have gotten away with it, too, if Mrs. Stuckey hadn't been such a terrible forger," I replied, stifling a laugh; it was crude to find mirth here, considering the woman was dead, but my relief at finding Morris and uncovering his innocence -- at least in the matter of murder -- had made me a little giddy. "No, I've seen the bill of sale that Mrs. Stuckey tried to draft and it's a monstrosity. The insurance agent saw right through her deception, and Randall fought over it, and I don't think the old man will get a single penny."

"Nor will he want the mask back," Morris replied. "Not if I can prove it's stolen."

"I saw myself that your father's signature had been forged on the bill of sale."

He grinned. "Then there you have it!" He clapped his hands in sudden glee, like a lost rambler seeing a straight path through a crooked wood. "I can identify my father's signature and prove that the bill is fake!"

Our moment of levity was short-lived.

No sooner had Morris finished speaking than a thundering blast ripped through the air as granite chips sprang from the spot between us.

Morris shunted himself backwards with a cry of alarm, pointing down through the trees to a spot where field met forest. We had been so engrossed in each other's tale, we hadn't paid attention to the pastures and hills, and five men on horseback stood along the edge of the pasture, looking up the ridge to the bluff. Francis Godwin stood in his saddle, lowering his rifle, then he urged his companions forward. They launched into a hard gallop directly towards us, plowing through ferns and underbrush, hooves scrabbling on the hard rocky surface.

"Come on," I said, grabbing Morris by the sleeve and hauling him after me. We sprinted up into the bushes, climbing higher on the hill.

The commotion of our pursuers dogged us over ridge and ditch, growing closer and louder. The vibrations of each hoof-strike rattled in my bones. Our path wove between the tangled, twisted oak groves and we tried to keep to the rockiest hollows, but neither Morris nor I were intimately familiar with this landscape. My instinct told me to stay to the low points in the woods, where tangled briars and salal bushes would mire the horses, but Morris cleaved left and headed for higher ground, hoping to out-climb them.

We were soon separated.

At last, I pressed my back to the rough bark of an oak, bracing myself to catch my breath, and I heard the riders race passed me, hidden from sight by a wall of sword ferns. Francis yelled directions. Another gun-shot echoed off the exposed rocks, scattering ravens from the high branches.

And then, in a frightened voice, Morris called out.

"Don't shoot me! For the love of God, don't shoot!"

They had him. My heart sank.

"Where is it?" shouted Francis. The man sounded unhinged. I followed the echoes of his crackling voice, creeping closer down through a rocky ridge with my pulse thumping in my ears.

"I didn't kill the lady," Morris pleaded, "Honest to God!"

I heard another blast. For a second, I thought they'd killed him, but then Morris cried out and I knew the shot had only been to startle him.

"Where is it?!" Francis screamed again.

I peered out between the bushes.

The riders had surrounded Morris in a semi-circle on a small bluff, segregating him from the cover of the trees, and with three or four rifles aimed at his head, he had no way of escape. We had circled back in our frantic escape and now stood only a few hundred feet farther along the hill, but on a spot that delved straight down, creating a sheer cliff; there was Buckley's silo on the other side of the sheep fields, with a few uneasy cows grazing in the pasture below us. The young man stood with his heels at the edge of the cliff, trembling, his hands pressed to the top of his crown. Francis dismounted, holding his rifle.

"Where's my father's mask?" he demanded.

Spurred by the question, Morris' face transformed: like glass melting before a roaring flame, his fear contorted and transformed into uncontrolled rage.

"It's not *your father's* mask," he bellowed, "None of the masks are! Randall Godwin has stolen and pillaged them from good people -- from families and caretakers and communities, from the lands they protect and the rituals they symbolize -- and he's ripped them out of their place and provenance for his own perverse desire!" Morris stepped forward and brandished his fists. "All those people from whom your father stole? The law says they got no rights to their own property, and they can't stand up to him to demand the return of their sacred belongings, but by God, I do! As an Englishman, I can stand before the law and accuse him of his crimes!" The young man's voice deepened and grew ferocious. "Randall Godwin is nothing but a thief and a liar, and a now he's a murderer, too!"

Francis gaped at the accusation, stunned into silence. Then he raised his gun and aimed for Morris' head. This time, there would be no warning shot.

"I know!" I called out, "I know where it is!"

I'd spoken before Francis could pull the trigger, but I hadn't thought clearly of my next actions -- I only knew I couldn't bear to see Morris' brains spattered across the hillside. When I stepped from the woods Morris glared at me as if I were a traitor, which I suppose I'd become in his opinion, but I couldn't stand by and watch Francis kill the man.

And believe me, I had no doubt that Francis hungered to destroy him. The look in his eyes was mad with bloodlust. This ragged, filthy roustabout had insulted his father's reputation and accused him of murder - by God, murder! - and Francis was unwilling to let that go.

But seeing me, the younger Godwin lowered his gun.

"I knew it was you from the first time I laid eyes on you," he sneered, "I should have known the criminal had an accomplice."

I bristled at the accusation but held my tongue.

"You know where the mask has been hidden?"

"I do," I replied. "And I'll tell you if you promise to let Morris go unharmed."

Francis looked between us, weighing whether he was willing to forego the reward or, more likely, the pleasure of shooting the man.

But his moment of hesitation showed that, while Francis did not trust me, a good amount of money hung in the balance and he was willing to consider my offer. The gun was still trained on Morris, and Francis still trembled with pent-up anger and adrenaline, so I decided to swing his decision in my favour. In a soothing voice reminiscent of Alex's hypnotic words, I reminded him, "How far can a $500 reward really help you? If the mask is worth as much as your father claims, you could sell it yourself and pay off all your debts."

A light dawned in Francis' eyes. He could finally be free of the old man's purse-strings! He'd never have to beg or scrape for his allowance again, he could choose to invest in as much liquor and entertainment as his heart desired. Francis lowered the gun.

"Where is it?" he growled.

But I would not budge.

"Let Morris go."

A sly smile slid across his lips as Francis gestured to his companions. The men on horseback reluctantly pulled up their rifles and shuffled aside, giving enough space for a single body to pass through the perimeter and escape into the woods. His tone turning congenial, Francis swung into his saddle and gestured with one hand towards the opening.

"Go on," he urged Morris, "Get out of here."

But Morris ignored him and stared hard in my direction, shaking his head slowly. "No, Miss Rose, you mustn't tell them!" he pleaded, "Please, you can't --"

"Leave, Morris, and don't look back until you're safe on the boats. You must tell Mr. Scott to prepare to cast off immediately, and don't you wait for me, understand?" I tried to muster a brave smile. "I'll be fine."

"You mustn't --"

"Go on," I said. Then, as he backed away and the forest swallowed him up, I returned my attention to Francis.

"I've done good on my end, madam," he said, "Now, you do good on yours."

I waited until Morris had scrambled down the rocks and bolted across the fields in the direction of Mr. Buckley's farm. Only then, once I knew he was safe, did I say to Francis directly, "Morris is right, you know. Your father is a murderer. When he discovered that Mrs. Stuckey had stolen from him, he stabbed her to death."

Francis bared his teeth to me as he studied me up and down.

"My father didn't know that he'd purchased stolen property. He's the victim in all this, not her." His horse reeled around, its ears flattened by the tension on the reins and the venom in his words. "You should be able to trust the people in your employment, the people who feed you and clean your house, the people who know every intimate detail about your life. She controlled his money, his home, his staff, but in the end, she conned him. Matilda Stuckey was a lying old bitch!"

"So, he killed her and dragged her body downstairs to stage the murder in the corridor, and decided to frame poor Morris for the act."

A few men looked to each other, startled by the accusation, but Francis didn't flinch.

The pit of my stomach dropped.

As I laid out each stage of the murder, I realized old Mr. Godwin didn't have the strength to carry Mrs. Stuckey's body all the way to the lowest level of the house, nor drag her into place before the empty case, nor hold the dense jade club high enough to crush her skull. That required the fortitude of a much younger man.

"Ah, but none of this is a surprise to you," I said evenly, "Because you were there, too."

He raised the gun and took aim at my head.

"Where. Is. It."

In that singular moment, I honestly couldn't predict how Francis would act. His expression was as knotted and intense as the devil mask, with eyes so wide and white that they seemed disconnected from their sockets. The man was fit and athletic, hot-headed and impulsive, drowning in debt and devoid of scruples; spurred by the depths of his desperation, he was capable of anything. Those raging, unblinking eyes stared at me like a cat stalking a mouse, and his thin lips had parted to show the flash of glistening teeth. His father had killed a woman because she'd made him look like a fool; perhaps that impulse was a trait that ran in the blood, and now Francis had the capability and motive to do the same.

Once more, I glanced across the fields. Morris had almost crested the hills. He'd be safe soon. As I'd demanded, he didn't look back, and I weighed the outcomes in my heart. What was more important: an object or a life?

Then I turned my attention back to Francis and said, "The mask is hidden in Buckley's barn."

An immediate bolt of regret shot through me.

But a greedy, hungry smile spread across his mouth. He slung his rifle back around and holstered it behind his saddle.

Before I could protest, he reached down and seized the collar of my robes, hauling me awkwardly up in the saddle before him. My skin crawled. I convulsed to get away but Francis clenched his arm around my waist so tightly that I could barely breath, and he kicked his horse. In one fluid motion the animal sprang to a gallop and flew along the trail, down the convoluted paths through the dead-handed oaks and the weed-humpy pastures and, flanked on either side by the rest of the riders, we raced across the fields, sailing over fences, splashing through ditches and heaving over the ridges as Francis, in his eagerness, lead us directly for the grain silo of Buckley's farm, which guided us in a straight line like a lighthouse in a storm.

Down through the gate and along the road we raced. Evening comes early in October, and already the strings of electric lights were on, their golden illumination pushing back the gentle violet dusk. The yard between the Big Top and the Ten-In-One was alive with jugglers, clowns, musicians, women, men, children, dogs and ponies, yet Francis and his wild group of hunters plummeted through it all with no regard for life nor limb, sending screaming figures scattering like geese before us, and as the posse reached the barn doors, the men pulled back abruptly on their reins so that hooves lifted from the ground and manes flicked forward. Francis reeled hard to the left. I was shoved to the ground, falling heavily, skinning my knees and slamming my shoulders into the biting gravel.

"Find it!" Francis ordered his men.

A kind hand cradled my elbow and helped me to my feet. "Miss Rose, my GOODNESS, are you alright?" said Mr. Buckley. He rounded on Francis as the men swarmed into the cow barn. "Young Mr. Godwin! What is the MEANING of all this?!"

"Call Turnpike, get him down here, along with my father," said Francis, "This is the thief and murderer! She's turned on her partner and gave up the mask to save her own skin!"

I tried to protest but I heaved for breath; the ride and the fall had knocked the wind out of me.

In all directions, the yard was a sea of churning chaos. Frightened parents tried to find their children in the melee, musicians had dropped their instruments, spooked livestock bolted in all directions. The noise was deafening. Alex burst through the entrance to the Big Top, wearing his red Hussar jacket and fur hat, brandishing his riding crop. When he saw me, still dazed, he hurried from the tent to step between me and Francis. "Damn it, man, you could have killed someone!"

"You'll hang for what you've done," Francis hissed at me.

"Step back, ya hacket feartie," Alex said as he slashed at Francis with the crop, "You think yourself so brave, roughing up a woman? Stand down, ya vile coward!"

The men of the hunting party had swarmed the barn, and I heard shouts coming from inside, followed quickly by the crash of equipment and lumber as they tore through cattle pens and hay loft. Someone slammed a hatch open from the grain silo. The rush and hush of grain pouring out of the silo hissed like water cascading over rapids.

The sound made Mr. Buckley cry out in alarm.

"You'll PAY for all of the damage, you imbecile!" he demanded.

"And when they find the stolen property hidden in your barn, Buckley, I'll have you brought up on charges of accessory to the crime," came the crisp reply, "You brought these reprobates to our town! You're just as much to blame as any of them!"

Mr. Buckley blustered and huffed, but as he rallied himself to argue, he suddenly paused.

A smell on the wind drifted through the crowd.

"Smoke!" someone yelled, just as the scent caught the attention of

Francis' horse. The poor beast reared back in instinctual terror, jerking the man backwards off his feet. In all directions, waves of terror flowed through the crowd, and they seemed to rise up like a singular entity, crushing and pushing and screaming as one. Alex grabbed my wrist and hauled me after him, away from the barn and the silo and the crowd, towards the open safety of the sheep field. I stumbled after him, still struggling for breath, but as we reached the field, I looked over my shoulder to see glowing tongues of flame lick through the barn planks, accompanied by thick billows of black smoke pouring from under the eaves. The electric lights, which had previously looked so pretty and festive, now became the villainous eyes of infernal creatures that peered at us through the gloom. They were the brothers, the sisters, the demonic cousins of the ooser, and I felt the weight of their gaze as they passed silent judgment on me: I had betrayed Morris. My desire to save his mortal life had condemned that sacred ancient mask to ruin -- along with centuries of magic, infinite layers of meaning and purpose, far beyond any monetary value. I alone had sent the priceless and irreplaceable ooser to its fiery destruction.

I collapsed on the grass.

"Are you okay, Rosie?" Alex said as he crouched beside me.

"The fire... the mask... "

"Rosie?" he said again, grabbing my face in his hands. "Rosie, are ye alright? Where did that rat-arsed bastard hurt you?!"

The roaring fire became a phoenix launching itself into the twilight sky. It was so beautiful, I began to sob. I struggled to contain myself, but eventually my breath slowed and my pulse calmed, and I said, "I'm fine, I'm fine," as I laid my hand upon his. "I'm just shaken. But poor Morris..." I looked back to the inferno, starting to cry again. "Morris had hidden the mask in the barn!"

The roar of hot rushing air swept through the night chill as families retreated, children crying and women screeching, paired with the relentless howling of the Geek in his cage. Men, both audience and performers, formed a line to the seashore and began hauling buckets of water to put out the fire, but the hay, grain and lumber were dry after the hot summer and they created the perfect fuel; spirals of hungry flame lifted high into the air, tendrils of smoke climbed up the outside of the silo, the lights and shadows flickering. Cinders and ash rained down. The bricks cracked and crumbling with the heat, causing a shower of grit and embers to cascade into the farmyard like falling stars in the night. It looked terrifying, like a nightmare made solid and real. It looked -- it looked --

My breath caught in my throat.

"The tower!" I whispered.

Alex still cradled my chin in his hands. He heard me but didn't understand the context.

"What's that?"

It was useless to explain. I pulled away from his touch, hypnotized by the vision that stretched out and upwards, humbled before the power of the disaster. The tower burned. It could not be stopped. To try was folly.

We watched in stunned silence as the fire illuminated the farmyard, casting shadows over the mass of sweating, seething bodies, and lending a horrid eroticism to the whole tableau. After a while, the heat on my face began to cool and the light of the flames began to dim. Alex still sat at my side, holding my hand, and I let my gaze drift away from the burning barn and towards the dreary fields.

There I caught sight of a figure walking away, climbing the knoll, head down and shoulders hunched. When it reached the top, it turned to survey the destruction, and the last beams of flickering firelight fell fully upon the soot-streaked face of Morris Cave.

Chapter Eighteen

The constable and the fire brigade arrived soon after but the barn and silo could not be saved, so people targeted their efforts to protect the house and animals as best as they could. A few embers landed on the Big Top but these were quickly extinguished. By midnight, the fire was fully contained, then controlled, then smothered completely. Smoke hung along the shoreline like silvery chiffon curtains, but a breeze was rising from the land and blowing out towards the sea; by morning, the smoke would be gone.

Constable Turnpike arrested Morris, who had stood in the field and watched it all burn without showing any impulse to escape. The police officer had dragged Morris as far as the motorcar when Francis Godwin noticed and rushed after.

"This is the culprit," Francis said, "And her, too!" He pointed to me, still seated nearby in the sheep field next to Alex. "Arrest them both and throw them in jail!"

Turnpike glanced at me. He narrowed his eyes as I stood and began to walk towards them.

"Miss Rose, you'll be interested to know, I had an illuminating visit today from Mr. Sully, the insurance agent," he said, "He brought a few accusations of his own against the senior Mr. Godwin who has attempted to defraud the company with a false claim."

Francis turned grey.

"And the counterfeit bill of sale," I began, "The one sitting on the desk in Randal Godwin's study -- did you find it?"

"How timely of you to ask. Why yes, I did, madam," said Turnpike. "I won't bother to ask how you know it was there. Miss Tanaka was kind enough to give me access, and I located the object of Mr. Sully's concern almost immediately."

Francis took a step back as if he might bolt.

"Your father is currently waiting for his lawyer in the Esquimalt police station," Turnpike said, "And if you know what's good for you, you'll come along with no trouble."

Alex looked between Morris and me. "Insurance fraud? This is the reason for the housekeeper's murder?"

I glared at Francis, massaging my sore shoulder, then turned to Alex to explain. "Back in 1901, Mrs. Stuckey and her cousin, Mr. Lawrence, sold a stolen artifact to Randall and made a good deal of money in the transaction, but neglected to provide the bill of sale. When that singular artifact was stolen, three nights ago, Randall recognized it as a stroke of good luck: with his finances in tatters after a series of poor investments, the elder Mr. Godwin saw an opportunity to make a bit of money by submitting a claim.

"Mrs. Stuckey felt differently. When she discovered the mask was missing in the morning, she knew her own crime would soon come to light. Without the bill of sale, she couldn't prove value or ownership, so in a fit of panic she decided to forge one. She had plenty of examples of Lawrence's handwriting. She traced out a reasonable facsimile and signed the bottom as Dr. Edward Cave, the legal owner.

"Using shoe polish to cover a scratch in a wooden floor is a common household trick, and the housekeeper knew that shoe polish made a good stain. She concocted a mixture to age the paper, but was applying the finishing touches when Randall discovered her in her room. When he realized she'd stolen ten thousand pounds from him, he fell into a fit of rage. Grabbing the letter opener, he stabbed her but, once the deed was done, he knew he must cover up one crime with the other.

"So, eager to get his money as soon as possible -- he had debts to pay, of course -- he roped in Francis to help move Mrs. Stuckey's body and stage the crime. Francis bashed in the head of her corpse to make it appear as if she'd surprised the thief in the midst of the burglary. Then, with the forged bill of sale in hand, Randall approached his agent to claim his money.

"But Mrs. Stuckey was a housekeeper, not an art thief. The insurance agent would've had suspicions, right from the start. And Randall was no criminal mastermind, either; he had no idea that the oily polish -- thinned down with turpentine -- would require a few days to cure."

I slid my gaze to Francis, who had turned red in the face.

"Perhaps your father hoped that the violence of Mrs. Stuckey's bludgeoning would keep anyone from looking too closely. If he'd only waited a few days, the bill of sale would have dried, and maybe he'd have been able to extinguish Mr. Sully's suspicions with a few well-placed lies." Turnpike seemed satisfied by my explanation, nodding slowly and arms crossed, so I glanced to Alex. "Mr. Godwin and his son wanted their money as soon as they could get it, and they were willing to pin the murder on one of us before we could leave."

"Then who stole the mask to begin with?" said Alex.

"I did," Morris admitted, "It belongs to my family. But I'll be damned if I let it fall back into Godwin's hands." He lifted his chin. "So, I burned the barn to the ground."

Mr. Buckley gave a piteous howl.

Alex groaned and rolled his eyes. "Oh, you foolish lad," he muttered.

"You destroyed the mask?" Francis moaned in despair, "You destroyed it just to keep me from selling it? You're insane!"

"I don't care. Put me in prison for theft and damage to property; that's the worst I've done." He glared at Francis. "At least I'm innocent of murder."

Turnpike slapped a pair of handcuffs on the younger Mr. Godwin, and led both men away to the police motorcar, to return them to town and sort out the details.

However, before he left, Turnpike glanced my way.

"I'll need a statement from you in the morning."

"Until then," I replied.

I watched the motorcar bounce and jostled up the gravel road, barely aware of the clamour around me; the smouldering beams of the barn hissed and popped, charcoal-stained men gathered in clusters to talk over the events of the night, and the Buckley family sat clinging to each other on the steps of their home, surveying the damage to their livelihood. Mr. Scott and Magda were there, too, giving their condolences. A few of the performers were trying to round up Nancy's ponies, which had gone insane with terror at all the flames and smoke.

Alex still stood at my side, holding his riding crop. "Well?"

I looked at him. "What?"

"I think it's safe to say, lassie, we'll never be invited back here again."

I gave a tired belly-laugh.

"That's okay by me," I replied. "People here are nuts."

I leaned against him, and he put his arm around me, and I'll be honest, the physical contact was very comforting after such a dramatic day. He smelled nice. I'd forgotten how good it could feel to be held in caring arms, and when Alex pressed a gentle kiss to my crown, I smiled.

"Thank you for coming to my rescue."

"My pleasure, Rosie. Ever since the poor mangy lion died, I don't get much of a chance to use the crop," he replied as we strolled back to the boats, his arm still slung over my shoulders. "It was a wee bit of fun to use it on that welly bastard."

"I'll need to answer Turnpike's questions, first thing in the morning."

"Fair enough, but don't dally," Alex replied. "Grover will be anxious to shove off before Mr. Buckley sets fire to our boats in retribution."

The constable listened and made notes as I explained myself, and he did not interrupt or dismiss my theories, for which I was grateful. I was concerned that Mr. Scott was going to weigh anchor and leave before I returned to the Circus Salmagundi, and I wanted to take as little time as possible with the legal particulars.

But when I was done, Turnpike set his notes before me and I signed them, and he nodded.

"You're help has been invaluable, Miss Rose."

"I'm glad," I said, "I like Morris, he's a fine young man. Who wouldn't share the very same passion to reclaim a cherished family heirloom?"

"He's been a model prisoner. Very amenable to the drunks."

"What will happen to him now that he's admitted to theft and arson?"

Turnpike leaned back in his chair and stroked his moustache with one hand. "It's tricky: the item in question had been stolen from Dr. Edmund Cave and Morris was in the act of reclaiming his father's property, so the offences against the man could be as slight as trespassing on Mr. Godwin's estate. But, on the other hand, Morris willfully destroyed the Buckley's barn and has caused them great financial hardship, for which he will need to be punished. Your boss, Mr. Scott, was able to procure a good attorney to represent him: I predict the young man will see a few years behind bars at the Saanich Prison Farm to atone for his actions. Difficult, perhaps, but nothing so severe as that which Randall and Francis Godwin will face."

"Will they hang for murder?"

"Randall will, most likely," said Turnpike. "Francis will spend a good long time behind bars." He shook his head sadly. "Randall always seemed like a decent chap to me. Francis had a temper on him, so the savagery he exhibited in bludgeoning Matilda is a little less surprising... and Matilda seemed like an honest woman, too. Well, one was a murderer, one was a willing accomplice, and the third was a thief." The constable tried to suppress a shudder. "You never really know a person, do you."

"I'm sorry that your wife will lose her second cousin."

Turnpike gave a snort of derision.

"It's not like Randall slummed with the likes of us. The most I ever got from the man was a bottle of cheap whiskey from time to time," he replied. "Justice is being served, Miss Rose, and I make no apologies for it." Then he paused before saying a humble tone, "But I do apologize for thinking the worst of you, Rose."

"It's understandable. You don't know me. I could've been any sort of person: good, bad, or otherwise."

He gave a knowing smile. "Ah, so you *don't* recognize me."

I sat a little straighter in my chair, suddenly feeling vulnerable.

He became very jovial at my surprise. "I served with your husband David at the Quarantine Station at Williams Head in 1917," he replied, "I was a few years younger then, of course, and clean-shaven. And I probably didn't have so much of a gut around my middle, either." Turnpike gave a chuckle as he slapped one hand to his belly. "I admit, I wasn't sure it *was* you when we first met: you're a bit more... colourful... than when David joined us at Williams Head, and you've cut your hair short, and that can change a woman's appearance quite a bit." When he looked at me, the light of recognition shone in his eyes. "But we met a few times at dinners for the officers, before the first battalions of Chinese fellows showed up."

"You were part of the group who trained the Chinese Labour Corps."

"Yes, I was!" he said, happy to hear me speak its name, "By God, David was a fine fellow to serve under. When we started training the men for the Chinese Labour Corps in April, your husband proved to be very precise, very particular. Those Oriental fellows could be troublesome but he was patient with them. Why, he even picked up a few words of their heathen tongue, if I remember right."

A cold trickle of dread percolated through my veins.

"I do remember you," I said, "We met at the Easter dinner, 1917, a few weeks before David shipped out."

"That's right! That's right!" Turnpike said, pleased to finally be recognized. "Can you imagine, chaperoning 80,000 young Chinese men to the fields of France, to dig trenches and build roads for the British? It must've been quite the adventure!"

"Yes," I said. "An adventure."

"Of course, we weren't allowed to speak a word of it to anyone -- top secret and all that. I still can't discuss it openly. But you know all about it, don't you?"

"Some," I replied, "David did not talk much about his time at the Front, once the war was over and he returned home."

"I heard it was all a nasty affair," Turnpike continued, oblivious to my clammy hands and trembling fingers. "I don't think too many of those Chinese fellows made it home to Shandong. There was malaria, accidents, German submarines -- the British officers enforced the rules and those poor fellows weren't allowed to fight, but damned if the war didn't kill 'em all the same."

"So I was told."

"And David? You said he's passed on?"

I nodded again, as if in a dream. "He succumbed to the Spanish Flu, not long after returning home."

Turnpike winced. "Oh, I am sorry to hear it."

"Thank you."

"He was a very good man, your husband. A dedicated soldier and an attentive officer, and there weren't too many that had his patience when it came to dealing with the foreigners. I know the government requests that we never speak openly about the Chinese Labour Corp and Canada's place in it, but you must be very proud of the fine work he did."

I swallowed hard.

You never really know a person, do you.

But instead of voicing any opposition, I said, "Thank you, Mr. Turnpike. It was lovely to see you again."

"And you, Mrs. Rosamund Irving." He winked. "Or should I use your stage name? Rose Ivy, isn't it? Good to see you, too."

I left quickly, bundled myself up in my scarves and robes to hide the tears that threatened to tumble down my cheeks, and I scurried out of the Esquimalt police station with my breath stuck in my throat. I was a fool to think I could come so close to my old home and not be recognized.

Every fibre of my being wanted to get back to the safety of the boats, but I was in no fit state to do it. I collapsed on a bench in the town square under the spreading branches of a maple tree, dropped my face into my hands, and wept.

For what, I can't exactly say. I suppose I wept for the loss of a future where I thought I would be happy, but that war and circumstance had thrown into confusion. I wept for the awful things David must have seen that had curdled him into a hateful and frightened shell of himself. I wept for the cruelty he'd shown, the pain he'd caused me, the distrust and fear I now felt because of him. I wept because everything was in bedlam and no one knew quite how to make the world feel stable or secure again.

I wept because I didn't know what the future held, and it bloody-well terrified me.

"Miss Rose?"

I looked up from my hands to see May Tanaka standing in front of me, looking fretful.

"Oh, May," I said, sniffling and trying to compose myself, failing miserably. "I didn't hear you come up --"

She sat down next to me.

"Are you okay? Of course, you aren't. I'm such an idiot for asking. Can I get you anything? A glass of water, perhaps?"

I shook my head. "I'm sorry, I'm just being sentimental."

"That's no reason to apologize," she said as she grabbed my hand and held it tightly. "You've been to see the constable?"

"I have."

"And Morris? Will they hang him?"

She looked gravely concerned.

"No, it sounds like he has a good lawyer to represent him, and the worst offence he'll be charged with is destruction of property. Turnpike seems confident that he'll have a short sentence."

Her smile of relief was like the summer sun. "That's very good news."

"I can't say it's so good for Randall Godwin," I replied.

“I guess not,” she agreed, “The cook has taken on Mrs. Stuckey's responsibilities for the estate, but of course it will be handed over to the elder Mr. Godwin's brother, and he plans to donate all the masks and artifacts to the museum. Who knows what shall happen to all the pieces?”

My heart broke. I thought of Morris, assuring me that the masks were not dead but only sleeping, waiting silently for their freedom. "I suppose now, they'll never return home where they belong," I said.

"I don't know about that," she replied, "Some of those masks are hundreds of years old; for them, what's a few more years to wait?" She squeezed my hand, imparting a little bit of optimism into me. "Let's hope that one day, each mask finds its way back to the people who love it and know it best."

"But what about you?" I asked, "If the house has been given away and the contents are all dispersed --"

"Oh, there's no longer any need for a full staff," she replied. "I was fired this morning."

"Oh, May!" I said, my own grief forgotten, "That's dreadful!

"It's alright!" she chirped.

"But what will you do?"

"Ah! I've already had a job offer, and it's an exciting opportunity. I'd be crazy to refuse!" She squeezed my fingers. "Mr. Scott has offered me a place in the Ten-in-One. He said, with Morris gone, there's an open cubicle waiting for me."

I laughed, mostly in disbelief. "Doing what?"

"My chicken show!" she replied, "I took the last of my money and bought the smartest chickens from the cook -- Big Mama and Pip and Uno -- and we have a routine that we can do, counting out seeds, adding and subtracting." A faint blush tinted her cheeks and a girlish giggle entered her voice. "Your ringleader, Mr. Alex McGee, spoke on my behalf to Mr. Scott and gave me a glowing recommendation."

"I'm sure he did," I replied to her fair face.

"And that's not all! I have a gift for you." She stood and pulled at my hand, guiding me to my feet. "I've already delivered it to the ship. I think you'll be very pleased."

We walked the whole way back without any indication of the nature of her gift, but May was electric with excitement and her giddiness was infectious. By the time we reached the *Atropos*, I'd left all my sorrow behind me.

The tents had been dismantled and folded, the ropes coiled and set in neat rows. The roustabouts were loading up the last bits of equipment, Gertie was leading her two horses on board the *Decimo*, and Nancy had taken her dogs for one last run around a pasture before we shipped out. Dr. Kane stood on the deck of the *Nona*, smoking a pipe, and when he saw us, he nodded his head in a demure greeting before strolling to the bow, to take one last lingering look along the pretty, rocky shore. Magda was hustling her children on board like a shepherd chasing wayward lambs, and I heard the Geek let out a few whoops from the bowels of the *Nona* where his cage had been secured in the cargo hold. The old, ram-shackled dock bustled with activity, shouting, and laughter. Almost every face was smiling and bright with the excitement of travel.

May led me up the *Decimo's* gangplank, along the outer deck, then down into the hold. In a dim corner on the starboard side were three bamboo cages stacked atop each other, and each one contained a chicken. Big Mama watched me with narrow, beady eyes as she clucked and purred in a low tone, but Uno was too busy pecking at a pile of seed to notice me. Pip's eyes were closed, sleeping. Next to the birdcages sat one of the huge barrels of seed from the Godwin's coop.

"I couldn't leave without bringing enough grain to feed them," May explained.

"Of course not," I replied. I liked May, but her dedication to her chickens was almost maternal, and certainly eccentric.

"Here," she said, handing me a screwdriver, "Why don't you take the top off the barrel and give them a bit of seed? Big Mama hasn't eaten anything since we left the Godwin estate."

Why did I feel like I was walking into a trap? I took the screwdriver with hesitation. The wooden top was quite secure, but I managed to lever the tool under the brim and pop the top off, pushing it up until the barrel opened with a squeak. I peeked inside.

I almost soiled myself with a jolt of sudden terror.

The barrel was only half-full of grain. Sprouting from under the soft blanket of golden kernels, one frightful duck-egg eye peered up at me, along with a wicked crescent horn and a scrubby scruff of moth-eaten piebald hair.

Epilogue

November 2, 1920

My beloved Morris,

I'm back to full health again, but I am absolutely crushed to hear that you'll be spending the next six years in prison. Six whole years! What a rum deal! I can't imagine you'll have a very good time; Mr. Buckley is furious, of course, but Mr. McGee has generously offered to provide a suitable character reference for you, and I hope that will lessen your sentence and preserve some of your reputation.

Take heart, my darling, I will wait for you. I look forward to our reunion when you are again a free man. I would've come to visit before you were sent off to the Saanich Prison Farm, but Mr. Scott (that wicked midge of a man, so frightful!) had us cast off almost immediately from the Buckley farm. I don't think Mr. Buckley will ever welcome us back. The friendship between he and Mr. Scott has certainly been destroyed -- torpedoed into oblivion! I trust you had your reasons for setting the whole place on fire, my darling, but it really has caused a good deal of hostility between the men. We may never be able to return to Esquimalt.

We're taking the winter season to regroup and rest. The weather will be nasty on the open sea, of course, so I'm happy for a chance to relax and to get my health back after that dastardly poison that Rosie administered to me. Wanda the knife-thrower's assistant has family who own a farm just south of Nanaimo, and they have generously offered for the Circus Salmagundi to stay in their cabins and board our horses, ponies, doggies and bear in their stable. It shall be wonderful to live on land again, even if it's only 'til springtime. We've all given the solemn promise to Mr. Scott that we will do our level best not to burn down their barn, too.

When I told Rose I was writing you a letter, she asked me to send you her regards. She's such a queer old thing. She keeps to herself, she doesn't like to be too conversational, and she can be dreadful snappy when she's tired. Goodness, I hope, when I'm in my forties and as decrepit as she is, I still have my looks and my sex appeal; she doesn't always make much sense to me, and she likes to keep her schemes to herself, and you just can't trust introverts. They're too odd and soft in the head.

For example, she asked me to pass along a message. She said, don't you worry. She hopes you'll forgive her for giving up the devil to the wild hunters in exchange for your freedom, and she promises to keep your uncle's dancing partner safe and sound until you are a free man again. I heard her and May talking about a pair of duck-eggs stashed in a chicken coop? I don't know what she's talking about. That woman is absolutely daffy.

Send me a letter when you can and tell me if you are well, and I will try to send you care packages whenever possible. I've included the address of our wintering farm at the close of this letter, and I will eagerly watch for your reply.

With love,
Calliope

Enjoy a sneak peek of 'The Vengeful Dead'

The sun had yet to rise over Baynes Sound. A few clouds gathered in the dark northwest, bunched together by a gentle breeze like wayward sheep in a wide meadow, but the rest of the pre-dawn sky remained clear, crisp, and speckled with brittle stars. Waves dimpled the surface of the water, dappled in shades of silver and pearl. To the east, the low-lying silhouette of Denman Island stretched flat along the horizon like a slumbering hound. Night retreated quietly with morning's calm arrival. By all accounts, the coming day promised to be beautiful.

Before leaving home, Teddy Wentworth had filled his pockets with enough bread for two boys to eat, while Billy Kagetsu had swiped a pot of sweet red bean paste from his mother's pantry, and the pair were in high spirits as they trudged along the edge of the sea with their homemade fishing poles slung over their shoulders. What a pleasure, to eat a Sunday's breakfast by the ocean, fish nibbling at the bait, not a single adult in sight! A few fairy lights bobbed on the water -- most came from fine-hulled purse seiners dragging nets for herring, but a few were simple lanterns hanging off the bows of rowboats, pit-lamping for spring salmon -- and the murmur of men's voices drifted over the water, muted with distance. This meant Teddy and Billy could talk freely about whatever 11-year-olds like best, without a care in the world, and without any fear that a father's hand might clout them for cursing. They headed southward into the dawn gloom. The bustle and clatter of Union Bay's gigantic coal pier faded into a dull roar behind them, but even seeking privacy and quietude, they kept the pier in sight. It wasn't wise to wander too far from town.

Billy was long and lanky for his age. His straight black hair fell in his eyes, so he swept it out of his way with a flick of his head. Teddy was shorter, more robust, with ruddy cheeks and a voice that had a squeak to it like a penny whistle. "So, the wife asks, 'Whatcha doing?' and the husband replies, 'I ain't doin' nothing', and the wife yells at him, 'God-damn, you did that yesterday!' and so the husband says --"

"The husband says, 'I weren't finished yet!'" Billy snorted a laugh; not at the joke, of course, but at the absent-mindedness of his friend. "You told me that joke already, Ted. Gimme one I haven't heard!"

Ted chuckled. "Alright, alright. Lemme think."

"While you're thinking, let's set up on that rock out there; it's good and flat and we'll both have a swell seat to cast our lines."

They crawled up onto the slab. The big wedge of granite was cold and damp with dew, and both boys knew it had sat here since time immemorial, washed with countless tides, so they gave it the same sort of respect one displays when entering a church or a temple. It was a holy thing, older than humanity. They removed their shoes and settled reverently at its edge with their naked toes dangling into the refreshing water.

Billy cast off his line as Ted struggled to recall a new joke. "Have I told you the one with the pig and the pie man?"

"Yeah."

"How about the gorilla that escaped from the zoo?"

"You told me that one, too," Billy said. Distracted, his eyes darted towards the dark trees, peppered with small boat sheds and a few cock-eyed cabins. "Jeeze, Teddy, is this spot safe, do you think? We ain't too far from the wharf?"

"Naw, we'll be fine." Teddy flicked his fishing rod and the cork bobber splashed into the water. "Why, you chicken?"

"Hell, naw!" said Billy with great offence.

"Has your sister been telling you ghost stories again?" He tugged at the line. "About the... what was the word she used... the yokai?"

"So what, if she has? I ain't scared."

Teddy smirked but said nothing else.

For almost half-an-hour they sat on the rock and gorged themselves, licking their fingers and laughing. Because March had been unseasonably warm, they removed their coats and pulled up their pant-cuffs to splash their legs in the cold water. They talked about catching a dog shark. The circus was coming to town, so they speculated on the quality of freaks it might bring. Billy spied a few treasures tossed up by the surf -- an old pomade canister with a picture of a lion on the top, a crumpled ladies' handkerchief, the stub of a pencil -- so he gathered up the junk and they laid out the flotsam in a line to devise saucy stories about their owners. Then Teddy performed an impression of their persnickety teacher, Miss Doyle, that was so perfect, Billy almost choked on his breakfast.

The velvety glow of dawn crept across the land. Boulders and bushes began to take shape. It was at that magical time, when the first confident rays of sun pierce the last lingering curtains of night, that a lumpy shape on the beach behind them caught Billy's attention.

"Hey, what that, over there?"

Teddy saw at once what Billy meant.

It wasn't uniform and straight like a log, or rounded and humpy like a worn stone. The surface had a soft texture, woven together like a big tangle of eel grasses, and it lay under a thick overhang of ferns and salal bushes a few feet above the high tide line.

"Don't know," said Teddy, "Maybe a dead seal? We must've walked right passed it. I'm surprised we didn't trip over it."

"Well, it wasn't there when we came fishin' yesterday," Billy replied as he set his pole aside and stood, stretching his arms over his head. "I'm gonna go see. If my line gets bit, you reel it in. Swear?"

"Yeah, yeah, I swear."

On his bare feet, Billy left the flat stone and crossed the twenty feet to the object. As he drew closer, he heard faint skittering sounds like glass marbles thrown across a tile floor, so he looked down to his toes. A swarm of green crabs, each one no bigger than a penny, scuttled back and forth across the gravel and seaweed. There were hundreds of them, maybe even thousands. A few were so bold that they hurried over the swell of his foot, their tiny legs prickling like nettles against his skin.

"Damn!" he said, trying to sound brave.

But a sudden sharp fear flared in his chest. Billy tried to smother the panic that was rising quickly through his body, chilling his fingers and arms. He almost turned back. Instead, he took a deep breath to muster his courage, and he reminded himself that Teddy would get a good laugh if he retreated from a bunch of tiny sea creatures. So what, if there too many to count? An unstoppable army of tiny spiders dressed in green armour? Their claws outstretched, their beady black eyes watching him from atop monstrous stalks? Billy knew he'd never hear the end of it, if he was a coward. There was nothing worse in all the world! Miss Doyle said they'd almost lost the war because of all the conchies and skirkers who refused to fight, and the older boys in the schoolyard were sure to give a good, patriotic pummelling to anyone branded a sissy. Billy wasn't about to let that happen! He straightened his shoulders, flicked the black hair from his eyes, and kept on course, following the river of crabs towards the curious lump, all grey and brown and solitary in the fresh, clean light of dawn.

When he reached it, he swallowed hard.

At first, the scene didn't make any sense to his eyes. The woven mat of grass was actually a sweater knitted of grey-brown wool. The woman lay on her side, youthful but not young, slim but not skinny. Her back was to the sea and her face was to the land with her arms crooked awkwardly under her, a crown of damp mousy curls covering the back of her head. She didn't stir as Billy approached; she lay as still as a statue on the beach without a care in the world. But if she was asleep, why was she lying with her head pushed down between two big rocks? That seemed a mighty uncomfortable place to rest.

Then Billy circled the woman, and his eyes followed the river of crabs to the patch of crimson that spewed from the side of the woman's head, and the breath snagged rough in his hitching lungs. The blood clung to the rocks like molasses, all chunky and gummy, black and red. The hole where her cheek had been was like a second gaping mouth, providing Billy with an easy glimpse of pink tongue and shattered teeth.

The opposite side of her head lay gently against the stones, but Billy could see that it had been transformed into a crater of hair and mush, surrounded by a shifting halo of swarming crabs. They crawled across the ragged edge of her flesh, over her face and through her curls, using their mandibles to nibble on the softest morsels. Some of them were crawling right inside, brazen little things.

Billy stumbled back, arms pin-wheeling. Cowardice be damned: the boy let out a blood-curdling scream.

Acknowledgments

Who would have thought, writing three novels back-to-back would demand so much time and dedication, not only on my part, but on those generous people who are supporting me on my writing journey? If writing a novel is a sprint, then this was a bloody marathon. I wish to thank everyone who has joined me on this Circus Salmagundi adventure.

Thank you to Cindy Bannerman, Tracy Jenneson, Jennye Holm, Jeff Holm and Kate Blood for reading the earlier drafts, pointing out the errors and missteps, and generally saving me from a great deal of embarrassment. Thank you, Zoe Pigott, for bouncing ideas around with me and showing me, with shining eyes and a gasp of surprise, what elements worked best.

Thank you, too, to those wonderful people whose research proved invaluable to writing 'Truly the Devil's Work': Dawn Copeman for steering me towards circus history on the West Coast of Canada; Jack Knox and Dan Black for their articles on the Chinese Labour Corps; Robert Turner's invaluable books on BC's nautical history; Sherri Robinson's Walking Tours of Esquimalt; and Daniel Patrick Quinn for his research on the history of the Dorset Ooser. Many thanks to Catherine Siba, Deb Griffiths, Joyce Johnston, Linus Pigott, Kailli Pigott, Julie Sabey, Marisol Laviolette Koubova, and Tony Grove, all of whom may or may not be aware that threads of our conversations are woven into this novel.

Thank you to Shawn Pigott for so many things: the wonderful cover design and technical support, the delicious dinners and long rambling conversations, your enthusiasm and creative thinking. I don't think it's too hyperbolic to say: without him, these books would not exist.

Lastly, thank you so much to the readers, supporters, book clubs, librarians, and gracious humans who have read my stories and told their friends. I am truly grateful to everyone who has visited book readings, sent emails, bought books, left reviews, and encouraged me to keep going. Just like running a marathon, writing a novel can be a lonely pursuit, but your appreciation makes it all worthwhile. If you've read this far, then a hearty thanks to you.

Manufactured by Amazon.ca
Bolton, ON

29830173R00111